Praise for
the *New York Times* Bestselling
Black Cat Bookshop Mysteries

Literally Murder

"Another wonderful installment . . . If you're anything like me and your life revolves around cats and books, you will never go wrong in picking up a Black Cat Bookshop Mystery!"
—Melissa's Mochas, Mysteries & Meows

"This book is fun! And scary, interesting, and hard to put down . . . It is a delight to read, with just the right amounts of mystery, tension, panic, and calm . . . [A] new adventure with Hamlet can't come too soon!" —Open Book Society

Words with Fiends

"Brandon again creates a lively whodunit . . . An endearing entry in a sturdy series, *Words with Fiends* should find many friends." —*Richmond Times-Dispatch*

"[A] finely tuned whodunit that quickly became a page-turner . . . Nonstop action . . . Great cast. This is one of the best books yet in this delightfully engaging series."
—Dru's Book Musings

"Really fun . . . Extremely clever . . . This is a sensational cozy mystery series that just gets better and better."
—Melissa's Mochas, Mysteries & Meows

continued . . .

A Novel Way to Die

"Our favorite sleuthing cat is back . . . This series really does have it all: [a] bookstore, cats, likable, relatable characters, and a strong mystery." —Cozy Mystery Book Reviews

"[A] delightful way to spend an afternoon. This book is fun, fun, fun! Ali Brandon is a great voice in the cozy mystery world!" —Socrates' Book Reviews

"Fun to read . . . The mystery was very good and the cat really added some interest to the story." —Fresh Fiction

Double Booked for Death

"A fun mystery that kept me guessing to the end!"
—Rebecca M. Hale, *New York Times* bestselling author of *How to Catch a Cat*

"Clever . . . Bibliophiles, ailurophiles, and mystery fans will enjoy *Double Booked for Death.*"
—*Richmond Times-Dispatch*

"A charming, cozy read, especially if cats are your cup of tea. Make sure the new Black Cat Bookshop series is on your bookshelf."
—Elaine Viets, national bestselling author of *Catnapped!*

"Hamlet is a winner, and so is his owner. The literary references in this endearing debut will make readers smile, and the ensemble characters hold promise for fun titles to come."
—*Library Journal*

"[An] outstanding debut to a very promising new series . . . The characters are interesting and smart, the mystery is clever and provides clues the reader will notice but [doesn't] let the cat out of the bag prematurely . . . I had such fun reading about Darla and her cohorts, and found Hamlet's antics made me smile . . . If you enjoy a cozy mystery, a clever cat, a bookstore setting, and smart, realistic characters, you are sure to enjoy *Double Booked for Death.*"
—MyShelf.com

"This first entry in the Black Cat Bookshop Mystery series is a harbinger of good books to follow . . . In case you are wondering, Hamlet fulfills his role as sleuth by knocking down books containing hints about the killer's identity. [Brandon] does a fine job with the plot and execution."
—*Mystery Scene*

"Those who like clever animals but draw the line at talking cats will feel right at home."
—*Publishers Weekly*

"The first Black Cat Bookshop Mystery is an entertaining whodunit starring a brilliant feline (who does not speak in human tongues), a beleaguered new store owner and an ex-cop. The story line is fast-paced as Hamlet uncovers the clues that the two females working the case follow up on . . . Fans will enjoy."
—The Mystery Gazette

Berkley Prime Crime titles by Ali Brandon

Black Cat Bookshop Mysteries

DOUBLE BOOKED FOR DEATH

A NOVEL WAY TO DIE

WORDS WITH FIENDS

LITERALLY MURDER

PLOT BOILER

Leonardo da Vinci Mysteries
writing as Diane A. S. Stuckart

THE QUEEN'S GAMBIT

PORTRAIT OF A LADY

A BOLT FROM THE BLUE

PLOT BOILER

ALI BRANDON

BERKLEY PRIME CRIME, NEW YORK

An imprint of Penguin Random House LLC
375 Hudson Street, New York, New York 10014

PLOT BOILER

A Berkley Prime Crime Book / published by arrangement with Tekno Books

For more information, visit penguin.com.

ISBN: 978-0-425-26155-2

PUBLISHING HISTORY
Berkley Prime Crime mass-market edition / November 2015

PRINTED IN THE UNITED STATES OF AMERICA

10 9 8 7 6 5 4 3 2 1

Cover illustration by Ross Jones.
Interior text design by Kristin del Rosario.

This one is for my nonwriter friends.
They may not understand the fear of a missed deadline,
or the horror of a terrible cover, or the thrill of a great
review, but they love me, anyhow. Thanks, y'all.

ACKNOWLEDGMENTS

The writing never gets easier, but the support seems to broaden with every book I publish. Thanks to my friends and family, who pretend not to notice when they catch me acting out an iffy scene or wrangling aloud with a pesky bit of dialogue. Gratitude to various random acquaintances who don't mind sharing their particular expertise when I need some oddball plot question answered. And virtual hugs to all the folks who follow me and Hamlet on Facebook and Twitter. Your comments, questions, and kitty pictures are greatly appreciated.

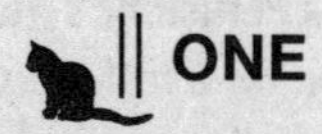

ONE

"I DON'T KNOW WHAT THEY SAY HERE IN BROOKLYN, BUT back home in Texas, they call it crawfishing on a deal. Fine, I'll be looking for it. Good-bye."

Had she been talking on a landline, Darla Pettistone would have slammed down the telephone receiver with a satisfying crash. But the call had come in on her cell phone, so she'd had to content herself with hitting the "end" key with more force than necessary. Then she slumped back in her vintage bistro chair and stared at her best friend, Jacqueline, aka Jake, Martelli, in dismay.

Jake raised a black eyebrow. "Crawfishing?"

"Crawfishing," Darla confirmed. "It means going back on your word. Which is what Johnny Mack just did to me."

"And Johnny Mack is—?"

"—the lead singer for Johnny Mack's Electric Trombone

Band. They're the ones my planning committee hired for our Fourth of July block party on Friday."

"Oh, yeah, the guys who play over at Oompah's," Jake replied, naming the biergarten-style restaurant across town where she and Darla had eaten a time or two.

The two women were sitting in the upstairs lounge of Darla's bookstore, a space that was now, after a recent remodel, somewhat unoriginally known as Pettistone's Fine Coffee Bar. The coffee bar had been open for a little more than four months now, but already Darla had seen a small if tidy uptick in her bookstore's monthly profits, which she directly attributed to this new addition. While previously their customers hadn't really started rolling in until noon, now she had a good ten or so regulars at her door each morning soon after opening time. After purchasing a newspaper or magazine, these newly minted regulars then rushed upstairs for a latte or other specialty drink crafted by her salesclerk-turned-barista, Robert.

Not that she had visions of competing with the local coffee shop, Perky's, when it came to cornering the coffee market. Still, it was already obvious that she'd made a sound business decision with the remodel. Of course, the entire project had been something of a leap of faith from the start, given that she'd been on a working vacation in Florida during the construction. In her absence, she had turned over responsibility for managing the remodel to her store manager, Professor James T. James. But James and the project both had come through with flying colors, even despite Darla's subsequent misgivings about the somewhat shady contractor she'd hired. What had previously been a lounge area was now a mini bistro complete with front and back service counters featuring lots of dark, glossy wood and copper.

Setting down her cup of latte, Jake went on, "What's the matter, kid, did they change their minds about trading in their lederhosen for red, white, and blue?"

"Worse! He cancelled the gig on me." Darla felt her redhead's temper start to flare. Taking a deep breath, she tamped down her indignation and managed a more even tone.

"It turns out Oompah's owner decided he wants to stay open on the Fourth, after all," she went on. "He offered Johnny double his usual rate to play. So Johnny is celebrating his independence a few days early by taking Oompah's money and running, while leaving us in the lurch."

"First things first," the ex-cop turned private investigator urged as she used a paper napkin to mop up a bit of the foamy drink that she'd sloshed onto the glass-topped bistro table. "Tell him you want your deposit back ASAP. He gives you any guff, call the credit card company and dispute the charge."

"Already taken care of," Darla gloomily replied as the sound of typewriter keys emanated from her cell phone, indicating an arriving text. "Johnny just returned the deposit electronically . . . less a processing fee," she added with a frown as she noticed her original transfer was a few dollars short.

"So charge the loss to the block party committee fund and book another band."

"It's not the money. In case you haven't checked the calendar this morning, today is Tuesday the first, meaning that the Fourth of July is only three days away. No way will I be able to find a replacement for them at this late date.

What are we going to do? What's a block party without a band?"

The pair considered the problem with mutual frowns for a few moments; then Jake snapped her fingers.

"Boom boxes," was the PI's practical suggestion. "I've got a pretty decent one stashed in my closet if you need to borrow it. And I'm sure some of the other store owners have some sort of sound systems. You can set up zones in front of the booths."

Darla shrugged. "I guess that could work, but it's not the same as live music, which is what we advertised."

"Aw, c'mon, kid. You could do patriotic music over here, oldies down the street, jazz across the way, and maybe some of that Auto-Tune/rap/Top 40 stuff for the kids at the end of the block. It'll be a heck of a lot cheaper than hiring a band."

"I guess that's better than nothing," Darla grudgingly agreed. "I'll put that down as plan B and run it by the committee. Thanks, Jake."

While Jake returned her attention to her latte, Darla penned a few notes on her aluminum clipboard—the heavy-duty type, like contractors used—which had been her ever-present companion since late spring. Fancy office supplies aside, budget had dogged Darla ever since she'd had the idea a couple of months earlier to organize the local business owners and put on a block party for the holiday—actually more of a street fair scheduled for the afternoon of July Fourth. The plan, as she'd originally pitched it to her fellow retailers, was to invite the public to shop and mingle out on the street in a partylike atmosphere. Though she suspected most of the attendees would be friends and family of the participating shop owners, she hoped the event also would draw in new customers while giving an advertising boost to their little business enclave.

Darla shook her head as she recalled how she'd jumped into this new project with both feet, even as James reminded her that they'd barely gotten past the coffee bar's grand opening. While he'd muttered about type A personalities and overachievers, she had shown him a list she'd compiled of independent bookstores that had recently shut their doors permanently. James had promptly hopped on board the block party train at that point.

While all the retailers would be chipping in a share of the expenses, Darla had ponied up the lion's share of the budget herself, meaning she was doubly invested in the event's success. The band was meant to be the biggest—as well as the most expensive—part of the attraction, along with door prizes and samples of food and drink from the local cafés. But she reminded herself that even without Johnny Mack and his boys, they'd still have plenty of other live entertainment.

TAMA—the Tomlinson Academy of Martial Arts, where Darla took a weekly self-defense class—was scheduled to give hourly karate demonstrations. And students from the nearby Brooklyn Modern Dance Institute were working on flash mob routines, where they would pretend to be part of the block party crowd and then break into highly choreographed dances. Penelope Winston, BMDI's owner, had shown the committee online examples of that kind of public stunt, and everyone had agreed it would be perfect for the block party.

And, of course, Darla wasn't about to leave Pettistone's Fine Books' official mascot out of the festivities.

She spared a fond look for the oversized black cat snoozing on a nearby bistro chair in defiance of health department ordinances. She had inherited Hamlet from her great-aunt, Dee, along with the three-story Brooklyn brownstone that housed the bookstore and her apartment (as well as Jake's garden apartment below). While moving from her native Texas to New York and taking over the book business had involved a definite learning curve, it was becoming a full-time cat owner that had practically required a degree in feline psychology. Frankly, Darla still considered herself an amateur in the field. But she was learning—mainly by making Hamlet the star of the show, so to speak. His silhouette graced the Pettistone's coffee mugs, and Robert even drew foam cat faces in the lattes.

For the first couple of weeks after the coffee bar was in business, she was sure it was the distinctive steam hiss of the frothing attachment that attracted the feline. Then she'd caught Robert pouring Hamlet a little saucer of steamed milk when he thought Darla wasn't watching. That, apparently, was the true lure. But as the occasional dairy offerings seemed to have no ill effect on Hamlet's digestion, and since it further cemented the "bro"-ship between cat and youth, Darla pretended not to notice.

"Oh, by the way, I've put Hamlet on the entertainment list, too," she told Jake.

"Don't tell me, you're going to play the Karate Kitty video, aren't you?" Jake said with a shake of her curly head and a mock groan.

"I was thinking about it. I have one of those electronic picture frames that plays videos, so I figured I could set that up at our booth."

Hamlet had been the star of a viral video on YouTube that featured him imitating Darla as she'd competed at a karate tournament. The video's popularity had then led to Hamlet being invited as guest of honor at a cat show in Florida earlier in the year. The cat show folks had taken one of the original cell phone uploads of Hamlet's antics and enhanced it, resulting in a clever montage put to the tune of "Eye of the Tiger." Darla had watched that video probably twenty times and, despite the fact that she basically was playing Odie the dog to Hamlet's Garfield the cat, laughed every single time.

"Hamlet's starting to gain a real following locally," she reminded Jake. "When people find out that he's also an Internet star, maybe they'll come to the store to meet him, and hopefully buy a book or two while they're here."

Her friend nodded. "This day and age, you gotta do what you can to draw in the business. That's why I'm offering free ten-minute consultations during the block party. You know, for all those people who are dying to hire a private investigator to check up on their cheating spouses but don't know how to go about doing it. Speaking of which"—she paused and glanced at her watch—"I've got a client conference in five, so I'd better get going. This one's a paying client, so I better not be late."

Darla checked her own watch.

"Have fun. The block party committee will be meeting here in about twenty minutes to finalize our last-minute items for Friday."

Then, knowing her friend's aversion to early mornings, Darla added with a mischievous grin, "You sure you don't want me to add you to one of the teams? We'll be hanging bunting starting at dawn, and we could use someone tall."

Jake snorted as she unfolded her six-foot frame from the bistro chair. "Kid, you'd have better luck rousting Hamlet at that hour. How about I stroll down the block sometime around nine and admire your handiwork, instead?"

With those words, Jake waved in Robert's direction and headed down the stairs to the bookstore's main floor. Darla, meanwhile, resettled herself at the table with her clipboard. Neatly stowed inside were the sheaf of handwritten notes, paid invoices, and paper napkin diagrams that she'd collected over the past few weeks. Clipped atop it was a bulleted list that detailed two dozen action items that had come of the committee's original planning meetings. As chair, Darla was in charge of delegating and follow-through.

Reluctantly, she erased the check next to the line that read *Arrange for a band*. Despite this setback, however, a satisfying number of check marks remained. In fact, the only other tasks still open were assigning the decorating team—to be resolved at the upcoming meeting—and collecting the participation fee from one final business owner. Although that last one might prove more difficult than Darla had originally anticipated. The holdout was George King, the decidedly un-perky owner of Perky's Coffee Shop.

"Hey, Ms. P., you want a latte?"

The question came from Robert, who had finished serving two giggling teenage girls, one a tall, light-skinned African American with a lion's mane of golden brown curls, the other a short, pale brunette whose hair had been cropped into a spiky pixie. Both wore yoga pants and long T-shirts and were drinking tall glasses of flavored iced coffee with a veritable mountain of whipped cream and shaved chocolate floating on top.

Slinging a white towel over the shoulder of his black Pettistone's polo shirt, Robert eased his way from around the counter and headed to her table. Picking up Jake's empty cup and giving the spot a swipe with his towel, he went on, "We got in that new Peruvian coffee blend if you want to try some."

Darla suppressed a smile as she caught the two girls giving Robert the once-over while his back was turned. Robert had been a tall, scrawny kid living on the streets when she'd first hired him, but he'd begun to fill out as the result of regular meals. His three-times-a-week lessons at TAMA had further refined his physique, so that he was turning into quite the handsome young man, Darla thought with a bit of surrogate maternal pride.

"Sounds good, but I think I'd better lay off the strong stuff for a while. How about a nice decaf with cream and sugar?"

"Coming right up."

Darla had noticed how adding Robert to her staff had slowly but markedly begun to change the customer demographic of Pettistone's Fine Books, as well. When she'd first assumed the reins following her great-aunt's death, the majority of the bookstore's customers were at least retirement age. Doubtless that had been reflective of the fact that Great-Aunt Dee had been in her eighties when she'd died, and her store manager, James—himself a retired university professor—was old enough to collect social security. Darla had felt like quite the spring chick in comparison at the ripe young age of thirty-five.

Bringing on board a teenager, however, had added a whole new vibe to the quaint if somewhat staid shop.

Hiring Robert had not been part of the five-year plan that Darla had written up within her first few weeks of taking over the business. When she'd first encountered Robert the previous autumn, he'd been homeless and antagonistic, recently kicked out of his indifferent father's house for the unforgivable crime of turning eighteen. It hadn't helped his cause that Robert embraced the goth look, with dyed black hair, black vintage clothing, facial piercings, and makeup that included black kohl eyeliner and black nail polish.

But then a few weeks after that incident, Robert—his "children of the night" appearance toned down to a slightly more business-acceptable version—had showed up at her store looking to fill a salesclerk job. To Darla's surprise, Hamlet had given Robert a literal paws-up as a candidate. The admiration apparently had been mutual, with Robert dubbing the cat his "little goth bro" because of Hamlet's inky fur. Since the finicky feline had previously chased away several other candidates whom Darla had deemed more suitable, she'd agreed to hire the youth on a trial basis.

And Robert had proved to be a model employee. Not only had he bonded with Hamlet, but he'd become protégé to the acerbic James, their relationship resembling that of grandfather and grandson. James didn't even seem to mind the youth's subtle manner of poking fun at him, like adopting a version of the store manager's ever-present sweater vest as part of his own personal uniform.

Moreover, it had been Robert who'd encouraged Darla to add an ever-growing section of graphic novels and comics that had helped draw in the younger crowd. And now as barista, he'd brought in a broad circle of friends.

All in all, Darla thought in satisfaction, hiring Robert had been a smart choice.

A short time later, Robert brought her a fresh cup of decaf. The two teenage girls were still dawdling over their own coffees, and Darla overheard one girl address her friend: "Too bad you can't get the Kona Blue Party blend here like you can at Perky's. Then this would be, you know, the most perfect place ever."

The other girl nodded. "Yeah, that stuff is the best. I get it at least once a week. But Robert is, like, way cuter than that guy at Perky's. And nicer, too."

Darla particularly agreed with that last sentiment, since the rival coffee shop owner had a notoriously foul temper . . . one reason she had yet to collect his portion of the block party funds. She'd already promised herself she'd remedy that situation today.

Right after the meeting, she decided. With that task weighing a bit on her mind, she went back to her clipboard and the papers gathered upon it. She needed to do just a bit more figurative housekeeping before the committee arrived.

She was reviewing the decorating teams list when she heard her name being called from the vicinity of the stairs. Darla looked up from her chart to see her store manager, Professor James T. James, gesturing in her direction.

"Sorry to disturb you," he went on in his usual precise, sonorous tones, "but Detective Reese is downstairs. He says he needs to talk to you for a few minutes. And he claims that the matter is important."

Important?

Darla frowned. Knowing Jake's pal, NYPD detective

Fiorello Reese, as she did, "important" could mean anything from something as innocuous as his wanting to tell her that their favorite deli had added a new variation of meatball sub to its menu, to asking whether she'd been witness to a crime somewhere in the neighborhood.

Not that anything like that ever happens around here.

As if hearing Darla's sarcastic thought, Hamlet slit open one emerald green eye and stared in her direction.

Just kidding, Hammy, she silently reassured him.

Or perhaps she was the one who needed the reassurance, given that Hamlet possessed an apparent talent for pointing the paw at bad guys. Fortunately, it had been some time since she and Hamlet had unwittingly stumbled across any sort of criminal activity. She had even reached the point of telling herself that she'd only imagined that Hamlet was a veritable Sherlock Cat when it came to figuring out whodunit.

Mentally crossing fingers that the detective's news was more of the meatball sub variety than otherwise, Darla called back to her manager, "Tell Reese to give me a second to pack up all my paperwork and then I'll be right down."

Hamlet, meanwhile, having overheard that his nemesis was in the store, opened the other eye and gave himself a long stretch that almost sent him tumbling off the bistro table. Then, with a quick paw lick that Darla translated to mean, *I actually did that on purpose*, he got to his feet and leaped to the ground.

"You behave now, you hear?" Darla called after him as, tail waving like battle flag, he purposefully marched toward the stairway as she stowed the paperwork that she'd spread across the small table back into her clipboard.

Unlike his immediate kinship with Robert, Hamlet had taken a dislike to Reese from the start. The feeling had been mutual, no doubt because they both considered themselves alpha males who liked things done their way. It hadn't helped that the pair's first meeting had occurred in Darla's darkened apartment when Hamlet attacked Reese in a case of mistaken identity. Fortunately, the detective had been wearing a leather jacket, which had protected him from four fuzzy feet worth of unsheathed claws.

The jacket had been less lucky.

Man and cat had managed a truce afterward, but it was an uneasy one. Darla typically found herself playing reluctant referee anytime the two crossed paths.

Now, as the cat paused and turned to give her a guileless blink of green eyes, she added with a mock-stern look, "Spare me the innocent act. I know you and Reese don't get along, but remember that you're on the clock. Save the cat-itude for after hours."

The green eyes squinted a little at her admonition. However, rather than flopping on the floor and flinging a leg over his shoulder to lick the base of his tail—Hamlet's patented "kiss off" gesture—he merely resumed marching in the direction of the stairs.

TWO

"CATS," DARLA MUTTERED IN AMUSED EXASPERATION AS the oversized feline slid like a silken shadow down the steps. Transferring her clipboard and coffee to the longer rectangular table designed for groups, she followed after Hamlet to make sure the ornery beast stayed in line.

Reese was standing near the cash register, leafing through one of the free newspapers piled there on the counter. He was dressed in his personal summer uniform of dark dress slacks and beige sport coat, the desecrated leather jacket (which Darla much preferred on him) back in his closet until cold weather hit again. As usual, his tie—a college-style striped one in blue and pale yellow—was hanging loose, though Darla forgave him that sartorial slip. With a bodybuilder's physique, doubtless it was uncomfortable having a heavy strip of silk knotted tightly around one's muscular neck.

He glanced up as Darla approached, and she realized that her heart, if not skipping the usual clichéd beat, was still pumping a bit faster than normal in his presence.

Don't be silly, she silently admonished herself. They were, after all, just friends. They'd tried the dating thing a couple of times in the past, but the relationship had never moved beyond the awkward stage, so they'd mutually agreed to keep things platonic.

Even so, she occasionally found herself wondering if she'd made the wrong choice in that decision.

"Hi, Reese. James said you needed to tell me something important," she greeted him, not bothering with the usual pleasantries as she searched his expression for some clue as to what it was that rated the designation "important." But, just as with Jake, she rarely could read him when he was in cop mode.

"How's it going, Red?" he asked as she joined him, his tone friendly if a bit subdued.

The greeting, while reassuring her that this was not an official police call, still made her wince slightly. The only other person who'd ever called her by that particular nickname had been her slimeball ex-husband, the memory of whom was better shoved into a very tiny recess somewhere at the back of her brain. Over the months, she'd finally given up protesting the appellation, grateful that at least the detective hadn't tagged her with the equally unoriginal moniker of "Rusty."

"Busy, busy, what with the block party. How about you?"

she replied, virtuously not whipping out her own secret name weapon. She'd once heard another cop jokingly call him "Little Flower," the literal translation of his Italian first name. As Reese had once explained to her, he took after his father in appearance—"Midwestern corn-fed," as Darla always termed his blond-haired, blue-eyed good looks—but his Sicilian mother had won the naming rights.

"Same old, same old," he replied with a shrug that strained the sport coat's already-taut shoulders. "You know how it is in the summer. The heat, it makes people crazy . . . and then you got the people with no AC, and they go even crazier. So we get some weird calls. Speaking of which—"

He paused and eyed Hamlet, who had leaped up onto the countertop and was eyeing him back . . . though, following Darla's earlier admonition to mind his manners, the feline had settled a good six feet away from him.

Darla arched a brow in fair imitation of Jake and gave him a mock-outraged look. "Are you calling my cat weird?"

"Hey, you're the one who says he's super-intuitive or something. All I'm doing is making sure I'm out of claw range."

Apparently satisfied he was beyond the Hamlet danger zone, Reese returned his attention to her. "So, uh, Red, you got a minute?"

"Sure, but really only a minute. The block party committee will be here anytime now. You want me to send up for a cup of coffee for you while we talk?"

She indicated the tiny bistro table against the far wall where a sliding door midway up the paneling hid an old-fashioned dumbwaiter. The sign taped to it read, "Place your to-go coffee orders here." A second sign propped on the table beside an order pad gave instructions on how to send up one's coffee request, which then would be sent down the same way.

Previously, Darla and her staff had used the ancient contraption as a mini elevator to transport boxes to the second floor stock area. It had been James's idea to use the dumbwaiter for its literal, original purpose. And given the number of elderly customers they had who might not be able to negotiate the stairs, Darla had agreed it was a brilliant notion.

Reese, meanwhile, was shaking his head, his expression now reflecting something that Darla could best peg as discomfiture. "Nah, I'm good. I just came by to give you a little update before you heard it from someone else. You see, I—"

"Star-spangled, my Brooklyn butt," a woman's voice from near the front door declared in strident tones, which—along with the jangle of the front door bells—cut short Reese's reply.

Darla smiled, not needing to glance over to recognize the speaker as Penelope Winston. At five-foot-nothing and perhaps one hundred pounds, with her salt-and-pepper hair cut short in a spiky do, the woman still resembled the New York City Ballet star she'd been thirty years earlier. These days, however, it was her brusque manner and smoker's rasp that often first garnered attention when she walked into a room.

Still, Darla had developed an affection for the woman over the weeks they'd been on the committee together. While Darla routinely overlooked her potty mouth, Penelope also had made a conscious effort to clean up her language in front of the group; hence the use of "butt" rather than a coarser body part term.

"No way am I going to let my girls dress up like Yankee-Doodle majorettes," Penelope went on, waving the bright red e-cigarette—or, more properly, as Darla had learned, pen vaporizer—that accompanied her everywhere. Addressing the three men who were crowded around her like her posse, she finished, "When they take off their hoodies and sweatpants, they'll be in red and white striped leotards and little blue shorts. Believe me, everyone will get the idea."

"Hey, leotards and little shorts work for me."

This grinning observation came from Doug Bates, owner of Doug's DOUGhnuts and another of Darla's committee members. Nearing fifty, and packing almost that many extra pounds, Doug favored the multiple gold chains and a tan that would put a Hollywood star to shame look. His genial, blond good looks always brought to Darla's mind an image of how Reese might look in another decade or so, if he gave up the gym for nights out in the local bar . . . or days spent sampling doughnuts. As usual on a working day, the man was wearing his baker's white drawstring pants and black-and-white checked newsboy hat, though he'd swapped the double-breasted chef's jacket for a black T-shirt with his shop's logo.

Catching sight of Darla, Doug waved and called, "The gang's all here. You want us upstairs?"

"Sure," Darla called back, acknowledging him with a return wave that also included Penelope and the other two men on the committee—Steve Mookjai and Hank Tomlinson. "I'll be up in just a minute."

She watched them start up the stairs, Steve and Hank at the head of the line, Penelope following, and Doug bringing up the rear. Darla turned her attention from her committee back to Reese, but not before she saw something out of the corner of her eye that made her do a momentary double take.

Had she imagined it, or had Doug just given the dance instructor a flirty swat on her "Brooklyn butt" as she climbed the stairs ahead of him?

Certain she must have been mistaken—as far as she knew, Doug and Penelope were nothing but casual friends—Darla turned back to Reese and said, "I can put them off for another couple of minutes. What did you want to talk about?"

The cop shrugged. "It'll keep. I know you're busy with this whole Fourth of July thing. I'll catch you later."

"Okay, if you're sure."

Darla frowned a little as she watched him leave, the string of bells on the front door jangling after him. She'd rarely seen the blunt-speaking cop at a loss for words, let alone looking so uncomfortable at not blurting out exactly what was on his mind.

"It was probably the meatball sub thing," she told Hamlet. The cat raised one side of his fuzzy mouth in what she could only interpret as a sneer before he plopped onto the counter, kicking a couple of free papers onto the floor in the process.

Great.

Darla shot the feline a dismayed look as she scooped up his handiwork. Obviously, he didn't share her assessment of the situation. And now that Hamlet had weighed in on the subject, it was going to nag at her until she finally found out why Reese had come by, though with Reese's schedule, that might not be until the block party. At least she'd made him promise to attend.

"James, I'm headed back up to the coffee lounge to meet with the committee," she called to her manager, deliberately dismissing the other subject from her mind. When James nodded from his spot where he was arranging books at the bestseller table, she added, "Since this is our last get-together before the block party, we might run long. Can you handle things by yourself?"

"I believe I can cope," was his wry reply as he looked about the nearly empty store. "And I certainly hope this event of yours helps business for all of us. I am not sure I have ever seen a summer here at the store quite this . . . quiet."

"Don't worry, James. After we knock it out of the park with our big bash on Friday, you'll be wishing for quiet."

Or so Darla hoped. She wasn't prepared yet to tell her manager that though she'd run the June numbers every way she could think to do, bottom line was that they hadn't hit their sales goal for the month. Even worse, unless the block party brought them the business boost she was hoping for, July was on track to end up much the same way.

Displaying more confidence than she felt, Darla headed upstairs. She saw that the other committee members had already gotten their various cups of coffee from Robert. Now, they were gathered at the big table where Darla had left her clipboard and drink, waiting for her to join them.

That was, all except one.

Penelope stood looming—as much as someone her height could loom—over the bistro table where the two teenage girls had been drinking their specialty coffees. The girl with pixie-cropped black hair sat frozen with her long coffee spoon halfway to her mouth, the blob of whipped cream it held gently dripping unnoticed onto the table as she stared up at Penelope. The other teen, with the mane of golden brown curls, was scrunched as low as she could in her chair, her expression one of outright misery.

"Emma, Allison, you know the rules," Penelope clipped out, shaking her vaping pen at the pair in a threatening manner. "You want to be in my troupe, there's no sweets, no junk food"—she paused and gave their coffee drinks a scornful look—"and no whipped cream with chocolate on top. Now, out of here, both of you."

"Yes, Madame Penelope," the pair obediently chorused. Grabbing up their purses, they shoved back their chairs and scampered for the stairway.

Penelope shook her head in disgust as she watched them go. Then, eyeing their abandoned drinks, she swiped a perfectly manicured finger through an untouched portion of whipped cream. To Darla's amused horror, she plopped that sizable blob into her own mouth.

"What?" the dance instructor demanded as she turned back to the committee table and saw everyone's attention was on her. Licking her finger clean, she explained, "The rules are for the girls. I paid my ducs years ago, so nowadays I can eat this junk if I want."

"Thank you, Penelope, for that unbiased review of our drinks," Darla said with a wry smile, earning outright chuckles from the others. Then they got down to business.

"Three day left," a smiling Steve Mookjai reminded them all with a celebratory lift of his logoed coffee mug.

Steve, the widowed, middle-aged owner of the Thai Me Up restaurant, had been Darla's first recruit for the July Fourth committee.

It's my favorite holiday, even before I finally become citizen a few years ago, he'd assured her, his words reflecting the faint accent that still colored his speech. Looking dapper with his short-cropped dark hair, very thin black mustache, and always spotless white chef's jacket, he ruled his establishment with polite panache. But it was his delicious cooking that kept Darla and the rest of the bookstore gang returning there on a regular basis. Like Doug, he'd doffed his white jacket for their meeting, wearing instead a New York Yankees jersey with Derek Jeter's number 2.

"Almost there, Steve," Darla agreed with a smile of her own. Then she acknowledged the rest of her team. "Everyone finish their action items from last time?"

"Canopies and signs are all delivered and sitting in the dojo storeroom ready to go up on Friday," Hank Tomlinson, the final member of the committee, confirmed with a satisfied nod that sent his short black ponytail bobbing. "Penelope, great job on the design. They look really professional."

He leaned back in the delicate bistro chair, muscular arms with their "sleeves" of Asian-style tattoos crossed over his broad chest. In his late twenties and co-owner of the TAMA dojo along with his fraternal twin brother, Hank was just the sort of entrepreneur that Darla wanted on her committee. He could take orders as well as give them, and he wasn't afraid to lay his opinion on the line. Not that she'd always gotten along with him; in fact, back when his late stepfather had been running the dojo, Darla had privately considered Hank and his brother Hal to be somewhat jerk-ish. But tragedy had brought out their better natures, and Darla now counted the pair among her friends.

"Perfect," she replied, checking off another item on her list. "If you and your student team can handle putting them up in the designated spots, that will free up the rest of us to concentrate on other things. Penelope," she addressed the dance instructor, "how are we doing on the rest of the decorations? Did those giant red, white, and blue pinwheels ever show up?"

Penelope took a drag on her e-cigarette and huffed out a vapor cloud that momentarily obscured her face. Darla resisted the reflexive impulse to wave away the fruit-scented mist, reminding herself that it wasn't secondhand smoke like with a genuine cigarette. She'd noticed several former smokers in the neighborhood going the vape pen route of late. Even Jake, who still snuck the occasional cigarette despite her assurances that she had quit, had toyed with one of those devices recently.

"Not yet," Penelope answered her question, "and I've been calling the idiot vendor every day this week. How hard can it be to ship a box of pinwheels? I finally had to go all Brooklyn on him. Scared him bad enough that he swore he'd send them out overnight tonight on his dime. So tomorrow, we'll have everything."

Darla smiled, while the men all chuckled in appreciation.

"Next time I have customer make trouble, I call you," Steve declared, earning a high five from Doug. Then, sobering he went on, "I finish my action item, too. The snow cone truck will be here before noon on Friday. My nephew, Mike, he promise to bring all his specialty flavors."

"Perfect," Darla agreed. "Snow cones and the Fourth of July go together like—"

"Like doughnuts and more doughnuts," Doug declared with a grin broad enough that his eyes almost disappeared into his red cheeks. "You should see the new firecracker doughnut I came up with. Blue icing topped with shredded coconut and red hots. It'll be a bestseller."

"Sounds pretty," Darla agreed, not quite sure how well cinnamon candies and coconut would combine on the tongue but certain the visual would get lots of attention. "Will you still be giving away doughnut holes at your booth?"

"Absolutely. Oh, and my action item is done, too. The company will deliver first thing Friday morning while we're setting up."

"Portable potties, check," Darla murmured with a nod as she made an entry on her list. Looking up again, she added, "Great job, everyone. We're on track for a fabulous block party. The permits are all in place, and the police will start blocking off the streets around eight thirty on Friday morning. Just one last little bump in the road, though."

Briefly, she explained to the group how Johnny Mack had cancelled that morning, leaving them without live music for the event. She also ran down Jake's suggestion for filling in the audio void with boom boxes.

When she finished, Hank shook his head. "I guess that would work, but there's nothing like live music. Heck, you can drive down the street and hear plenty of recorded tunes blasting out of cars. I'm not really feeling this, you know?"

"I'd prefer a band, myself," Darla replied while the others nodded in agreement with Hank. "But we're down to the wire, here. Who can we possibly find to play on such short notice?"

"How about the screaming babies?" Robert piped up as, coffeepot in hand, he came over to the table intent on refills.

Darla slanted the youth an exasperated look. "Cute, Robert, but not much help." Turning back to the committee, she went on, "Here's a thought. Maybe if we all posted something on our social networks—"

"Seriously, Ms. P., that's the band's name, the Screaming Babies," the youth protested as he poured her more decaf. "I know they don't have a gig this weekend because I'm, like, friends with the lead singer, Pinky. You should hear them. They're really sick."

Which, Darla knew, was teen slang for really good. But given that Robert was a fan, chances were the Screaming Babies were a metal or goth band, not exactly the vibe she and they committee were looking for. Still—

"I don't know, Robert. We wanted someone who could play something a bit more Top 40, plus we'd want some patriotic music," she told him. "Any chance they could do something like that?"

"Heck, yeah. Sometimes they call themselves the Babies and just play covers of other groups' hits."

His tone enthusiastic, Robert went on to name several bands that the Babies presumably covered, none of whom

Darla—a fan of eighties and nineties rock—had ever heard of before. And since most of them featured "blood" or "death" or "night" as part of their names, she doubted that said hits included anything that would be appropriate for a family event.

On the other hand, she told herself, Pinky and his screaming cohorts would probably make for perfect entertainment at a Halloween soirée.

"So what do you think, Ms. P.? Should I, you know, tell Pinky you're interested in hiring them?"

"I don't know," she repeated with a questioning look at the others at the table. "What do y'all think?"

"Beggars can't be choosers," Penelope shot back. "I say, have this Pinky person come by for an audition this afternoon. If he can get through 'The Star-Spangled Banner,' hire him."

"I second," Steve said, raising a hand, while Hank and Doug both nodded their approval.

Darla shrugged. "I guess it can't hurt to give him a tryout. Robert, can you call Pinky and see if he can come by the store later today? No promises, though . . . just to talk."

"I'm on it," was his cheerful response as he reached into his jeans pocket with his free hand and pulled out his smartphone. "It's after noon, so he should be up by now."

As Robert headed back to the coffee bar to make his call, Darla allowed herself a wry smile. She'd thought it odd enough that the committee had wanted what was basically a biergarten band for their entertainment. Now they were gung ho on someone whose specialty was heavy metal. Who knew what they'd agree to if the Screaming Babies weren't a good fit?

"All right, that takes care of the action items. Now, a final bit of old business. One of our merchants still needs to pay up."

"Let me guess," Hank said. "It's gotta be Mr. Perky himself, Brooklyn's very own King of Coffee."

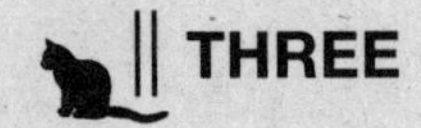

THREE

"KING OF COFFEE? MORE LIKE THE BARON OF B.S.," WAS Doug's muttered response, drawing a stiff nod from Steve and a frown from Penelope.

As for Darla, she suppressed a wince. "King of Coffee" was the same inflated title that Mr. George King, owner of Perky's, had given himself a few months earlier when she'd first made a courtesy visit to him before her coffee bar's grand opening. He did rather resemble the paintings she'd seen of his almost-eponym, King George III. Like that ruler, he possessed a large nose, doughy cheeks, and extra chins, along with snowy hair receding almost to the halfway point of his scalp. But where His (historical) Majesty was usually portrayed with a calm gaze, this petty tyrant had roasted coffee beans for eyes.

I'm King of Coffee around here . . . me, Georgie King,

he'd blustered in a heavy Brooklyn accent. *You come waltzing around my kingdom, you're gonna get crowned.*

Teeth gritted, Darla had tried to politely point out to him that her new coffee enterprise was only a sideline for her bookstore. That explanation, however, had made him puff up even more.

Yeah, here's an idea. How's about I sell some of them trashy paperback romances here with my coffee—you know, just as a sideline?

While Darla had struggled with which to address first, the implicit threat to her well-being or his prejudice against romance novels, Mrs. King had made a tentative appearance from the back room. Half his girth and age, the gamine-featured Livvy King was a dark slip of a consort to her husband's pale, portly ruler.

Georgie, she had ventured, patting the messy black braids pinned atop her head, *some delivery guy is at the back. He won't let anyone sign for the box but you.*

While Georgie snorted and trudged off to handle the paperwork, Livvy had managed a tremulous smile for Darla. *Sorry, he gets a bit snippy when his blood sugar is low*, she'd said to excuse her spouse. Darla had politely accepted that bit of fiction even while she wondered how the unlikely pair had wound up husband and wife.

Ultimately, it had been Livvy she'd dealt with a couple of months later in drafting Perky's to be part of the block party, and getting a deposit and signature on their merchants' mutual agreement. It was only when the time had come to hand over his remaining share that George had gotten involved . . . and not to the betterment of everyone concerned.

Now, Darla replied, "That's right, George King is our holdout. When I stopped by over the weekend to collect the rest of what he owes to the block party fund, he told me he's not sure it's worth his time or money to take part in something that, quote, unquote, 'will probably turn out to be a big-ass bust.' And as of today, he still hasn't paid up."

"Count on Georgie for that," Doug replied. "Always gotta pee in everyone's Cheerios. Heck, you should have seen him when I first opened the doughnut shop and he found out we served hot coffee. He accused me of poaching his business."

"Ah, he's not so bad," Penelope began, only to be interrupted by a harsh laugh from Steve.

"Not so bad?" he broke in, repressed anger seeping past his usual air of friendly reserve. "You should hear what he say to my kids yesterday when they buy coffee at his shop."

Darla knew both of Steve's offspring: son Jason and daughter Kayla, all-American teens who worked part-time in their father's restaurant. They came by Darla's store on occasion as well, lured by their love of anime and recent friendship with Robert.

"They are good kids," the man went on through gritted teeth. "All they want was lattes to go. No trouble, no nothing. But what he say to them . . ."

While Darla and the rest listened in dismay, Steve repeated the coffee shop owner's subtly racist taunting as they attempted to place an order. While not blatantly derogatory, Darla could see why Steve was upset; the sly innuendo was just as cruel as any outright slurs.

"At first, they think he make bad joke, and they laugh. But when he keep on talking, they know he mean it. They run out, no coffee. The only reason they tell me is because I see that Kayla is crying," he finished, hand clenching and unclenching in impotent outrage.

Grim faced, Hank shoved back in his chair, the tattooed koi on one bicep and the inked tiger on the other both bulging. "How about we take a little field trip down to Perky's and explain to Mr. King that his kind of bigotry doesn't fly in our neighborhood."

"I'm in," Doug agreed, looking equally irate.

"No need for violence, guys," Darla clipped out, flipping back through her notes. "If my numbers are right, I think we have just enough reserve cash to give Mr. King back his deposit. As soon as we're finished here, I'll run down to his shop, pay him back, and tell him we don't need a racist jerk like him taking part in our block party."

"No, no, my friends." Steve held out a restraining hand and shook his head. "Your support is appreciated, but I was wrong to speak up. This belongs to my family. If there are trips to be made and words to be said, I do them."

"If you're sure," Hank grudgingly agreed, while Penelope gave Steve's arm a reassuring pat.

"Maybe they misunderstood," Darla heard the dance instructor whisper to him. "I don't think Georgie, er, Mr. King, is really like that."

Penelope's unexpected vote of confidence notwithstanding, Darla frowned. "Well, there's still no reason we can't boot him out of the event, anyhow, since he hasn't paid up."

"No, Darla, not necessary." Steve summoned a humorless smile. "Go see him, like you plan, and if you can get his money, take it. The party should not suffer because he is idiot."

"Steve's right," Doug added, though his tone was still resentful. "Georgie-boy is already in all the advertising, so it would look strange if Perky's didn't have a booth on game day. Besides, making him pay his fair share would probably hurt more than anything else we could do."

"Yeah," Hank said with a smirk. "And knowing that jerk, even if he didn't pay up, he'd probably still set up a booth outside his shop for the block party."

Then, turning to Penelope, who'd said no more during the exchange, he asked, "You on board?"

"Hell, might as well let him stay." She puffed out another stream of vapor and added, "Darla, are we done? I gotta rehearse my girls again and do a final costume check."

Darla spent a moment looking over her notes and then set down her clipboard. "I think that's it. See everyone bright and early Friday morning!"

With a few final words among them, the committee members got up from the table and headed toward the stairs.

Darla followed more slowly, feeling oddly guilty over the situation. She reminded herself that King's boorish behavior had no connection to the event she'd spearheaded, and that he doubtless had been spouting his mean-spirited dogma ever since he'd opened the coffee shop a decade earlier. Then she frowned. If that last were the case, then his coffee really had to be outstanding to compensate for his business to continue flourishing. Remembering the two teenagers who'd earlier been singing the coffee shop's praise, she decided she might do well to try out one or two of his blends to see just how good his product really was.

By the time she made it downstairs and waved her committee out the door, Darla had decided on her course of action. She'd head over to Perky's with a heaping helping of Texas charm and attempt to bring this obnoxious sheep back into their diverse fold. He might be a jerk, but what mattered was the success of the block party.

James was waiting on a pair of matronly women who had stopped in while Darla was busy with her committee. She waited until her manager had finished ringing up the two before briefly explaining the "King George" situation, drawing a commiserating nod from him.

"I want to get over there before they close, since they're only open until four on weekdays," she told him. "No point in letting this drag out."

Then, with a glance over at her store mascot, who was still lounging on the counter and now snoring loud enough to riffle the newspaper stack, she added, "If you can hold down the fort again, I think I'll take Hamlet with me as backup. If Georgie doesn't cooperate, I'll just have him speak to my associate."

"You do realize that Hamlet will likely not be allowed inside the coffee shop?"

"Yeah, health code and all that," she said with a dismissive wave. Then she added with a smile, "You do realize I was kidding about the backup, right?"

"I am not always certain with you. And, never fear, you may consider the fort held."

"Thanks. And if we're not back in a reasonable amount of time, go nose around Perky's for signs of foul play. With that man's attitude, he might toss me and Hamlet into his coffee roaster, just to say he can."

"If that happens, you may be assured I will see to it that your tombstone reads 'Roasted in Peace' as an appropriate epitaph." Then, as Darla chuckled a little at this bad bit of wordplay, he added, "While you are in the lion's den, perhaps you might do a bit more corporate spying, so to speak. I am hearing rumors that Perky serves a particular blend that is especially appealing to the younger crowd."

"Kona Blue Party," she promptly confirmed. "I've heard about it, too. I was already planning to buy a pound of it so we can try to figure out why it's so—"

The splat of newspapers hitting the floor cut her short. Once again, Hamlet had decided that his comfort outweighed the customers' convenience of a free local read. Tsk-ing, Darla scooped the newspapers up and neatly squared them back on the counter again.

"I know, Hamlet, the news is depressing," she told him as she glanced at the headlines while stacking them again. *Apartment Fire Leaves Three Homeless. Teen Recovering from Drug Overdose. Vandalism Spree Ends in Arrest.* "But that doesn't mean you have free rein to toss the papers all over the place."

Hamlet blinked and lifted a paw, as if about to dispute that statement. Then, apparently deciding it wasn't worth the effort to educate her, he settled back to resume his nap.

"Not so fast," Darla told him as she reached beneath the counter for his leash and harness. "I might not be able to use you as my muscle, but at least you can walk over to Perky's with me."

A few minutes later, Darla had buckled a protesting Hamlet into his harness and, clipboard under her arm, started off toward the coffee shop. Hamlet, after his initial bout of grumpiness over being rousted from his comfy spot near the register, seemed to enjoy the outing. While not exactly prancing, he strolled with purpose, black tail lazily following after him. He'd learned to walk on a leash a few months earlier, courtesy of a "feline behavioral empath" whom Darla had consulted to help Hamlet out of a funk. To her surprise, the curmudgeonly cat had taken to his new harness like a champ, and daily walks were now part of their routine. And Darla had to admit that she rather enjoyed the attention the two of them drew while out and about. How could one not feel elegant and adventurous when accompanied by an oversized panther of a cat?

The afternoon was hot by Brooklyn standards, but Darla was used to Texas's sweltering heat and so didn't even break a sweat as they headed up the street. Besides, she was dressed for the weather in lightweight khakis and a yellow Pettistone's polo shirt, and had a water bottle tucked into her shoulder bag. It helped that the street was also nicely shaded by dual rows of brownstones and a few strategically placed small oaks, taking the sidewalk temperature down a few degrees.

Even so, Darla had still done her usual barefoot check of said walkway before starting out. Only after she'd determined that the concrete was cool enough for her bare flesh—meaning it also was safe for feline paws—had she set Hamlet down for their walk.

A few minutes later, they arrived at Perky's. The independent coffee shop was located in a staid brownstone similar to Darla's building. Like most other brownstones nearby, this one also had been converted into living spaces above and retail below. A glass entry door there at ground level led to the former, while Perky's occupied all of what was a converted garden apartment. Reaching it required taking several concrete steps below street level.

Just as with Darla's building, those stairs were enlivened with a sturdy wrought iron balustrade that served both as a handrail and as a comfortable place to lean while sipping one's coffee. George, however, had cleverly added a matching wrought iron gate that, when closed and locked, would effectively bar all but the most athletic from heading down to the coffee shop after hours. Of course, at this time of day the gate was open. With Hamlet at her side, Darla descended into King George's realm.

FOUR

A FAINT AROMA OF BREWING COFFEE BEANS WAFTED UP AS Darla and Hamlet walked down. Since the last time she'd been there, someone—probably Livvy—had taken time to throw a fresh coat of mango-colored paint on the peeling front door, and there were now two oversized terracotta pots each holding a fragrant bush with pink blooms that she recognized as oleander. No doubt Livvy had been responsible for those, too. The bold colors put a cheery bit of chic back into the shabby kingdom.

Too bad no one had bothered to re-gild the Perky's name onto the window at the same time, Darla thought. It looked like most of the "P" from the mottled glass had been scraped off, so that the name on the door now read "erky's." Given that the establishment's owner had a definite knack for irking people, perhaps the revised name was appropriate, she thought with a silent snicker.

But she also noticed with approval the addition of a little glass-and-wicker bistro table and chairs on the sunny narrow landing area outside the coffee shop. Since the place was more of a retail venue, it offered little inside seating other than a few high barstools at the counter and a couple of wooden benches where customers could wait for their to-go orders. The table was a nice little touch. *Maybe,* Darla wondered, *these recent curb appeal touches mean that George is now on board with the July Fourth festivities?*

Darla hesitated at the door, wondering if she dared try to skirt the health code—and George's bad temper—by bringing Hamlet inside with her. Technically, he wasn't even allowed to hang out in her bookstore's upstairs loft now that the coffee bar had been installed there, either.

Of course, Hamlet had never been a stickler for rules.

Darla, on the other hand, was . . . at least when it came to other people's establishments.

"Sorry, Hammy, but you're going to have to wait here."

Darla set down her clipboard and detached his leash long enough to thread the end through the loop she'd wrapped around one of the decorative iron bars; then she refastened the snap-hook to his harness, giving it a final tug to be certain he was safely secured there in the shade. That accomplished, she reached into her bag and pulled out her water bottle and the folding pet bowl she always took on their walks.

"I promise I'll be inside for only a few minutes," she told the cat as she poured a couple of inches of water into his travel bowl and set it beside him. "Meow if you need anything in the meantime."

By way of answer, Hamlet flopped onto the cool concrete, back deliberately turned to her. Darla rolled her eyes but didn't let this display of cat-itude sway her as she turned the knob on the coffee shop door and walked inside.

The previously faint coffee aroma was now a full-fledged cloud that enveloped her as she walked to the counter. She gave an appreciative sniff while glancing around.

The shop's layout was similar to many coffee establishments Darla had patronized before, the public portion of the coffee shop a rectangular space the size of a traditional living room. A work counter complete with sinks and refrigerators took up most of the back wall, but was mostly hidden by the rough-hewn service counter in front of it. Rustic shelves ran floor to ceiling on two side walls.

The wooden planking displayed blends of bagged coffee—both beans and ground—along with coffee mugs and espresso cups in various colors and configurations. Another shelf displayed herbal concoctions: teas, infused oils, and so on, which she knew was Livvy's specialty. One shelf even held official Perky's gear: T-shirts, mugs, and reusable shopping bags.

A pleasant enough place despite its owner, Darla mused as she walked up to the counter. Just enough retro vibe to be interesting, but not so kitschy that it would scare off traditionalists.

The shop was currently empty of customers, however. The King himself was the only one besides her in attendance. Wearing a tent-sized short-sleeved blue shirt with a jumbo Perky's coffee cup embroidered on the back, he was bent over the antique coffee roaster in the corner.

Unlike the small, sleek stainless steel unit that Robert

sometimes used at the bookstore, this was an embossed copper machine. It was similar in size to a meat smoker like her father used back in Texas, but topped by an oversized funnel-shaped feeder. A few stainless parts appeared added to the equipment as an afterthought, no doubt automating the machine for modern-day use and lending it a definite steampunk look.

As she watched in interest, George released the door on the roasting drum, spilling out a steamy caramel-colored waterfall of roasted beans into a spinning cooling tray.

"Looks wonderful," she exclaimed, drawing the man's attention.

George grunted and straightened. "Oh, it's you. What, you need a real cuppa coffee, and not that swill you pour over at the bookstore?"

"Our coffee is top-notch, thank you very much," she replied, her initial smile pulling taut. Their coffee ought to be good, she told herself, given that they bought most of their beans pre-roasted from a couple of well-known outlets. "Actually, I'm following up one last time to see if you're still planning on taking part in the July Fourth block party. We'll need the balance of your contribution if you're going to have an official booth on Friday."

"Wha'did I tell you the other day? You ask me, that block party is gonna be a big bust."

"Well, things look like a big bust in here right now," Darla reflexively replied with a pointed look around the empty shop. Then, recalling her original intention to kill the man with kindness, she made a swift mental reset to "charm" mode.

"Seriously, George, I really think this event will do a

lot for the entire retail neighborhood. And everyone on the committee thinks it's important you take part."

"Yeah, I bet they do," the man said with a snort. He reached into the spinning cooling tray and snatched out a couple of beans.

"Here, try this," he demanded, handing her one and then popping the other into his mouth. "Just like a cuppa the best coffee you ever had."

While George crunched loudly, Darla cautiously bit down on the still-warm bean he'd offered. She wasn't yet used to the idea of popping roasted coffee beans like breath mints, but she knew that Robert did the same thing anytime he roasted a day's worth of product, assuring her it was an important part of the quality control process.

As the robust coffee flavor filled her mouth, she gave an appreciative nod. George might be a jerk, but he definitely knew his way around a roaster.

"Really good. Now, about your share of the sponsorship . . ."

"Eh, talk to Livvy about it," he exclaimed as his wife peeked her head around the open door at the far side of the back counter. "I'm gonna go take a walk."

To her surprise, he grabbed a red vapor pen identical to Penelope's from beneath the counter and, leaving the cooling coffee beans still swirling in the tray, clomped to the door.

Darla felt a brief instant of panic, recalling that Hamlet was tied outside. What if George wasn't pleased to find a cat on his landing and aimed a kick Hamlet's way, or something equally heinous?

Instinctively, she rushed to the door and caught it

before it closed after him. She saw in relief that George had ignored the black feline now curled beneath one bistro chair (and who, Darla noted, was giving the man his patented evil green stare). Instead, George was intent on his vaping pen. Puffing on it like a hookah and trailing a stream of aromatic vapor behind him, he started up the concrete steps.

Her concern for Hamlet resolved, Darla sent a quizzical look after George. Somehow, the blustering coffee shop owner didn't seem the type to give up his cigarettes. On the other hand, maybe he'd decided that, as a master roaster, he needed his sense of taste and smell at full peak.

Darla shut the door after him and turned back to Livvy, who gave her a small smile. The young woman was dressed as if she might have just come back from yoga class, wearing capri-length black tights beneath a man-tailored pin-striped shirt, too small to have been borrowed from George. As usual, her black hair was scraped up into a messy topknot, giving her the look of a disheveled pixie.

"Please don't think I was eavesdropping, but I overheard your conversation with Georgie," she said in a soft voice, taking a sip from the oversized coffee mug she held. "No matter what he says, we both think your block party is a marvelous idea. How much do we still owe the committee?"

Darla told her, and Livvy set down her mug and reached beneath the counter, pulling out a leather-bound check register that looked as if it was a contemporary of the coffee roaster. She wrote out the check with a ballpoint pen and ripped it from the ledger, handing it with a flourish to Darla.

"There, all paid up. Now, what do we need to know about the event?"

Smiling, Darla opened her clipboard and tucked the check away, then pulled out the information sheet that she and the committee had drafted for the vendors. She and Livvy went over the details for a couple of minutes before Darla glanced back at the door.

"Sorry, I'd better go. Hamlet—my cat—is waiting outside. You can call me or any of the committee members if you have more questions." Then, recalling one of her other motives for coming over to Perky's, she added, "Oh, before I forget, I wanted to pick up one of your special blends to try out."

"Sure thing, which one do you want? We've got a really nice Jamaican that sells well. Oh, and if you like a medium French roast, Georgie has one he calls *Oui, Oui*. And if you want to try a dark roast—"

"Actually, I was hoping to try the Kona Blue Party blend."

Livvy choked a little, and her pale green eyes opened wide. "You want Kona Blue Party? Y-You're sure?"

"I'm sure."

Livvy frowned. Then, looking from side to side as if expecting to be overheard by someone, she leaned closer. "Darla, do you know what Kona Blue Party is?"

"Of course," Darla said, a bit puzzled now. It occurred to her that perhaps George had instructed his wife not to sell his special blend to the competition. That possibility made her even more determined to try it.

Summoning a no-nonsense smile, she assumed a confidential tone. "I'm sure you don't sell it to just anyone, but a couple of girls at the bookstore said it's the best they ever had. And since I'm in the coffee business"—she put finger quotes around the words to downplay any sense of her as competition—"I really want to try it for myself."

"Coffee business," Livvy murmured. "Good one. All right, if you're really sure."

Her attitude still reluctant, Livvy nodded and reached beneath the counter. "We have one bag left. Will that be enough?"

"I'm sure that will last me a couple of days," Darla agreed as she eyed the small, plain brown bag, which, somewhat to her surprise, lacked the usual gold Perky's sticker in the shape of a coffee cup. Enough for one pot, tops. "How much?"

Livvy named a sum that made Darla raise her brows, the more so when the woman added, "Cash only."

"What is this stuff, gold?" Darla muttered, digging into her purse.

Not that she wasn't familiar with coffee that commanded a king's ransom. Certain Brazilian and Guatemalan coffees were easily fifty dollars or more a pound. Not to mention the so-called civet cat poop coffee that cost more than three times that. But despite the outrageous price, she was more curious than ever now to try George's special blend.

"Thanks," Livvy said as she took the money and handed over the bag. "Enjoy."

"I will."

Tucking the small bag into her purse, Darla grabbed up her clipboard again and made her good-byes. *Mission accomplished*, she thought with pride as she headed out the door to where Hamlet waited.

The cat was still curled up beneath the bistro chair

looking sulky as she set down her bag and clipboard to unfasten his lead.

"Sorry, Hammy," Darla told him. "I know you don't like our friend George, but you're just going to have to chalk this one up as taking one for the team. I've got a check from his wife, meaning I can put another check on my list. Get it?"

When Hamlet gave her a sour green look at this weak attempt at humor, she meekly emptied his water dish and looped the leash around her wrist before gathering her things again.

"Oh, and look," she added, reaching into her purse and plucking out the small sack of coffee, which she dangled like catnip before him. "I picked up some of the competition's prime roast so Robert can reverse engineer it and figure out why people like it so much."

"Me-ROOOW!"

With that outraged sound, the cat whipped an oversized paw in her direction and smacked the bag of coffee right out of her hand.

"Hamlet! What's wrong with you?" Darla scolded as she scrambled after the wayward small paper sack and stashed it back in her purse. Fortunately, his claws had been sheathed, so that coffee beans hadn't spilled everywhere. She didn't want to antagonize him further at the moment, so she opted to overlook the ornery feline's behavior.

Seemingly appeased by the bag's removal, Hamlet deigned to rise and pad alongside her for the short walk back to the store. To her relief, George apparently had taken a different direction for his own little stroll. One encounter with him per day was her limit.

Then she frowned, remembering Steve Mookjai's

account of the recent incident between his teenagers and the coffee shop owner. Did they really want someone like George King representing their retail neighborhood? What if he tried his insults on one of the block party guests? Maybe she should simply have given George back his money, and then told the committee that he'd decided to bow out of the event.

Darla was still second-guessing herself when she reached the bookstore. Determinedly putting those thoughts on the back burner, she hurried up the steps, Hamlet bounding ahead of her. A college-aged man in cutoff shorts and retro tie-dyed tee was leaving just as she headed in the door. She gave him a pleasant nod, encouraged to see that his reusable Pettistone's tote appeared half full.

Robert was behind the front counter, which meant the coffee lounge upstairs must be empty. Reminding herself to meet with her young barista at the end of the day so they could try out the Perky's blend, she unfastened Hamlet from his harness. Free of the collection of straps, the feline gave himself a shake, sending a fine dusting of black fur over Darla's running shoes. Then he made a beeline for the children's section, where he likely would settle into the oversized beanbag chair that was one of his favorite lounging spots in the store.

Darla, meanwhile, gathered up her gear again and joined Robert at the counter. "Any luck with your friends, the Babies?"

"I talked to Pinky. He doesn't have a gig for the Fourth, so he said he'd, you know, come by and talk to you. He should be here any minute."

"Perfect. I just hope you're right, and that his band is

as versatile as you think," Darla replied as she bent to lock her purse and clipboard into the drawer beneath the counter. "Otherwise, it's back to Jake's plan B."

DARLA FROWNED AT HER WATCH. THE "ANY MINUTE" ROBERT PROMISED had morphed into three quarters of an hour. Was this Pinky person going to be another Johnny Mack? If he didn't show in a few more minutes, she'd let Robert know they needed a backup to their backup band.

Shaking her head, she pulled out some paperwork from beneath the counter and began going through invoices and billings while James dealt with a father and his young son who'd just walked in. She could smell the new batch of coffee Robert was roasting up in the coffee bar . . . an aroma faintly reminiscent of old, wet socks being burned. *Not* the odor that she'd expected when they had first begun the coffee venture; she'd expected something reminiscent of the intoxicating scent of freshly ground beans. In fact, the first time that smell had permeated the store, she'd been more than a little concerned that something was wrong with the process; this, despite Robert's reassurances that he was following the roasting directions to a T. Darla had been relieved when Livvy had later explained her theory that if the roasting beans actually smelled like fragrant roasted coffee, it meant they were losing aroma and, thus, flavor. Still, the smell tended to bother those customers who weren't coffee aficionados.

She bent to search the shelves beneath the open counter for the neutralizer spray she used downstairs to counteract the roasting smell. Someone—quite possibly a certain large, black feline—had knocked the canister over, and it had rolled all the way to the back of the shelves. Grumbling to herself, Darla half crawled beneath the counter trying to reach the spray, aware as she did so that the string of bells on the store door had jingled. Hopefully, James would take care of whoever it was, since she literally was in no position to wait on a customer at the moment.

"Gotcha," she muttered a moment later as she dislodged the can from where it had been stuck between two boxes of returns. Mindful of hitting her head, she wriggled back out again and straightened, only to find herself face-to-face with a reject from horror movie central casting.

She gave a startled little cry and took a reflexive step back, only to realize a heartbeat later that this must be Robert's tardy friend, Pinky.

At least she assumed so, given that the young man sported a single bright pink braid sprouting from the top of his otherwise shaved head. The pink theme carried to his beard, which had also been braided into two long dyed plaits that clung like colorful lampreys to his rounded chin. He sported black eyeliner and black lipstick, as well as piercings in his eyebrow and his nose. But even all those goth accoutrements couldn't completely camouflage the youthful plumpness of his pleasant, round face.

"Are you Pinky?" she managed, recovering her composure.

"Yeah. My friend Robert told me that someone here is looking to hire the Screaming Babies for a gig?"

His voice was young and pleasant, too—hardly what she'd expected, given his band's name. "I'm Darla Pettistone, Robert's boss," she went on, putting out her hand.

"The band that was supposed to play at our July Fourth block party on Friday cancelled on us, and he suggested you might be able to fill in."

"Depends," Pinky told her as they shook. "What's the pay?"

She gave him the same figure they'd budgeted for the Electric Trombone Band, and the young man nodded. "Yeah, that would work. So how late you want us 'til? Three, four in the morning?"

"Actually, this is a daytime, uh, gig."

Doubt creeping in—she should have known better than to take advice on hiring a band from a nineteen-year-old—Darla gave Pinky a quick overview of the block party schedule.

"I know the Screaming Babies are a goth group, but Robert said you were a cover band, too. The block party will be a real family event, so we're hoping for more traditional music . . . maybe even patriotic songs."

"Sure, we can do patriotic. So, are we hired?"

"I thought Robert mentioned that we wanted to, well, audition you first." Darla hesitated; then, remembering Penelope's suggestion, she went on, "Can you sing a few bars of 'The Star-Spangled Banner' for me?"

Pinky frowned, his eyebrow ring twitching. "That's, like, the song they always sing just before the football game starts, right?"

"Yes, that's the one. The national anthem. You know, the one that begins—"

"*O say can you see, by the dawn's early light . . .* ?"

A bell-like tenor belted out of the young man's mouth, stunning Darla into silence. As she listened in growing amazement, Pinky sang a flawless a cappella version of the anthem, pink chin braids bobbing rhythmically as he hit every note. He finished a few moments later with, "*and the home of the brave*," drawing a burst of applause from James and his customers, who had stopped on their way to check out at the register to listen along with Darla.

"Dude! That was, like, totally sick!"

Those words came from Robert, who was hurrying down the stairs. "I told the boss lady you were, you know, really good."

Darla gave an enthusiastic nod of agreement. "Robert was right. You are wonderful!"

Pinky shrugged, the rosy braid atop his head slipping down over his face. "Yeah, I guess," was his modest reply before he repeated, "So, are we hired?"

"Most definitely," Darla declared and reached beneath the counter for her clipboard. "Let's fill out the agreement, and I'll write you a check for the down payment."

A few minutes later, all the paperwork settled, Darla smiled in satisfaction as she re-checked the *Arrange for a band* line item on her list. *Johnny Mack's cancellation might well turn out to have been a blessing in disguise*, she told herself. Meanwhile, Robert and Pinky went upstairs to the coffee lounge to celebrate the gig. First, however, the latter had signed an autograph for the awestruck boy who'd overheard Pinky's *American Idol* moment.

"Dad, Dad, I want to join the school chorus this year," she heard the boy exclaiming as he and his father headed out the door with a bag of books.

In fact, the only one who hadn't appeared impressed by the lead singer's performance was a certain oversized feline.

Midway through Pinky's performance, Darla had glimpsed from the corner of her eye a black shadow slinking away from the beanbag and heading toward the travel section. Nap time obviously took precedence over the arts, at least in Hamlet's case.

On the other hand, the impromptu musical performance had seemingly met with James's approval. He was smiling as he rearranged the shopping bags and then turned to Darla.

"As you know, I am quite the patron of the arts."

Darla nodded, aware that her manager also sat on the board for a small musical theater group.

James went on, "I have attended every major musical production that has opened in this city for the past thirty years. Yet I have to say that this Pinky person is perhaps the finest tenor I have had the privilege to hear . . . with the exceptions, of course, of Placido, José, and Luciano."

"He was fabulous, wasn't he?" she agreed. "You know, James, after all this hard work, it seems that things have finally come together. Not only do we have a talented singer on board, but I was able to get the rest of the Perky's money, so all our sponsors have paid up."

"Prodigious job, Darla. Now, let us just hope that we can get through the next few days without any more drama and have an enjoyable block party."

FIVE

"ROBERT," DARLA CALLED IN A WARNING TONE THE NEXT morning, "you know the rules about Roma. She's allowed in the store, but only if she's on a leash or you're holding her."

"Sorry, Ms. P.!"

Sounding a bit out of breath, the youth rushed down the stairs in the direction of the sales counter where Darla was powering up the register for the start of another business day. "I had her leash hooked to one of the bistro chairs. She must have, you know, figured out how to untie it. And then she wouldn't come when I called, so I've been chasing her."

As proof of that last, a small white and gray blur that was a ten-pound Italian greyhound came flying over to where Darla stood. Smiling despite herself, Darla promptly dropped to one knee and gave the tiny canine a hug.

"What a bad little girl, running off from Robert like that," she told the pup, laughing as she tried without luck to avoid Roma's long pink tongue frantically washing over her face. Then, with a glance at the children's section, she went on, "Look, Hamlet, here's your favorite dog friend. Why don't you say good morning?"

From his spot on the green beanbag in the kids' story area, Hamlet opened one green eye at Darla's announcement and let loose a soft hiss.

The sound was enough to distract Roma from her spa duties. With a pleased little yip, she promptly wriggled free of Darla's grasp. Rose-shaped ears tucked tightly to her tiny head in racing mode, she turned and bolted in Hamlet's direction, leash flapping behind her.

Robert rushed after her. "Sorry, again, Ms. P.," he called over his shoulder. "I think she's, you know, just excited to see everyone."

Hamlet, however, did not share that same sentiment. As Roma skittered to a stop before him, Hamlet sprang up and clambered to the highest point of the beanbag, staring her down like a panther encountering a wolf cub.

Roma yipped again and with one tiny paw tentatively touched the cat's squishy refuge. This time, Hamlet's answering hiss sounded like an oversized tire rapidly losing air, and he raised a paw, as well. But rather than a delicate canine foot, his was a large, fluffy mitt complete with unsheathed claws.

"Hey, little goth bro," Robert lightly scolded Hamlet as he caught hold of Roma's leash and scooped her up again. "All Roma wanted to do was say hi. She's smaller than you, so, you know, be nice."

To make up for the rebuke, he leaned over and gave Hamlet a swift scritch under the chin. The gesture apparently mollified the cat, for he settled down upon the beanbag, paws curled to his chest, though he kept a watchful eye on the tiny hound that Robert held. For her part, Roma's long pink tongue lolled out in a wide doggie grin that seemed to say, *I won that round, cat!*

Darla gave her head a rueful shake. "I have to say, I admire Hamlet's restraint. It can't be easy for him, putting up with a pesky little dog after all these years of being the four-footed boss around here."

Robert grinned. "I think Hamlet's just putting on a show for us. I think deep down he really likes having a buddy."

"Right. And George King secretly wants to be besties with me," she said with an answering chuckle.

While Robert hurried back upstairs, Roma safely tucked beneath one arm, Darla returned to her opening routine. Despite a few lingering worries about the block party on Friday, she had started the morning in a hopeful mood. She had a final get-together with Penelope scheduled for that afternoon, but otherwise she was looking forward to a relatively quiet day.

Which expectation was, she knew, an open invitation to a major smackdown from the Fates. Last thing they needed was for Penelope's giant pinwheels to go astray, or her dancers to all come down with a nasty twenty-four-hour bug.

Fortunately, the rest of the morning proceeded smoothly. It was just before noon, while Robert was still busy upstairs cleaning up after the morning coffee rush and James had not yet arrived for his shift, when an unexpected customer dropped in.

"Livvy, what brings you by?" Darla greeted her. The young woman had only been by the bookstore twice before during Darla's tenure as owner, so her appearance there was a surprise. Maybe the coffee business was slow enough that she needed a distracting book during the lulls.

Then another thought occurred to her. *Please don't be coming to get your vendor fee back because George changed his mind again*, she thought in sudden dismay. She'd already deposited the check, and the sum was already earmarked for the pinwheel vendor.

Fortunately, Livvy didn't appear to be on any sort of recovery mission. Moving as silently as Hamlet in her black yoga pants and a long, pale blue embroidered smock that appeared to be vintage, the woman joined her at the register. As always, she appeared not to have glanced in the mirror before she went out, for her dark hair was caught up in a messy bun, the slash of pink lipstick she wore was decidedly crooked, and her short pink nails were decidedly chipped.

"Hi, Darla," Livvy returned her greeting, smiling as she glanced about the store. "I'm glad I caught you while it's quiet. I'm on my way to pick up lunch for me and Georgie at the deli, but while I have a minute I wanted to see if you could special order something for me. I tried to buy it online, but I think it's out of print."

Relieved that this wasn't related to the block party, Darla nodded and went over to her computer. "I'll give it a shot. What's the title and author?"

Livvy dug into the shapeless red linen hobo bag slung across her flat chest and pulled out a torn-off slip of notebook paper. "The book is called *The Medicine Woman's Guide to Herbal Remedies*."

"Sounds interesting," Darla said as she typed that title and the author's name Livvy gave her into one of her book search sites. Within moments, she had some hits.

"Last edition was published in 1977," she confirmed after scrolling through the handful of results. "You're right, the book is out of print and it's pretty much a collectible now. But it does look like a used copy or two is out there on the secondary market. James is our rare and collectible guru. Do you want him to scout around and see what kind of deal he can get you?"

At Livvy's swift nod, she added, "But just to warn you, the prices I'm seeing start at around two hundred fifty dollars. Before I send James out looking, I need to make sure first that you're willing to pay that kind of money for it."

"I'll pay anything!"

The vehemence in her tone made Darla widen her eyes. She'd seen avid collectors before, but they were rarely that overt in showing interest in a particular object lest someone hike a price on them. Livvy's reaction was like someone tossing out a thousand-dollar bid for an item when the auctioneer's opening was only fifty bucks.

Noticing Darla's reaction, the young woman promptly tried to make amends.

"I'm sorry, Darla, I didn't mean to raise my voice like that. But, yes, I really need that book, no matter what it costs."

She hesitated, brushing back straggling strands of

outgrown bangs from her face and looking like she was debating saying more.

Then, taking a deep breath, the woman went on, "It's not a state secret or anything, so I might as well tell you. You see, I have RA—rheumatoid arthritis—and traditional medicine isn't helping me much anymore. I was already selling herbal products at the store, mostly for cooking, but I've been doing a lot of research into herbal cures to get some relief for my symptoms. You know, the old self-medicating thing. I read at one of the online RA forums that this book has some really good home remedies."

"Oh, Livvy, I'm so sorry," Darla softly exclaimed. "One of my friends back in Dallas has that, and I know she's always up and down about how she is feeling."

"Actually, I've gotten some relief so far from my own concoctions, though Georgie tells me it's all in my head. But I'm still pretty much an amateur at this whole herb thing, so I need a solid reference book."

"So, do you make herbal teas or tinctures or something?" Darla asked, curious.

Livvy smiled again and whipped out a red vapor pen like the one her husband had used the day before.

"Teas are old-school. I'm turning all those old recipes into e-juice."

"E-juice?"

"That's what the liquid—actually, it's oil—is inside these vape pens. Most people use juice that has nicotine in it, since they're trying to give up regular cigarettes. I make my own, put my herbs into oil, and let them steep until I've got a strong mix. And then I smoke it."

She started to raise the vapor pen to her lips and then

paused. "You don't mind, do you? It's not really smoke; it's just water vapor that smells like herbs."

"No worries. Penelope uses her vapor pen here in the store all the time."

"Penelope Winston?"

She grimaced a little, and Darla gave her a quizzical look. Livvy shrugged in return. "She and I go back," was her cryptic explanation. And from her sour look, apparently "back" wasn't a pleasant place. Darla's curiosity was piqued. Livvy wasn't young enough to have attended Penelope's studio, so it couldn't be a student/teacher clash. But if they'd crossed paths here in the neighborhood, it was more than possible that she and the crass-spoken dance instructor had managed somehow to butt heads.

Reminding herself it was none of her business, Darla changed the subject. "I guess those vapor pens are quite the trend here in the neighborhood. And I think that everyone I've seen has this exact same model."

"Yeah, it's top-of-the-line if you're on a budget," Livvy said through a cloud of woodsy-smelling mist, waving the pen in demonstration like a shopping channel hostess. "Easy to clean and fill, nice finish, not too lightweight and not too heavy. What kind do you have?"

"Me?" Darla gave an amused snort. "Sorry, nonsmoker here."

"Really? I assumed . . . Oh, never mind," Livvy cut herself short. "But if you decide you want one to use for something besides, um, nicotine, the cheapest place to go is Bill's Books and Stuff. At the price he sells them, he must have bought a truckload of this style. That's where all the kids get theirs."

Now it was Darla's turn to grimace. "Bill's Books and Stuff?" she repeated. "You mean, Porn Shop Bill?"

The man who was nicknamed "The Not-So-Great Ape" because of his hunched form and copious carrot-hued body hair owned an adult bookstore in a rougher neighborhood a few blocks from Darla's store. Prior to coming to work at Pettistone's, a desperate Robert had worked there. He'd even rented a dismal room from his sleazy employer, only to be fired and left homeless when he defended an underage girl from one of Bill's favorite customers.

Darla had clashed with the man when Bill came to her store soon after, demanding Robert return overpayment from his final paycheck. She'd shoved cash from her own register at Bill and then thrown him out, fervently vowing as she did so never to lay eyes on the adult-bookstore owner again if she didn't have to.

Livvy apparently saw the distaste Darla didn't bother to hide, for she shook her head and smiled a bit more broadly.

"Yes, I know, he's disgusting, but sometimes you can't pass up a great deal. But whatever you do, don't buy any e-juice from him. It's probably contaminated with who knows what. There's a really nice vapor shop on Kent Avenue that Georgie goes to—" She broke off and slapped a hand over her mouth. "Georgie! I forgot! I need to get his lunch. He gets so grumpy when he doesn't eat. You'll call me if you find the book, right?"

"James will put a verbal hold on it if he finds a good deal, but we won't buy it until I get hold of you and we get the official okay back from you."

"Perfect," Livvy agreed, trotting off toward the door. "I'll see you Friday at the block party."

She gave a quick nod to James, who was entering as she was rushing past. While the string of bells on the door jingled after her as she shut the door again, James inquired, "A new customer?"

"That's Livvy King. She's the wife of our good friend George from Perky's."

Which reminded her that they'd not yet tried the Kona Blue Party blend of coffee she'd bought yesterday. *Note to self—have Robert brew it up before we shut down for the night.* The youth was working a split shift that day, so he would be back again late in the afternoon when they'd have time to experiment.

James, meanwhile, was nodding. "Ah, yes. I hope she was not here to terrorize you on her husband's behalf."

"Not at all. She's Good Cop to George's Bad Cop," Darla said with a wry smile. "And, actually, she was here as a customer. She's got an out-of-print book she wants us to find for her. I'll email you the details."

"Fine."

James pulled out his travel mug from his leather messenger bag—despite having a full coffee bar and barista at his disposal, he preferred to brew his own coffee at home—and set it on the counter. "Anything else specific for this afternoon?"

Darla shook her head. "Everything is status quo for the rest of the day . . . Oh, except that I have to run out around four to Penelope's studio for a few minutes. I need to leave her a couple of checks, plus we're doing a final scheduling of the dance routines. But Robert is working a split today, so he'll be here to cover while I'm out."

"I must admit, I will be glad when your block party is

over," James observed as he stashed his bag beneath the counter. "First the construction, then the coffee bar grand opening, and now a July Fourth party. Did anyone ever tell you, Darla, that you are—how shall we put it?—an over-achiever?"

"It's a curse," she agreed with a chuckle, "but I get what you're saying. And I promise, no more projects once this block party is over with."

"JAMES, I'M HEADED OVER TO PENELOPE'S STUDIO NOW," DARLA SAID A few minutes before four o'clock, picking up her purse and phone. "Robert will be here in a couple of minutes. Do you want me to bring something from the deli on the way back?"

"Actually, I will be dining with Martha this evening after we close. She has found a new Italian restaurant that specializes in Northern cuisine, so we agreed to give it a try."

"Sounds like fun," Darla agreed. "And remind Martha she'd better be at the block party on Friday, too."

Martha Washington—*no relation to the First Lady of the same name*, as that woman would laughingly tell new acquaintances—had been dating James for the past year, though it had taken James almost that long to admit their relationship was more than just friends. Part of it had to do with the age difference: Martha was in her late thirties, while James was a few years shy of seventy.

Darla originally had been a bit skeptical of James and Martha's May-December relationship, but soon enough she had determined that the pair seemed well suited despite the age difference. They had numerous shared interests—books and music and food—but even their differences were complementary. Where the ex-professor was stuffy, Martha was down-to-earth. And when he got on his helium-inflated high horse, she didn't hesitate to let a bit of air out of it.

"Meow!"

That comment came from Hamlet, who knew that purse and phone in hand meant Darla was on her way somewhere. She gave the cat a fond look but shook her head.

"Sorry, Hammy, but I'm going to the dance studio. You wouldn't like all that music and thumping around. We'll see about a walk tonight."

Leaving James to hold down the fort, she started off in the direction of Penelope's studio. She arrived to find that the afternoon class was still in progress, the dancers' silhouettes visible through the sheer white curtains spanning the broad front window. She'd been inside the Brooklyn Modern Dance Institute a couple of times in the past, so she was already familiar with the studio.

Most of the original interior had been torn down to create a single large room with custom mirrored and barred walls on two sides. An expensive sprung dance floor had been laid over the existing hardwood, covering three-quarters of the space and raising that portion of the studio by a good half foot. On the remaining walls, framed dance art—including several black-and-white photos of Penelope in her dance prime—lent inspiration to all levels of would-be ballerinas.

Darla knew that, in her office, Penelope displayed the slightly less conventional photos. A teenage Penelope riding on a camel against a backdrop of pyramids. A slightly older version of her in arabesque upon an ocean sand dune. And, Darla's favorite: Penelope wearing denim shorts and a bright green cropped blouse grinning as she climbed to the top of the mast of what appeared to be a banana boat.

Pleased at the chance to see the students in action, Darla hurried inside and took her silent seat along the far wall reserved for spectators.

Perhaps twenty students of high school age—almost all of them girls in pink tights and black leotards, though three boys in black tights and white T-shirts completed the class—moved in groups of three across the dance floor. Their graceful images were reflected in the mirrored walls to either side of them—some tall, some short, but all far more polished than any ballet class Darla had ever seen. Two of the students she recognized as the girls, Emma and Allison, whom Penelope had shooed from the coffee bar.

While Darla watched, the girls performed one short combination of steps, the boys following with a complementary routine. They danced to what Darla recognized as a piece by Tchaikovsky, which a frumpy middle-aged woman in powder blue slacks was coaxing from an old upright in the studio's far corner. Stationed not far from the piano was Penelope dressed in a dark blue leotard and matching overskirt.

Like a pint-sized drill sergeant, Penelope kept time to the piano music, shouting out a cadence and thumping the sleek black cane she clutched against the sprung wooden floor.

"And one and two and—chin up, Megan!" Penelope rasped out. "And seven and eight—Lindy, you're supposed to be a swan, not a pelican! And three and four—Josh, you're not hailing a cab. Keep those arms steady and graceful!"

Darla stifled a smile. She'd taken ballet for a semester back when she was in grade school, and Mrs. Miller had been a similar harridan in tights, regularly reducing some of the more sensitive children to tears. But as Darla recalled, quite a number of the old battle-ax's students had made the cut at regional and national dance companies. From what she'd heard, Penelope's longtime students were at a similar level.

"Stop!"

At that command, the piano abruptly fell silent, while the dancers stumbled to a swift halt in a ballet version of red light, green light. Shoving her cane into the hands of the short blond girl closest to her, Penelope strode to the center of the room and waved the students back toward the walls. Her tone imperious, she said, "Apparently, a few of you girls think you're at a school dance. Let me demonstrate once again for those of you who didn't bother watching the first time. Madame Pianist . . ."

She gestured toward the woman at the piano, then struck a willowy pose, one arm curved overhead and the other extended. The pianist ran her fingers across the keys, and a delicate stream of notes spilled across the studio. While her students watched, Penelope launched into a graceful series of pirouettes and small leaps, all but levitating above the sprung floor.

Darla watched, too, transfixed for a few magical seconds. Gone was the crude-mouthed pixie she knew, replaced by a delicate swan gliding across unseen water. *Compared with Penelope, the student dancers were pelicans, indeed,* Darla told herself.

With a final flutter of a kick, Penelope ended the combination in an arabesque, one leg extended behind her at a right angle and swanlike arms frozen in midflight.

"All right, you think you can manage it this time?" she demanded of the class, dropping the pose and snatching the cane back from her student as she strode in a quite un-swanlike manner back to her spot near the piano. "Now, line up, and let's try it again."

The class proceeded in much the same fashion for another quarter of an hour, before Penelope called a final halt.

"Dismissed," she said with one last thump of the cane. "Go cool down. And those of you who are part of the block party flash mob, be sure you're here Friday morning at ten on the dot for makeup and costume!"

While the class hurried over to the barre along one mirrored wall and began the cooldown stretches, Penelope went over to the piano for a few words with her accompanist. Then, leaving the other woman to gather her sheet music before departing, the dance instructor plucked her red vape pen from a vase atop the upright and strode in Darla's direction.

"Those kids will be the death of me," she muttered, taking a long drag on the pen and exhaling a cloud of vapor that almost obscured her face. "When I was a student, we had discipline."

She gave her cane a threatening shake, glaring in the direction of her class still gathered at the barre. "When I screwed up, Monsieur Lavoisier wasn't afraid to whack me in the leg with *his* cane. I learned to listen."

"Well, I think these days they call that child abuse, and there's a law against it," Darla reminded her with a mild smile. "Besides, I think they were pretty darned good. And you, you're brilliant. I could watch you dance all afternoon!"

Penelope dismissed the compliment with a snort of vapor, but a smile twitched momentarily on her lips, so that Darla guessed she was pleased by the praise. Then, in a calmer tone, she went on, "The girls are all set for Friday. We've got three different choreographies that we'll repeat once each, so that's six performances. That'll take us from noon until six."

"Perfect. We'll stick with the original plan, on the hour each hour," Darla agreed as she reached into her bag. "And here are those checks the committee owes you. I'm almost afraid to ask, did those pinwheels ever show up?"

"Back in the storeroom. It's amazing what you can do with a few well-placed threats," she answered with a grin. "Speaking of which, did old George ever come through with his share of the vendor fee?"

"Actually, Livvy—his wife—was the one who paid up for them. It's like Beauty and the Beast with those two," Darla observed with a wry smile. "He's king of the jerks, and she's just as nice as she can be."

"You think?"

Penelope's expression twisted into the same sour look that Livvy had worn earlier that day when speaking of the dance instructor. Darla belatedly recalled how Livvy had said she and Penelope "went back."

Her voice growing more strident, Penelope went on, "Well, Miss Livvy might play like she's all sweetness and light, but she's the one who calls the shots with George. Don't let that delicate and helpless look fool you. Believe me, Livvy King is a first-class b—"

She broke off before finishing the epithet, since a few of her younger students were in earshot. Taking a calming breath, the dance instructor finished with a G-rated version.

"—Backstabber, a first-class backstabber. Watch yourself around her."

Apparently, the "going back" thing went both ways. But when it came to the two women, Darla intended to play Switzerland. Channeling said neutrality, she hurriedly changed the subject.

"Okay, we've got the pinwheels and checks taken care of, and we're in agreement on the flash mob schedule. Anything else we should go over?"

"Nah, I think we're covered. But I tell you, Darla, after this I think I'm going to take a couple of days off. Trying to get all these kids ready for tryouts on top of teaching all the classes by myself is starting to be too much. I think I need my guy to take me on a little road trip to wind down."

"Your guy?"

Darla raised her brows, curious. Had she been right about that little incident with Doug in the bookstore, after all? Or maybe the guy in question was someone else, altogether. Either way, she was glad to know that Penelope had someone.

But instead of the coy smile that Darla expected from her, the woman's expression once again turned sour. "Yeah, my guy, and the SOB owes me. I just found out he's been seeing someone on the side."

Definitely not Doug, Darla swiftly decided. He might look like a player with the gold chains and all, but she knew he was as softhearted as they came.

Aloud, she said with a sympathetic nod, "Been there, done that, got the T-shirt," recalling a similar incident toward the end of her marriage. "But maybe a nice romantic couple of days somewhere will fix things."

"We'll see." Then the woman brightened. "Anyhow, Darla, I think our block party is going to knock off everyone's socks. And when everyone is talking about it after Friday, we'll make sure you get all the credit for everything that happened."

SIX

"ROBERT, YOU READY TO PLAY CORPORATE SPY AND TRY TO figure out what's so special about this coffee?"

Smiling, Darla shook the bag of roasted beans that she'd bought from Perky's a couple of days earlier for an outrageous price. It was about thirty minutes until opening time on Thursday morning, meaning it was just Darla, Robert, and Hamlet upstairs at the coffee bar—and, once again, Hamlet seemed overly interested in the special blend. He had leaped onto the bar top and was moving cautiously toward the bag she held. Ignoring Darla, he put out a large fluffy paw so that he was almost—but not quite—touching the sack.

Like her sister used to do on road trips when they were kids, just to start a fight, Darla thought with a shake of her head.

"Crazy cat," she murmured as she set the coffee beans down out of paw's reach. "I wonder why he's so obsessed with this bag."

"I think Hamlet's turning into a coffee expert," Robert said, chuckling. "Maybe I can teach him how to use the roaster so he can, you know, help me out."

"Sure, but who's going to teach him to be nice to the customers?"

Picking up a squirming Hamlet and setting him on the floor, Darla reached again for the bag. Only when she held it right to her nose could she make out the faint, satisfying scent of perfectly roasted coffee. She had read that a cat's sense of smell was fourteen times better than a human's; still, the hint of coffee aroma through a lined and sealed bag shouldn't be enough to send Hamlet into such a tizzy.

Moreover, what was it about Perky's blend, in particular, that raised his feline dander?

"All right, Robert, let's go about this scientifically. How about a little bean sampling first before we brew it up?"

"We can make it, you know, a cupping party, like they taught us about in barista school," Robert countered. "It's like a wine tasting, except with coffee. Hang on; I'll get the stuff."

While he rummaged behind the counter, Darla carefully unrolled the bag's sealed top edge. As she did so, a more pungent coffee aroma began spilling out, but hardly anything she thought should offend His Royal Catness's delicate nasal passages.

"All right, here we go," the teen said, setting out two small coffee cups and two spoons. Handing Darla a small silver scoop, he went on, "Measure out a scoopful into each cup. Usually you'd measure out more to do it right, but we, like, just have the one bag."

Once she'd done that, he plucked a bean from the cup nearest him and squinted at it intently.

"Full City roast," he determined, and then went on to explain, "You can tell by the deep chestnut brown color. And, see, there's hardly any oil on the bean surface."

Darla nodded, taking a bean from the other cup and studying it herself. She'd picked up enough of the coffee lingo to know Full City was the lightest of the traditional roasts. And when she drank her coffee black, it was what she preferred.

Moving over to the espresso grinder, Robert poured in his cup of beans and gave them a quick, coarse grind before dumping the now-ground coffee back into the cup. He did the same with Darla's beans, then took a glass measure and drew some steaming water. He filled each cup to a bit beneath the brim, then said, "Okay now we let it cool for a minute."

While they waited, Robert related a few more things he'd learned in regard to tastings—such as the fact that coffee was like dark beer, meaning that it was better served at room temperature. And he also explained that at a full-fledged cupping party with lots of samples, everyone spit out the coffee after tasting, just like they did with wine at a tasting.

"If you didn't, you'd be awake for, like, a week afterward," he finished with a grin.

Then he picked up a spoon. "Okay, time to try the coffee. You want to dip all the way to the bottom and get a spoonful. Then you slurp it like soup."

Feeling a bit silly, Darla followed his example and did the soup thing. After smacking her lips a moment, however, she frowned. Apparently, she wasn't a coffee connoisseur, for this particular brew wasn't knocking her socks off despite its price tag.

"What do you think, Robert?"

He frowned a little, too. "Well, it's medium body, fruity overtones . . . aroma a hint of chocolate and caramel," he intoned, sounding a sommelier.

Darla waved away his comments. "Sure, sure—but, bottom line, does this taste to you like it's worth what I paid for it?"

"You want the truth, Ms. P.? It's not bad, or anything, but our coffee is, like, one hundred percent better than this."

She gave a relieved sigh.

"Thank goodness it's not just me," she exclaimed. "I thought my taste buds were defective or something, because this reminds me of something you'd find in a diner. But how do George and Livvy get away with charging so much for this dinky bag of average coffee?"

Darla grabbed the bag and opened it up again, peering inside for the secret. Then she paused, and her eyes opened wide. "What the—?"

Dropping the bag onto the counter again, she hurried around to the back of the coffee bar and pulled out a serving tray. While Robert watched, expression puzzled, she set the tray on the counter and spread a clean towel across its surface. Then she reached for the bag of coffee again.

"Robert, I have a bad feeling I know why this coffee costs so much."

She carefully poured the bag's contents onto the towel,

then gave the tray a little shake, so that the beans spread neatly into a single layer. Using the spoon with which she'd just been slurping, she poked at the small, plastic-wrapped bundle of something distinctively leaflike that sat atop the brown mosaic of roasted coffee beans.

"Like, wow," Robert muttered, leaning in closer. "Is that what I think it is?"

Hamlet leaped back onto the counter. "*Meow*," was his opinion on the matter.

Darla shook her head. "I guess this is why Livvy kept asking me if I was sure I wanted to buy the Kona Blue Party blend. For what she was charging, I thought it was one of those handpicked coffees from some bush that only bloomed every ten years under a full moon. I never would have guessed she was dealing drugs."

"So what are we going to do?" Robert asked.

Darla reached into her pocket and pulled out her cell. "Let me ask Jake what she thinks. I want to get this settled quickly."

A few minutes later, Darla was letting in a yawning Jake, along with the usual morning regulars who mumbled their hellos before making a beeline upstairs to the coffee bar. Fortunately, she'd had the presence of mind to cover the tray with another towel and had stashed what she was already thinking of as "the evidence" outside in the brownstone's private courtyard.

"Wait, can't I grab some coffee first?" Jake protested as Darla led her to the back of the store.

"Come with me first, and then Robert will brew you up a fresh mug," Darla promised. Leaving the door between store and courtyard open so she could hear any other customers coming in, she walked over to the tray she'd left on the white wrought iron bistro table where she often ate her lunch. "I can't believe Livvy and George are dealing drugs," Darla lamented as she whipped off the towel to reveal the tray of beans with its damning bundle.

"Don't feel bad, kid," Jake told her. "A while back, the cops busted an eighty-year-old guy who was supplementing his social security by acting as a mule for some cartel. Times get tough, and people do stupid things for extra cash."

"Maybe so, but they aren't supposed to do it in my neighborhood." Frowning, Darla gave the bundle another poke with the spoon. "So is this what I think it is, marijuana?"

"No way to tell for sure unless we open it up."

So saying, the PI carefully undid the small baggie; then, clearing all the coffee beans to one side, she poured the leafy contents onto the tray. The baggie hadn't held much, perhaps a couple of tall tablespoons' worth.

"Not pot," Jake promptly declared.

Since Darla had never actually seen marijuana except for on television, she took Jake's word for it, though she asked, "How can you tell?"

"The leaf is the wrong shape and texture for cannabis," her friend explained, picking up a bit of the plant material to examine it more closely. "Also, the color is different, as is"—she paused and sniffed the leaf—"the smell. On top of that, it looks like there's more than one type of plant mixed in here."

Jake picked at more bits of dried, broken leaves and then shrugged.

"To be honest, this looks kinda like the herbs I remember

Ma tying up in cheesecloth and tossing into her soup stock, to flavor it. In fact, if I'm not mistaken, this"—she held up one bit for Darla to look at—"is actually catnip."

"Me-ROOW!"

Startled, Darla glanced toward the open door. She'd left Hamlet upstairs to hang with the morning crowd, but apparently the persnickety feline wasn't about to let anyone else take credit for his detective work. Before she could shoo him off, he came trotting out into the courtyard and leaped up onto one of the bistro chairs, big paws planted on the table's edge as he stared at Jake. She, in turn, looked over at Darla, who nodded.

"Give it a try."

Grinning, Jake held out the leafy bits toward the cat. "All right, Hammy, we need an expert's opinion here. Catnip, yes or no?"

Hamlet's whiskers twitched as he sniffed at Jake's hand. His green eyes widened and he promptly bumped his head against her fingers, then reached up an oversized paw and began batting at her.

"I think we have our answer," the PI said, brushing her fingers together to dislodge the remaining crumbles, which Hamlet promptly pounced upon.

Darla, meanwhile, gave a snort of disgust. "Catnip! At least now I know why Hamlet was so interested in the Perky's bags."

"Yeah, my guess is that we've got nothing more than your basic backyard herbs here. Along with the catnip, there may be a bit of sage or lemon balm."

Darla picked up a few crumbles of leaves and gave them a tentative sniff herself.

"Definitely some sage in there," she agreed, and then sighed. "I can't believe it. So Livvy and George were running a scam? You know, I'm not sure which is worse, thinking that they're drug dealers, or finding out that they're run-of-the-mill con artists."

"So, what do you want to do about it, kid—blow the whistle on them, or chalk it up to a learning experience and let it go?"

"I'm not just going to let it go. At a minimum, I want my money back," Darla declared, her redhead's temper beginning to simmer. "After that, I'm not sure, maybe talk to Reese about it. You want to go with me to confront them?"

Jake shook her curly head.

"Sorry, I'm tied up today," she replied, tone apologetic. "I've got to do a little work for a client, and it might take most of the day. But if you're going to go over there, at least take James as your backup."

"He's not in until after lunch again today," Darla grumbled, scraping the herbs back into the baggie for safekeeping again, "but I guess things can wait until he gets here."

She glanced down at Hamlet, who was busy rolling about in the catnip crumbs Jake had dropped on the brick patio. Apparently Mr. Flying High Kitty wasn't nearly as distressed over the situation as she was!

Jake followed her gaze and grinned a little at the usually reserved cat's antics.

"Uh-oh. Looks like someone has a new vice. Better watch it, Hammy, or you'll end up in kitty rehab." To Darla, she said, "All right, kid, I'm off to get my coffee and then I'm out of here. Let me know how it goes."

Halfway through the door, however, the PI halted and turned.

"I know you're pretty ticked right now, but keep in mind that scammers don't take kindly to being called on their scams. Maybe you should wait and talk to Reese first. It could get a little nasty if you and James just go barging in there."

Darla shook her head. "I want to shut this little operation down before tomorrow. What if they try selling this stuff at the block party? If word gets around and they get busted for fraud, it could hurt a lot of the neighborhood businesses, not just them."

"I understand your concern; I just don't want you getting hurt. If you insist on doing this, at least have Reese's number on speed dial, just in case."

"I'll do that. Or," she added with a small smile, "I could bring Hamlet with me for backup to James's backup. Worst case, I can send him running for help like Lassie."

That last drew an eye roll from Jake, who gave her a wave good-bye and headed back inside the shop. Darla finished repackaging the coffee beans and faux drugs back into the bag and grabbed up the tray.

"At least they could have used a better grade of coffee," she muttered. "Come on, Hammy, the party's over. Get back inside and sleep it off."

"*Meow-rumph*," the cat replied, his tone decidedly peeved. Even so, he scrambled to his feet and trotted after her.

Once back at the register, Darla stuck the offending bag in her purse, while Hamlet made a beeline for the green beanbag chair. Darn straight she was going to get her money back from the Kings, she told herself, still fuming. As for taking any further steps, she'd decide upon that later, once she had her cash in hand again. But no matter how things went down, no way was she going to let a pair of coffee con artists ruin her Fourth of July block party.

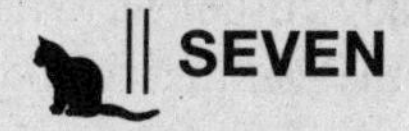

SEVEN

"ACTUALLY, SWINDLING THE ILLEGAL PHARMACEUTICAL-using public is a time-honored practice," James assured Darla that afternoon soon after he arrived for his shift and she'd gotten him up to speed on the situation.

Though appropriately appalled at the Kings' tactics, the ex-professor also seemed a bit amused by the entire situation . . . much to Darla's dismay.

"I recall a friend of mine back in the early seventies who once placed an advertisement in the back of the local street newspaper," James told her. "He offered 'lids'—which was the slang term for small baggies of marijuana—for ten dollars each, mail order only, to his post office box. Considering that this amount was below the going rate, he received numerous responses."

"Pretty trusting, weren't they, mailing money to a PO box to buy something illegal?" Darla wryly observed.

James nodded. "It was, as they say, a kinder and gentler time."

"Right. So, don't tell me . . . these folks sent in their money and got zilch back."

"On the contrary. My friend mailed a lid to each and every customer, per the terms of his advertisement. What he did not spell out in advance was the fact that the lids he was supplying were literal ones."

Darla gave a disbelieving laugh. "You mean, like jar lids?"

"More specifically, they were the plastic snap-on covers designed for cat food cans. He had found a discarded case of them behind a Dumpster, and those are what he sent. Of course, his customers could hardly complain that they had been swindled, and so he had a tidy revenue stream going for several months."

James paused, his expression wry. "Unfortunately, one disgruntled customer finally traced him to his post office box and had a rather nasty 'come to Jesus' moment with the lad. Let us just say that, once he was discharged from the hospital, my friend decided to get out of the mail-order business permanently."

"All right, James, I get the point of your story—I think. But, don't worry. I don't plan on administering any beat downs."

"But are you sure you wish to do this? As Jake pointed out, those of questionable ethics often react poorly when called on it."

"I'm sure. Let's wait until after four, so they'll be closed.

I wouldn't want to confront them in front of customers, just in case it does get ugly."

THE AFTERNOON SPED ON BY, SO THAT IT WAS ALREADY A FEW MINUTES after four when Darla stopped what she was doing.

"Ready to head over to Perky's?" she asked her manager. At his nod, she added to Robert, "James and I are going to resolve that Kona Blue Party issue from this morning. Do you mind covering for a little bit? We'll be back in less than an hour, and Hamlet will help you keep an eye on things."

Hearing his name, the cat yawned and stretched from his post atop the front counter. His catnip high had long since worn off, but he'd made up for it with extra naps throughout the day. Now he scrambled to his feet, looking ready for action.

"Sorry, Hammy," she told him. "I checked outside, and it's too hot for you to go walking this afternoon, after all. You're going to have to play bodyguard another time."

The cat gave her a sour look but settled back onto the counter again. Then, with Robert's assurances that all would be well in their absence, Darla and James headed out.

Traffic, both pedestrian and auto, was relatively light on this day before a major holiday. Most of the shops already flaunted festive red, white, and blue in preparation for the block party—which was appropriate, given that the day had turned out to be hot as a firecracker, Darla thought with an inner sigh.

If anything, the afternoon had grown steamier since lunch, so that even in her cropped pants and polo shirt she now felt overly dressed for the weather. James's only concession to the heat, however, was to roll up the sleeves of his crisp white dress shirt and to dab at his forehead with his starched handkerchief. And since she had never once seen him break a sweat before, she knew that the day was hot, indeed.

With luck, maybe the weather gods will shave a few degrees off the temperature tomorrow, she thought with a hopeful sigh.

"So, how was the new Italian place last night?" Darla asked James as they waited on a passing car to cross the street.

"The chef is actually from Brooklyn but apparently attended culinary school in the Piemonte region for a time," he replied. "The specialty last night was a prosciutto Alfredo dish that was more than adequate. As for the wine list, it was a bit lacking, but their reasonable prices made up for the stingy selection."

"And what about Martha? Did she think the food stacked up to Saucy's menu?" Darla asked as they stepped off the curb, naming a local Italian place that she knew was Martha's favorite.

"She appeared to enjoy her meal, as well."

His tone was uncharacteristically glum, and she shot him a concerned look. "James, what's wrong? Martha didn't break up with you, did she?"

"I fear it is even worse. She indicated—quite subtly, of course—that she wishes to take our relationship to the next level. I believe she wishes to cohabitate with me."

"You mean, move in with you? I have to say, that doesn't really sound like her."

Darla had been to Martha's apartment once before, and had been more than a bit impressed with how the woman had transformed what obviously had been a nondescript one-bedroom walk-up into a charming loftlike apartment. With ample use of lace, sheer curtains, and pastels, the place reflected both Martha's tea-and-crumpets heritage, courtesy of her English mother, and her father's magnolia-scented Georgia roots.

You don't have to say it; I know it's girlie, Martha had confided to Darla with a rueful laugh, *but it's me, deep down. And, I can't imagine living anywhere else.*

James, meanwhile, was shaking his head.

"During the course of our meal, Martha mentioned the downside of living alone in the city. She also said that if her situation does not change in the foreseeable future, she might be forced to bring in a cat to keep her company. I do not know about you, but I cannot see any other way to interpret her remarks."

"Don't panic, James," Darla assured him. "We single gals all go through that stage on a regular basis. I doubt she's trying to rope you into living together. If anything, she's probably worried you might want to move in with her so she can take care of you in your dotage."

As she'd hoped, the friendly insult was enough to draw a smile from the ex-professor.

"Touché. I will take your advice, Darla, and try not to dwell on the subject."

By now, they had reached Perky's. The gate to the steps leading down to the coffee shop was shut, and a "Closed" sign hung on the door. Darla glanced at her watch. Four thirty. The Kings must already be back home.

"Let's try their apartment," Darla said, her insides suddenly a bit shaky now that the confrontation actually was at hand.

"Perhaps I should ease into the conversation by mentioning the book Mrs. King asked us to order," James suggested, obviously sensing her discomfort. "I called her back last night with my best price, and she gave me her credit card number."

Darla bit her lip and shook her head. "No, according to Livvy, George doesn't think much of her herbal treatments. For all we know, that might set him off. Let's just get down to business and let them know we're onto their scheme."

To the side of the glass entry door were mounted three buzzers, each labeled with a different name. "King" was neatly printed under apartment number one. With a final glance at Darla, who nodded, James pressed the bell.

"Yeah," came a mechanically distorted voice that Darla recognized as belonging to George.

"Hi, it's Darla and James from the bookstore," she replied through the nearby intercom. "Can we talk with you for a minute? It's kind of important."

For a moment she thought he was going to ignore their request. Then the door buzzer sounded.

"Quick, before he changes his mind," Darla said to James, and grabbed the handle.

The tiny entry hall was a pleasant twin to Darla's own brownstone, the walls paneled below and painted a neutral sand above. A narrow occasional table hugged one wall and held a lighted ginger jar lamp whose cheerful lavender shade coordinated nicely with its darker purple belly.

Apartment number one was just a few steps away, giving George a commute as short as hers to the bookstore.

James knocked, and the door opened a crack. George stuck his florid face out, his expression one of annoyance. "Is this about that stupid block party again? I thought Livvy took care of it."

"Actually, this has to do with coffee," Darla replied.

George's expression morphed from annoyance to suspicion, but to Darla's relief he pulled the door open.

"You can sit over there," he said, gesturing them toward an overstuffed love seat strewn with vintage crewelwork pillows.

Darla took her seat beside James and spared a look at the apartment's main room. Livvy's influence was apparent here, too . . . a little modern décor enlivened by quirky "found" and vintage touches. Except for the empty pizza box on the small dining table in the corner, the apartment was neatly maintained.

"Yeah, so whaddaya want?" George demanded, spinning a ladder-back chair around and straddling it. Someone else might have pulled off the clichéd move, but not George. With his puffy features and pale, hairy legs poking out from a pair of baggy blue cargo shorts, he reminded Darla of a certain doughy advertising icon stuck behind bars.

He gave them an expectant frown and added, "If yer looking for advice running yer coffee bar, you come to the wrong place. I ain't helping the competition."

"Actually, this involves both you and Mrs. King," James smoothly interjected. "Is she available?"

"Nah, she's off gallivanting around somewhere." Then,

squinting in James's direction, George asked, "Now, who are you again? I don't know that many black guys."

"James is my store manager," Darla told him, praying that the Coffee King wasn't about to spout off with any inappropriate remarks.

George gave a braying laugh. "I thought that cat of yers was in charge."

"He thinks he is," James said with a polite smile, "but I can assure you that is my job."

"Yeah, yeah, that was just a joke. So, why are you guys here?"

Darla took a steadying breath and reached into her shoulder bag. Maybe it was just as well that Livvy wasn't around. Better that the odds be two against one . . . even if the "one" was George.

She pulled out the sack of roasted beans, plopping it onto the glass-topped coffee table before her. Then she summoned a coolly pleasant smile to match James's and said, "Here's the deal, George. We want to talk to you about Kona Blue Party."

George squinted a moment at the bag, as if uncertain what it was. Then his coffee bean eyes hardened, and he glanced back up at them. "So, you don't like the coffee? What, yer looking for a refund?"

"You know darned well we're not talking about the coffee. We're talking about the little prize included with every purchase," Darla shot back, plucking the rolled baggie from the sack and tossing it onto the table beside it. "So, come clean, George. What's the deal here?"

"You guys ain't supposed to buy that stuff," he protested. "We only sell it to them kids that vape."

"Well, I didn't know the rules. I heard from several of my customers that your best product was Kona Blue Party, so I shelled out a hundred and fifty dollars for what I thought was some exotic coffee. What I got was a cheap Full City roast and a baggie of catnip."

"Hey, hey, don't get yer panties in a twist," George protested. "So we make a little money on the side with the stuff. Nothing in there is illegal."

"Yes, but I surmise that your customer base is under the impression that it is, that they are purchasing illicit drugs," James interjected. "It appears you are selling common kitchen herbs, which you are representing as marijuana or some similar intoxicating drug."

"Fine. So sue me."

"I'm not going to sue you, but I might have to discuss this with my friend, Detective Reese of the NYPD," Darla countered, pulling out what she hoped was her figurative ace in the hole.

She must have trumped him, for some of George's bluster seeped away at that. Then, with a snort of disgust, he lowered his voice and said, "Look, this don't have to get out, you know what I mean? Besides, it ain't my fault if them kids is too dumb to know the difference."

"That might be true," James agreed, "but the bottom line here, as they say, is that even if you are not peddling illegal pharmaceuticals, you still are perpetrating a fraud."

"Nah, it's not like that. Livvy just did it as a joke, at first." Then, when James gave him an encouraging nod, he went on, "Some Asian kid came in a couple months back asking her if she had some herbs he could vape that would get him—what did he call it?—'happy.' He never says in words what he wants, but she knew what he meant. So she tells him no."

He shook his head.

"So then, the same kid, he comes back a coupla days later. Livvy, she tells him no again, but he thinks she's just blowin' him off. And he keeps coming back, askin'."

"So she finally did something to get rid of him," Darla guessed, feeling sudden sympathy for the woman. She'd had a customer or two herself who wouldn't take no for an answer.

Of course, none of that excused the fact that Livvy had ripped Darla off for more than a hundred dollars.

George nodded and leaned forward against the chair rails, immersed now in his account.

"So now it's, what, four times the idiot comes back," he went on, "so Livvy, she decides to fix him for good. She tells him she has a special blend she'll sell him under the table, but that he has to swear not to tell anyone where he bought it. So she mixes him up a little baggie of catnip with some sage and hops, tosses in a little tea. And then she charges him a hundred and fifty bucks. He paid it, and you know what? He came back the next week saying it was the best high he ever had, and he wants to buy more."

"Seriously? He got high vaping that?"

The man shrugged. "You got your caffeine in the tea to give a buzz, the hops gets you going, too, and the other stuff relaxes you. So, yeah, you vape it and you feel a little something. But mostly, it's—whaddaya call it?—the Placido effect."

"I believe you mean placebo effect," James corrected

him. "One has an expectation of reacting a certain way to a certain substance, and so one does."

"Yeah, that." George nodded. "It's like thinking you're getting drunk off them nonalcoholic beers. It's all in your head. Anyhow, instead of staying quiet, that idiot kid tells all his friends. So we figured, what the heck? Them kids got money to burn, and it's not gonna hurt them. So we made up a name for the stuff, and after a while, we had four, five kids a day looking for the Kona Blue Party."

"Good Lord," James muttered, "*Breaking Bad* comes to Brooklyn."

George, meanwhile, reassumed his belligerent air. "Hey, like I told you, it wasn't nothing illegal. Besides, I didn't sell nothing to no one. It was Livvy who did all that."

Right, blame the wife, Darla thought with a snort. *You just count the money.*

Aloud, she said, "It's happening under your roof, so you're equally responsible, George. But maybe if you swear to me that Perky's Coffee Shop is officially out of the Kona Blue Party business, we can forget this conversation. Assuming you give me my money back, that is," she added when she noted the little spark of triumph in his tiny eyes.

George shoved himself off the chair and stalked over to the dining table, where he picked up a bulging wallet. He pulled out a handful of bills and strode back to where she and James sat.

"Fine, here ya go," he exclaimed, tossing the money onto the table.

While a startled Darla gathered the scattered bills,

George reached stubby hands for the coffee and bag of herbs that she'd left unattended. James, however, was faster than the other man.

"I believe we will hang on to this," James said as he got to his feet, coffee beans and baggie safely in hand. With a glance at Darla, who had shoved the cash, uncounted, into her bag, he added, "It seems we have overstayed our welcome, Darla."

For a moment, she feared that George might wrestle her store manager for the bag of coffee. But to her relief, he merely blustered, "Yeah, you have. Now why don't ya get outta here?"

Agreeing that discretion was the better part of valor, at least when dealing with the King of Coffee, Darla hurriedly stood and followed James to the door. It wasn't until they were safely on the sidewalk outside the brownstone that she heaved a sigh.

"Thank goodness that's over."

"I second that," James agreed in ironic understatement, handing back Darla her bag of Kona Blue Party as they started down the sidewalk. "You might wish to keep this as proof of the Kings' business sideline, just in case Mr. King attempts to claim later that you somehow took advantage of his wife in a business deal."

"Do you really think George would do that? I mean, he's the one in the wrong, not us."

"Yes, but in my experience, people like him 'do not go gentle into that good night,' as Dylan Thomas would say. I suggest that we keep our distance from Mr. King for the foreseeable future. He is—how should I put it?—a live wire."

"What about tomorrow at the block party? Do you think he'll try to cause any trouble?"

"Actually, he should be worrying that we will cause the trouble by reporting his fraud to the proper authorities."

Darla considered that while they waited on traffic. "You're right," she said as they crossed the street, "but even though George is a jerk, and he and Livvy are ripping kids off, I'd feel kind of bad turning them in."

"Then I have a suggestion," James told her. "Remember that Detective Reese should be at the block party tomorrow. Perhaps you should ask him what he thinks . . . without naming any names, of course."

James's proposal made sense, and Darla nodded.

"I guess that's as good a plan as any. If I can get a private minute with him, I'll ask him. But, I tell you, James," she finished with a grimace, "I'll be glad when this block party is over, and the only drama I need to worry about is on the theater reference shelf at Pettistone's."

EIGHT

"OH, DARLA, THIS REMINDS ME OF MY CHILDHOOD," MARY Ann Plinski exclaimed as a dozen children under the age of ten each came trotting down the middle of the street gripping a tablespoon upon which was balanced a red- or blue-dyed hard-boiled egg.

The Plinskis, Darla's septuagenarian neighbor and her brother, owned Bygone Days Antiques and Collectibles. Their store and apartments were housed next door to Darla's in the connecting brownstone. Robert lived in the garden apartment under the shop, receiving a cut-rate rent in return for doing odd jobs for the elderly pair.

"First a gunnysack race, and now an egg-and-spoon relay," Mary Ann continued to gush from her chair beside Darla and Hamlet, under one of the street canopies. "My goodness, I haven't seen this sort of old-fashioned fun in years. What a marvelous way to spend the Fourth of July!"

"You haven't seen everything yet," Darla warned her with a grin. "Next up, we're going to have a genuine pie-eating contest for the grown-ups. I hope you like blueberry."

The old woman gave an approving chuckle that echoed Darla's own high spirits. In fact, so far the block party was a smashing success—at least, in Darla's estimation. Beginning at eight thirty that morning, the police had begun closing down the two-block area where the event was to be held. Darla had been ready for them, already dressed in red denim capris and a vintage red, white, and blue tie-dyed shirt that she'd found in a thrift store. To beat the heat, she'd braided her auburn hair into twin pigtails that she'd looped back over themselves, so that she looked like she was wearing oversized red earrings. *A bit hokey*, she'd told her mirrored reflection, *but perfect for a July Fourth event.*

The decorating committee had promptly gone to work hanging streamers, bunting, and flags from every conceivable pole and awning, while the volunteers from TAMA began putting up a series of canopies down the center of Darla's block. By the time the block party officially began at ten, almost two dozen people were already milling about. By noon, when the competing aromas of fresh doughnuts and Thai food and smoked deli sandwiches hung heavily in the warm air, almost a hundred people were strolling the street and sidewalks.

Everything was going so smoothly that Darla was almost willing to forget yesterday's unpleasantness with

George over the Kona Blue Party coffee-that-wasn't and not bother Reese about it. That was, assuming the detective showed up as promised.

Resisting the temptation to call and find out where Reese was, Darla instead peered over to see how the bookstore's booth was faring. As planned, shop owners along either side of the street had set up tables or booths to showcase their wares and services. Darla's own offering (overseen by James and Robert at the bottom of the shop steps) was a stack of remainders and advance reader copies to give away, along with coupons for future visits. They also were handing out discounted cups of iced coffee to help beat the heat and promote the coffee bar. Roma, in a star-spangled harness and lead tied to the bannister, delivered the canine cuteness factor, sitting prettily on the shady stoop next to a big red bowl of water.

In addition to the tables that most of the retailers had set up outside their respective establishments, even more activities were taking place under the canopies that Hank and his crew had raised. One area served as public relations, where the various retailers were taking turns handing out fliers from the participating shops and restaurants. In another, the two owners of Child's Play, an upscale toy store, were teaching children's crafts to a handful of eager grade-schoolers. The final canopy, where Darla and Mary Ann were currently sitting, had been designated a rest area with tables and chairs. This was where the event-goers could relax with their food, or simply kick back with a cold drink.

The next street down, however, was where the action

was. Darla and Hamlet had just come back from watching another exhibition by TAMA. Rather than more canopies, several of the dojo's older students had assembled a makeshift ring of heavy red tumbling mats arranged in a large square in the middle of the street. One of Hank and Hal's classes was scheduled to give a demonstration of martial arts skills every hour. This time, it had been the advanced karate students demonstrating falls and throws. Hamlet had watched in particular fascination . . . *no doubt remembering his glory days as the Karate Kitty,* Darla thought in amusement.

"You've done a wonderful job with the block party," Mary Ann gushed on, clapping as another round of spoon-toting kids raced past them—much to the disdain of Hamlet, who flopped from his seated position onto his belly and refused to watch. "And what a clever idea you had for my booth, offering free appraisals. Brother has already looked at five different items, plus we're almost sold out of all the vintage Independence Day memorabilia we had."

She paused and waved at her sibling seated at a bunting-draped table across from them. Mr. Plinski—whose first name Darla still didn't know; he was only ever referred to as "Brother" or "Mr. Plinski"—waved a feeble hand back. He wore one of those bucket-style fishing hats like Henry Fonda in *On Golden Pond*, which, combined with his white long-sleeved shirt topped by red suspenders, looked appropriately summery. Mary Ann, in a vintage red and white striped shirtdress, coordinated quite nicely, Darla thought.

Then the old woman gave Darla a puzzled look. "But I do have to wonder, my dear, where you found those, er, interesting young men dressed in black playing the music."

"Great band, aren't they?" Jake exclaimed from behind them and slipped into the seat next to Mary Ann. Like the rest of them, she was dressed in patriotic hues: blue walking shorts, a white boatneck top, and a chunky necklace of red, white, and blue stars and beads.

Jake nodded her curly head in time to the beat, which was pulsating from the block beyond where a makeshift stage was set midway between the intersection and the martial arts ring. "These guys are awesome. Robert said they're called the Shrieking Kids, or something like that?"

"The Screaming Babies," Darla corrected her with a sigh. "Robert found them. They agreed to play mainstream music, but it sounds like they've reverted to their original material."

Darla had had her first inkling of a musical rebellion when Pinky and his fellow Babies had shown up at noon. All the young men had their black eyeliner and black nail polish in place, and were wearing all black instead of the patriotic red, white, and blue that she'd suggested. Still, they'd started off their set with a credible version of Springsteen's "Born in the U.S.A.," followed by a couple of vintage Beatles hits. Darla had relaxed, certain that the Babies were firmly with the program. She'd even gotten a big thumbs-up and a quick riff on the air guitar from Steve as she passed by his restaurant's booth.

But about thirty minutes after their first number, the band launched into a few verses of a song she didn't recognize. Heavy on bass and an electric organ, it featured

Pinky giving a raspy croon to lyrics that, if one listened carefully, were dark to the point of suicidal.

Thankfully, the band had taken a break right afterward. Darla had been busy helping Doug hand out doughnut hole samples at the time, so she hadn't been able to check in with Pinky to make sure that the last song was an aberration. It wasn't until the band started in on their second set that Darla realized that she'd been sold a gothic pig in a nice black satin poke. Not that the Babies weren't talented; even though the music wasn't to Darla's taste, she could still recognize their skill. But their moody, sonorous music wasn't exactly providing the upbeat background sound she had hoped for.

Jake, meanwhile, was still raving.

"Seriously, they sound like the Cure's little brothers," she proclaimed. Darla wasn't surprised that Jake liked the music; her friend had a known preference for dark heavy metal groups, though these guys were more emo than thrasher. "I can't believe they're not under contract somewhere. I wonder if they have any CDs for sale."

"Actually, I think they do," Darla told her. Then, glancing at her watch, she went on, "Say, Reese said he was going to stop by this afternoon, and maybe even bring a friend. Have you seen him?"

"Not yet. But I've been pretty busy at my own booth. This is the first break I've had." Jake paused and chuckled. "I set up that whole ten-minute-free-consultation thing kind of as a joke, but you wouldn't believe how many people have stopped by for advice. Heck, I might even get some actual clients out of this."

Darla smiled, too. She could easily see Jake's booth

from her vantage point beneath the canopy. It was a dozen feet away from the Pettistone's table, and situated in front of the wrought iron railing at the stairs that led down to her garden apartment. In homage to Charles Schulz's acerbic comic strip character from *Peanuts*, Lucy van Pelt, Jake had set up a table with a big sign reading, "The PI is IN." Jake normally gave free consultations in the privacy of her office (which was also her apartment), but Darla could see how some people might not be comfortable taking that first rather intimidating step of setting up an appointment with a real-life detective. In a festival-like setting like this, however, some of those barriers might be lowered.

Mary Ann, meanwhile, rose. "I'd better get going. I promised Brother I'd bring him a lemonade and some of Steve's Thai appetizers to try. And maybe I'll run down and pick up one of those Screaming Babies CDs for myself, while I'm at it."

"You go, girl," Jake said in approval, giving the old woman a clenched-fist salute. Then, turning back to Darla, she launched into a different subject. "I almost forgot, Robert mentioned you had a little run-in with George King at the Perky's booth this morning. What happened?"

Darla suppressed a groan. "Typical George, acting like a bully. It wouldn't have been so bad, except he threatened Hamlet."

While Jake listened in concern, Darla gave her a quick rundown of that morning's encounter. As a good event coordinator, she'd made the rounds of all the retailers right before the block party began. Hamlet, wearing a red, white, and blue harness that matched Roma's, had accompanied her, giving his own approval by means of a meow or a head rub against the booth. Everyone had met with the finicky feline's approval . . . that was, until he reached King George's booth.

To his credit, George—or more likely, Livvy—had gotten into the spirit of the event and set up one of the nicest booths of the event, a long wooden table covered in cloth doilies instead of the usual card table gussied up with a tablecloth. Displayed upon it were vintage coffeepots, along with a small batch of logoed Perky's merchandise and, of course, carafes of various brewed coffee offered by the sample and by the cup.

Once again, probably all Livvy's doing, Darla had told herself as she nodded her approval of their setup. She had hesitated going any closer, until Livvy had given her a swift if friendly wave. Apparently, George had yet to tell his wife that they were out of the faux drug business, she decided in relief. Assuming a nonchalant air, she had gone over to their table and greeted the couple.

George wore another of his tent-sized blue Perky's shirts, meaning that, intentionally or not, he fit the day's color scheme. Livvy had made a greater effort, wearing a bright red T-shirt over her usual black yoga pants and a red, white, and blue bandana tied over the two short, spiky braids she wore in place of her usual messy bun.

George had given Darla a hard look, but all he said in response to her greeting was, "Eh, it's gonna be a scorcher." His prediction was borne out by the fact that the armpits of his Perky's shirt were already soaked through, though the morning was still pleasant.

Livvy, however, shook her head. "It won't be any hotter than usual, and we're in a nice shady spot here," she assured her husband. To Darla, she said, "All the decorations on the street look great. I feel like I'm in a Norman Rockwell illustration."

"That was the idea," Darla replied with a smile. "Everything should go smooth as silk, but if you need me for anything, I . . . *Hamlet!*"

That last had come out in a shriek as, without warning, Hamlet leaped onto George's table. Before she could stop him, he had cocked one large front paw and sent a bag of coffee beans flying, like a major league batter hitting one out of the park.

"Hamlet!" Darla shrieked again as she tried to catch the airborne bag before it hit the sidewalk. Her athletic skills were not on a par with those of the feisty feline, however, so the coffee beans had landed with a splat.

Fortunately, George hadn't cheaped out with his packaging, for the bag did not spill its beany guts all over the sidewalk as she'd expected. Heaving a sigh of relief, Darla grabbed up the bag and set it back on the table, only to see George cocking a big mitt of his own.

"Darn cat," he exclaimed with a threatening shake of said mitt in Hamlet's direction.

Darla promptly snatched Hamlet off the table and set him safely behind her on the ground.

"Don't yell at him; yell at me. I forgot there's something about your *coffee* that irritates his nose," she shot back in exasperation, though she doubted any of the bags on display were adulterated. Chances were Hamlet was only acting reflexively. A bit more calmly, she added, "It's my fault he was near the table in the first place."

"Don't worry, Darla," Livvy interjected, grabbing her husband by the arm and obviously not getting Darla's veiled intimation. "No harm done. Besides, George wouldn't hurt an animal. He's just putting on a show."

"Eh, I shoulda knocked his furry block off," the man muttered, though he lowered his fist and instead started rearranging the merchandise.

Dismayed by the outright threat to her pet, Darla had been tempted to stomp off and recruit the Tomlinson twins to do a little block-knocking on Hamlet's behalf. But Livvy had shot her a pleading look, so Darla had contented herself with a stern glare before gathering up Hamlet in her arms and finishing her rounds.

Now, as Darla finished her account, Jake gave a commiserating nod but reassured her, "Believe me, kid, I've run into dozens of guys like George over the years. Like Livvy said, his type of bully is all bark and no bite. He talks a good game, but he's not going to do anything about it. So don't worry about Hamlet."

"I hope you're right," Darla replied, reaching down to give the feline in question a fond pat. "Not too many people get under my skin, but Mr. Perky sure knows how to do it. If he's not careful, I still might blow the whistle on their fake drug scheme."

"That's up to you," Jake replied with a shrug, "but if you go for it, at least wait until after the block party wraps up." Then, glancing at her watch, she added, "I'd better get back to my booth. I've got another of my ten-minute clients showing up soon."

They headed back across the street to their respective

booths. Darla sent James and Robert to take their well-earned breaks, while she spent the next twenty minutes handing out books and letting children have their pictures taken with Hamlet. The latter obligingly posed on the table next to the electronic picture frame that was looping his "Karate Kitty" video. Doug stopped by the booth, as well, trading one of his firecracker doughnuts—"Last one, girl!"—for a cup of iced coffee.

"You seen Penny, er, Penelope around?" he asked over the distant music.

Darla shook her head and looked at her watch. "Not recently, but if we're on schedule her girls should be performing again any minute, so she'll be wherever they are."

Nodding his thanks, Doug swallowed down the rest of his coffee and, tossing the empty into the nearby trash bin, headed back through the crowd toward his shop.

James and Robert returned a couple of minutes later, both bearing rainbow snow cones courtesy of Steve's nephew. At the same time, the faint sounds of goth music abruptly faded. That music was replaced by the canned playing of a bouncy hit from a well-known pop diva.

"Boom box tunes," Darla exclaimed. "I bet that means the dance troupe is about to perform nearby. Guys, hold down the fort. I need to get Hammy his window seat before the girls start. The last number scared him a little, I think."

Slinging the feline over one shoulder, she puffed her way up the half dozen concrete steps to the bookstore's front door. She unlocked it and entered the darkened shop, setting Hamlet down with a whoosh.

"Time to switch over to diet kibble," she told him as

she unbuckled his harness. "Now, why don't you watch things from the window? I cleared a nice spot just for you so you can lounge right there and have a cat's-eye view of the action."

Apparently unimpressed by her efforts on his behalf, Hamlet made a sound suspiciously like a harrumph but wandered toward the window, anyhow. Darla, meanwhile, had already turned to the door.

"I'll be back later," she promised as she slipped outside again and joined James, Robert, and Roma at the booth.

"Look, I bet those are Ms. Penelope's girls," Robert said, pointing to a couple of teenagers who were strolling in their direction. One of the girls swung an oversized boom box in one hand, which explained the music they'd been hearing. Both girls wore high red and white stockings, and short blue dresses, and what appeared to be red yarn wigs tied up in twin ponytails. As for their makeup, rather than a heavy-handed application of bright red lipstick, they instead sported mere cherry-sized dollops of red in the center of their mouths. Even as Darla noted an unfortunate similarity between the girls' hairstyles and hers, James spoke up.

"Children's literature is not my specialty, but I would venture to say that these girls have been reading Johnny Gruelle."

"Johnny who?" Robert asked in confusion, obviously unfamiliar with the author James had mentioned.

Darla grinned a little. She'd been a fan of the Raggedy Ann stories when she was in grade school and recognized the homage; moreover, now she saw other similarly dressed girls moving among the milling festivalgoers.

Having watched the two earlier flash mob dance routines that Penelope had choreographed—both variations on vintage 1980s rock—Darla had a feeling about what was coming next.

Sure enough, the boom box–toting teen set down the player and pressed a few buttons. The Auto-Tune female voice abruptly shut off. In its place came the familiar one-two, one-two bang of a drum, that rhythm followed by an equally recognizable whine of guitar that was pure Aerosmith.

"Rag Doll!" Darla exclaimed in delight as the classic hit song of that name came blasting from the boom box's speakers.

"*Yes, I'm movin'!*" she sang to herself, grinning as the red-wigged girls came together, a dozen matching live rag dolls in a line. Everyone around them paused, attention now fixed on the troupe who thrashed, wiggled, and swayed in choreographed precision to the raucous lyrics. Perhaps the song was a bit R-rated for a family-oriented event, Darla conceded, but the boom box's cheap speakers disguised the worst of the racy language, so that the music took priority.

A few minutes later, the song abruptly ended with the living rag dolls flopping to the ground into limp heaps. Darla and the other spectators burst into applause, which signaled the girls to pop back to life and scamper off down the street.

"While I am not a fan of that particular musical group," James said, "the dance routine was quite well performed. Kudos to Ms. Winston and her troupe."

"That was, like, totally sick," Robert decreed with a

vigorous nod, while Roma gave an approving bark. Darla glanced back up at the shop window to see if Hamlet had also enjoyed the show.

Apparently not, she decided with a smile, since the only view she had of the ornery feline was that of his back leg flung high in the air. At least from this angle, the people on the street couldn't tell he was signaling that the act hadn't met his entertainment standards.

Turning back to the street, Darla spotted Penelope coming out from beneath the PR canopy. She caught the woman's eye and waved. "Great job!"

Penelope nodded and waved her vaping pen in Darla's direction. But instead of coming over to chat, she headed off in the same direction the girls had gone, her expression distracted. *Must be the heat*, Darla decided.

"Hey, kid, look who decided to show up," she heard Jake call to her.

Darla looked over toward the PI's booth to see Reese standing beside her friend. She smiled. The detective was wearing tan slacks and a navy blue NYPD polo shirt, a sexy yet professionally casual look that she'd always liked on him. But barely had she registered all that when Darla also noticed the woman standing next to him, possessively clinging to Reese's heavily muscled biceps.

Darla felt her smile slip a little.

The female in question looked to be a little younger than Reese, likely in her late twenties, though the thick application of bright makeup on her overly tanned features made judging her actual age difficult. With her four-inch strappy white sandals and short, straight black hair teased to stratospheric heights, the young woman topped Reese's almost six-foot height by a good two inches. But most eye-catching of all was her outfit: a tight, capri-length jumpsuit in a shiny red and white tiger-striped fabric, its bustier-style top revealing more than necessary of her assets.

Hey, lady, this is a family-friendly event, Darla wanted to shout, but contented herself with a mental eye roll. Even the usually unflappable James looked slightly taken aback. As for his part, Robert simply appeared mesmerized by Miss Tiger . . . or, rather, by the bustier portion of her outfit. But in contrast, Reese's expression was one she could only peg as unenthusiastic—hardly the face of a guy out to have a good time with friends.

James was the first to break the momentary lull in conversation.

"Detective Reese," the store manager greeted him in his usual sonorous tones, "nice to see you here. It has been a glorious day so far. Now, are you going to introduce us to your companion?"

"Uh, yeah, sure."

He and the woman started toward them, trailed by Jake, and Darla realized that Reese was being careful not to make eye contact with any of them. Obviously, this wasn't his long-lost cousin he was squiring about. The thought made her heart start beating faster . . . and not in a good way.

They halted in front of the Pettistone's booth, and Darla caught a strong whiff of vanilla and violet scent. She grimaced a little as she recognized the perfume from an accidental spraying at a department store makeup counter. If she recalled correctly, this fragrance was the one named for a certain *Sex and the City* actress.

"Everyone, this is Connie. Uh, Connie Capello." Reese

paused and visibly swallowed. "Connie, this is James, Robert, and, uh, uh . . ."

"Darla," Darla supplied with a tight smile as he struggled over her name. She stuck out her hand, all at once glad that she'd splurged for a manicure the day before at the nail shop down the street. "Nice to meet you."

Connie grasped her hand in a surprisingly firm grip. "So pleased to meet you, too," she said in a nasal accent that, in Darla's opinion, made her sound just like that actress from the movie *My Cousin Vinny*. "Fiorello has told me all about you guys. You're the bookstore lady with the cat, right? Sorry, I can't stand cats and I don't read books, but I'm sure you're a very nice person, all the same. And your Southern accent, it's *so* cute."

Before Darla could explain that a Texas accent and a Southern accent were not one and the same, Connie had released Darla's hand and turned on Reese with a mock pout.

"But, Fi"—she pronounced it "Fee"—"you didn't introduce me right to your friends. Here, I'll take care of that."

Red-lipsticked mouth parting in a wide smile, Connie whipped around to face Darla and the others again, all the while flapping her left hand meaningfully before her. A sparkler's worth of refracted light bounced from the vicinity of the other woman's third finger, and Darla's overly frantic heartbeat was now accompanied by a sudden twisting feeling in her stomach.

Surely that wasn't . . .

"The name's Connie Capello," the woman declared, "but come Christmas you can call me Mrs. Fiorello Reese!"

NINE

AN ENGAGEMENT RING? **DARLA HOPED THAT SHE DIDN'T LOOK** as shell-shocked as she abruptly felt. *Reese, getting married? It had to be a joke.* Yet one look at the detective's sheepish expression assured her that it was not.

Well, she told herself firmly, it wasn't as if she and Reese were anything more than pals. So why in the heck did the announcement make her feel like Hamlet suddenly had sunk sharp claws into her heart?

This time, Jake was the first one to jump in to alleviate the awkwardness.

"You're engaged? Hey, that's great. Congratulations, you two," she exclaimed, smiling brightly, though Darla caught the slanted look she shot Reese's way. "So, how did old Fiorello pop the question?"

Connie preened just a little.

"It was so romantic. Last weekend, we was doing A.C."—Atlantic City, Darla mentally translated—"you know, checking out some of the fancy casinos before they close down for good. We was walking back from Caesars to the motel, when we passed a jewelry store. I stopped to look in the window . . . you know, just for fun. The next thing I know, we was inside, and Fi was putting this ring on my finger!" She shrugged and winked. "You know what they say: 'diamonds are a girl's best friend.'"

"Let me offer my felicitations, as well," James said, holding out his hand to Reese, while Robert vigorously nodded his agreement. "How does the old saying go? *Married in days of December cheer, Love's star shines brighter from year to year.*"

"Well, we figured the holidays would be convenient for all the relatives," Reese mumbled as he shook the store manager's hand. "And Connie's favorite color is red, so she wants to go with that whole poinsettia and cranberry theme."

"Yeah, I got it all planned out already. I'll have all my bridesmaids dress in red, and the guys can all wear red bow ties and cummerbunds." Then, fluttering her false lashes at Reese, she added, "Of course, my dress will be traditional virginal white."

Right, Darla thought, and then swiftly turned a reflexive snort into a cough. Plastering an innocent smile on her lips, she said aloud, "Wonderful news. I'm sure you two will be very happy. So, tell me, Connie, how long have you and Reese—er, Fiorello—known each other?"

The woman waved a dismissive hand, her ring flashing.

"Oh, we grew up in the neighborhood together, so we've

known each other since we were kids." Then, snuggling still closer to the man, she added, "But I have to say, even though we only really started dating a few weeks ago, I always knew even when I was a little girl that me and Fi would end up together. It was, you know, Fate."

"Hey, why don't we go check out the rest of the street fair?" Reese interjected. "If we're going to watch the fireworks tonight, we need to be outta here pretty soon so we can get to the river before traffic is too backed up."

"Yeah, you're right." Dropping her voice to a conspiratorial stage whisper, Connie added for Darla and the others' benefit, "Since Fiorello is a cop, we get to watch the show from one of the police boats."

"Wow!" Robert spoke up. "That would be, like, totally great. I wish I could go."

"Robert, remember, we're going to be watching from the rooftop of our building," Darla told him. "And if we don't have a good enough view there, I'll have the television tuned to the live broadcast."

To Connie, she said, "I'm glad you two could stop by. It was nice to meet you, and congratulations on your engagement. Y'all should go walk around some more and have fun. Our retailers have lots of freebies and good deals at their booths. And the TAMA dojo should be putting on their last demonstration of the day in about thirty minutes."

"Sounds like fun. Nice meetin' everyone."

The pair headed down the sidewalk, Connie still clinging to Reese's arm. Darla watched them go, scowling a little when she overheard Connie say, "Your friends are really nice, Fi, especially that Darla. And wasn't it cute the way she did her hair? She looked just like those little girls who were dancing."

I was just trying to beat the heat, Darla thought defensively, not that she hadn't made the same comparison herself earlier. And it wasn't as if she couldn't have made a crack about Connie's teased do, if she'd wanted to. She decided to take the other woman's words as a compliment, however, vowing to take the high road in the situation.

"So is Detective Reese really getting married?" Robert asked with a puzzled look.

Jake shrugged. "Looks like it. And before anyone asks"—she paused and shot a look at Darla—"no, I didn't know anything about this. Talk about a surprise."

"Hey, it's a nice surprise," Darla was quick to declare, wondering as she did whether this bombshell was the subject Reese had wanted to discuss the other day. *Note to self*, she wryly thought, *when someone is trying to tell you something, shut up and let them.*

"Connie seems like a nice girl," she went on. "Still, I have to admit I never expected to see Reese, of all people, tying the knot."

"Technically, the pair are only affianced at this time," James pointed out before Jake could respond. "Much can happen in six months."

Darla gave him a quizzical look. "What do you mean?"

"Let us just say that, like Ms. Capello, I am a believer in Fate."

With those cryptic words, James turned to a couple—a middle-aged woman and her elderly father—who'd approached the booth and were checking out the Hamlet-logoed coffee mugs. Darla, meanwhile, couldn't help a baffled look in his direction.

Fate?

She'd known the pragmatic James long enough to be certain he wasn't the type to give credence to anything that smacked of Destiny or Providence. So what was he really trying to say, in his roundabout way?

She glanced at her watch and promptly gave Fate the symbolic heave-ho. Reese and his relationship status would have to wait. The block party still had two more hours to go, and that was where her attention needed to be.

She summoned a smile for Jake and Robert. "Okay, back to more important matters. It's almost time for the pie-eating contest. Robert, are you going to give it a shot? Come on, I'll be your official cheerleader."

"Pie eating?" Robert shrugged and grinned a little. "Yeah, sure. Free food, right?"

"Great. What about you, Jake? You up for some blueberry pie?"

Jake snorted. "Not in your dreams, kid. How about I keep an eye on Roma while you two go play county fair?"

"Deal," Darla replied, glad for a legitimate excuse to exit stage left before Jake had a chance to turn the conversation back to the subject of Reese's announcement. Doubtless the PI would have more—much more!—to say on the matter.

Thirty minutes later Darla and Robert were back at the Pettistone's booth, with the latter looking like a male version of the purple girl from *Willy Wonka and the Chocolate Factory.*

"I thought you were supposed to eat the pie, not wear it," Jake commented with a friendly smirk as she handed over Roma's leash to the youth. Robert settled on the stoop, and the little dog promptly began licking the sticky berry residue from his face.

"And did you prevail?" James wanted to know.

Robert gave the older man a blue-tinted grin between dodging Roma's long pink tongue. "Not a chance. Believe it or not, one of those rag doll dancers won. She, like, left us all in the dust. I came in third after Mr. Plinski."

"You should have seen it," Darla exclaimed with a laugh, as James gave them both a genteel look of disbelief. "We had a couple of beefy guys who looked like they ate pie all day long, and they both got beat out by our top three. Emma, the girl who won, weighs maybe ninety pounds, but she never missed a bite. And Mr. Plinski was a champ. I swear, he didn't even get a spot on that white shirt of his. I suspect the only reason he didn't win was because his dentures slipped. And you should have seen Mary Ann cheering him on."

Darla waved at both Plinskis, who had returned to their booth and were settling into their respective chairs. Mary Ann gave a wave back, while her brother gave a sedate nod, his features still shrouded by the bucket hat. At least she'd finally gotten a close-up look at the old man who, save for his neatly oiled and surprisingly thick gray hair, looked uncannily like his sister.

Then, with a pat for Roma, whose white and gray snout now had a distinctly blue tinge to it, Darla headed up the steps, adding, "I'm going to grab Hamlet and make a final round of all the booths. We'll be winding up the block party soon, and I want to be sure all our retailers and guests are enjoying themselves."

"I am sure that you will receive nothing but kudos," James assured her. "I realize that you had a committee assisting you, but you certainly did the lion's share of the work. You can be very proud of yourself."

"Thanks, James." Darla felt herself blush. A compliment from Professor James was, as he would term it, quite the rara avis. She would make certain to pass on the sentiment to the rest of her team.

Opening the bookshop door, she called, "C'mon, Hammy. Time to let your public get one last look at the Karate Kitty."

Hamlet was still sitting in the window, though he seemed to have gotten over his previous disdain and was now facing forward and snoozing quite comfortably on the broad display sill. At Darla's summons, he yawned wide, showing an alarming expanse of pink inner mouth and two rows of sharp teeth. She clipped his lead onto his harness, and they walked back out onto the street, leaving James and a still-sticky Robert to keep an eye on the booth.

Alone now except for Hamlet—and a few dozen milling block party attendees, some of whom stopped her for a better look at her feline companion—Darla had time to consider just what Reese's bombshell announcement meant to her. It wasn't like the two of them had had any sort of understanding. Heck, they'd only gone out a couple of times, after which they'd both apparently come to the unspoken agreement that they worked better as friends. Even so, she had always felt some sort of a spark between them—maybe not the sort of spark that set off a raging forest fire, but enough of a spark to summon up a decent campfire.

On the other hand, maybe that whole spark business had been a figment of her imagination. After all, Reese hadn't been concerned enough about sparks to make a second attempt to give her a heads-up about the situation before the block party.

"Quit it," she muttered aloud, the words earning a questioning glance from Hamlet, though he quickly returned his attention to the sights around them. In the distance, she heard Pinky and his Screaming Babies start up their final set, their doleful sound feeling more than a bit appropriate given her present mood.

Darla headed in that direction, giving a wave to Steve as she passed the Thai Me Up booth. His smile in return was a bit flustered since, even with his son and daughter to help him, the line to his booth stretched several people back. *Good problem to have*, she thought in approval.

A few shops down, Doug's doughnut booth was temporarily unattended, but two display platters held fresh doughnut holes, the glass lids steamy from the still-warm samples. She snagged a bite-sized red velvet cake one and popped it in her mouth. But even that bit of gooey, sugary bliss wasn't enough to dispel her melancholy.

"Hey, kid."

Jake's voice from behind her made Darla halt in midstep. *So much for the alone time*, she told herself, suppressing a sigh. Hoping to postpone the inevitable interrogation, however, she quickly said, "I thought you had clients. Who's minding the store?"

"Eh, the PI is 'out' for the rest of the day," Jake replied, falling in step beside her. "Anyone else needs advice, they can make an appointment during regular business hours. So, you want to talk about it?"

Darla gave her friend an innocent look. "You mean, about the block party? Sure, why not? I think everything has gone great, even with the wrong band. Everyone I've talked to so far says—"

"You know what I mean," Jake cut her short with an exasperated shake of her curly head. "Do you want to talk about the whole Reese-getting-engaged deal? I know you and he had some sort of a thing going a while back, so having him lob this kind of news at you out of the blue has got to sting a little."

Sting a little? How about sting like an onslaught of killer wasps?

Darla frowned at herself. Where had *that* idea come from? The whole marriage situation must be getting to her more than she'd expected. Abandoning her plan to play dumb—no way would Jake let her get away with that, anyhow—she simply nodded.

"Yeah, it kind of does."

"Well, kid, let me let you in on a little secret. I've known Reese for a long time and, ring or no ring, I don't think he's found what he's looking for yet."

"So, are you and James both playing soothsayer today?"

Jake grinned a little. "Just playing student of human nature, kid . . . and I have to say, I've got an advanced degree in it."

Darla didn't doubt that, given Jake's years on the police force before her early retirement and reinventing herself as a private investigator. But she, Darla, was no stranger to the vagaries of the male species (exhibit one being her slimeball ex-husband). She was pretty certain that Reese *had* found what he was looking for . . . or, at least, what he *thought* he was after.

"It is what it is, Jake," she replied in a firm tone. "If I'd really wanted a shot with Reese, I would have tried harder. And same thing on his part. I think I'm just suffering from a bit of wounded pride."

"Yeah, I know that one. The old 'I don't want you but I don't want anyone else to have you' routine. Better known as 'dog in the manger' syndrome."

"Well, I'm not going there," Darla resolved with a stout nod. "All you're going to hear from me is congratulations. If they invite me to the wedding, I'm there with a big present and a smile. Let's just pray Connie doesn't want me for one of her bridesmaids."

"Agreed." Jake rolled her eyes. "Did you get a load of that tiger-striped outfit she had on, like she was a refugee from a J. Lo music video? I can only imagine the bridesmaid gowns she'll pick. She's already said red, and they'll be strapless, for sure. And split so high in front that one wrong move and your whole . . . everything is on display."

"Oh, and don't forget the wedding photos," Darla exclaimed, getting into the spirit of things as they continued down the sidewalk. "She'll have to have one taken with all her bridesmaids with their backs to the photographer and their skirts stuck in their undies so they're flashing their butts. And one where everyone is hanging out their tongues and making dirty hand gestures that the parents and grandparents won't get."

Jake snorted. "And wouldn't you love to be the bridesmaid

who catches the bouquet? Then you get to have Connie's second cousin—the one with sweaty hands and acne—slide the garter he caught as high on your thigh as he can get away with before you deck him."

Darla laughed, cheered by this bit of silliness. "Well, even though I decline the bridesmaid honor, I'll still show up at the wedding, just to watch the shenanigans. Now, how about we forget Reese and Connie for a while and see if we can pry some free iced coffee out of George. Remember, he owes Hamlet an apology from this morning."

The Babies, meanwhile, had launched into a new song as the women approached, and Darla was pleased to realize the band was back to doing covers again.

"Santana," Jake said in an approving tone as the lyrics to "Black Magic Woman"—slightly speeded up—drifted to them. "Those fellas are pretty darned versatile, aren't they? Reese and Connie ought to hire them for . . . oops!"

Jake gave her forehead a melodramatic slap, and Darla laughed a bit ruefully.

"That's okay, you get one free pass. And, I agree, the Babies would make for a pretty interesting wedding band."

They found a shady section of street curb not far from the stage and settled there to listen to the rest of the song. The music was too loud for talking, for which Darla was grateful. *Fake it 'til you make it* was her motto for the moment, but faking it took more energy than she realized.

As the last twangy notes of the seventies hit faded, Darla rose from the curb and swiped a bit of sweat from her brow.

"I need to talk to Pinky for a moment before we grab that coffee. Do you mind watching Hamlet a sec? I think he needs to rest up another minute from the walk," she told Jake, nodding in the cat's direction as she handed the leash to her friend.

Hamlet lay sprawled on his back against the curb, looking unsettlingly like a drunk sleeping it off in the gutter. At Darla's words, he slit open one green eye. *Not moving*, his expression confirmed.

"Go ahead, kid, we'll be here when you get back. And tell the band I'll be back for one of their CDs after their set."

Leaving the pair, Darla headed toward the makeshift stage. The Babies had paused for a needed water break, and she saw in sympathy that their black T-shirts were soaked through with sweat. She also made a mental note to ask Pinky the brand of his eyeliner. Despite the heat, it hadn't melted into a broad smear beneath his eyes as she suspected hers had.

Of course, his might be permanently tattooed on.

"Hey, y'all, you've done a fantastic job," she told them as they sucked down their water. "Several people mentioned they wanted one of your CDs."

"Yeah, we already sold, like, four of them," Pinky said with a proud smile. "That's better than most nights at the club."

"Well, save one for my friend"—she gestured toward Jake, who was fanning herself and Hamlet with a discarded block party flier—"and save one for me, too. I'll get it when I write you the check for the rest of your fee."

Pinky gave a triumphant little fist pump. "Six!"

"Hang around awhile after you finish the set, and I'll bet you sell a couple more. Speaking of which, do you mind ending up with a special request? I think it would strike the perfect note for the Fourth if your last song was 'The Star-Spangled Banner.'"

"Sure, we can do that. Right, guys?"

Grunts of assent greeted that declaration, and Darla gave a satisfied nod. "Perfect. Just be sure you announce it beforehand so everyone can stand at attention."

Leaving the Babies to finish their break, Darla rejoined Jake and Hamlet. "All right, time for that iced coffee. Hammy, we'll get you a nice water."

They crossed the street toward Perky's, passing Hank and his brother Hal, who were disassembling the mats in the makeshift demonstration ring. The last demonstration of the day was finished, and a handful of Darla's TAMA classmates were milling about, still dressed in their TAMA T-shirts and white gi pants. They were gathering the stanchions and rope that had enclosed the ring, and picking up stray trash.

"Hey, Darla," Hal exclaimed, his biceps bulging as he lifted a pile of mats and heaved them atop another stack. Unlike his brother, who wore his hair in a ponytail, Hal shaved his big head smooth. Like Hank, however, he'd cut off the sleeve of his karate gi jacket, the better to show off said biceps.

"This block party was a great idea," he said with an approving nod, sweat making his bald head gleam. "We already had five new students sign up this afternoon."

"Wonderful! That's what this event was about, giving us all some good publicity and getting our names out there."

Leaving the group to finish dismantling the ring, Darla, Jake, and Hamlet headed down the sidewalk to where the Perky's booth was situated, and where His Highness was seated alone behind the table. Perhaps there had been a lull in customers during the karate demonstration, while everyone had gathered near the ring to watch, and George had apparently decided to take advantage of the break. He was slumped back in his chair, arms crossed and chin on his chest, giving every appearance of napping.

Darla slowed her pace.

"What do you think? Should we wake him up?" Though she suspected that rousing a snoozing King of Coffee would be akin to poking a sleeping bear with a stick. Definitely not recommended.

Jake shrugged. "That depends. How badly do you want that iced coffee?"

"Not enough to listen to him roar for fifteen minutes. Maybe we can wait for Livvy. I'm sure she's around here somewhere."

The squeal of feedback decided the issue, however, when Pinky's voice came from the stage speakers. "Ladies and gentlemen, this is, uh, our last song today. So give it up for the, uh, national anthem!"

Mike in hand, Pinky leaped high into the air and landed back on the stage with a thud, arm whipping around to dramatically cue his band. An abrupt shriek of guitar even worse than the feedback split the air, and Darla's mouth dropped open.

"Oh no, don't tell me," she said with a groan. "He's going to do the Jimi Hendrix version."

Sure enough, with a growl and a clash of electric strings Pinky launched into a sixties rock-and-roll-inspired "Star-Spangled Banner."

So much for the world's greatest tenor, Darla thought

in dismay as she and Jake dutifully stood with hands over hearts even as she winced at the discordant notes. Darla glanced George's way. Amazingly, the man was still sleeping through the rage of minor chords and Pinky's shouted lyrics. He had to be wearing earplugs . . . that, or he was partially deaf!

It definitely sounds like bombs bursting, Darla thought as Pinky reached that line of the song. *Good thing there's no law against blowing up the national anthem.*

And then, abruptly, the music stopped. Pinky's clear tenor rose over the silence, the bell-like tones giving Darla sudden chills as he sang the final phrases a cappella.

"O say does that star-spangled banner yet wave, o'er the land of the free and the home of the—"

"Me-OOOW!"

Hamlet's sudden caterwaul startled Darla so much that she almost dropped his leash.

"Hammy, what's wrong? Are you hurt?" she exclaimed, forgetting standing at attention as she swiftly bent toward the cat. She barely heard the rousing applause from the fairgoers as Pinky and the Screaming Babies took their bows, and she almost missed the announcement about CDs for sale.

Jake leaned closer to Hamlet, too, and frowned. "Maybe that last note hurt his ears."

"I doubt it. There were lots of other notes earlier that should have sent him scampering before—*wait!*"

This last was directed back at Hamlet, who was tugging against his leash in the direction of Perky's. Darla straightened and glanced that way again. George still slumped unmoving behind the table, and a sudden bad feeling gripped her.

"I think Hamlet is trying to say that something's wrong with George," she exclaimed, pointing toward the motionless man. "Quick, we need to check on him!"

The three of them rushed in that direction, though Jake put out a restraining arm as they reached the table. "Let me," she softly told Darla, then called in a louder voice, "George, can you hear me? George?"

When the man remained unmoving, Jake moved closer to him and gave his shoulder a gentle shake. "George, are you—?"

His arm abruptly swung loose, dangling now so his knuckles grazed the sidewalk. Jake gave her head a grim shake and reached out a hand to George's neck to check his pulse.

"Oh no, it can't be!" Darla gasped. "Jake, is he—?"

"Whaddaya want?" George roared, eyes flying open as he straightened in his chair.

Reflexively, Darla shrieked and jumped back. Even the usually unflappable Jake looked startled before she shook her head and chuckled.

"Sorry, George," she told him, while Darla heaved a relieved sigh. "We wanted a couple of iced coffees, and it looked like you were sleeping."

"Just resting my eyes," he grumbled, shoving back his chair and rising. Then, catching a glimpse of Darla, he nodded in her direction and sourly added, "Why don't you drink *her* coffee that she says is so good?"

Reminding herself that thirty seconds earlier, she'd been giving thanks that the man was still breathing, Darla summoned a serene expression. "Because we—*Hamlet!*"

All at once, the leash that had been looped over her wrist

went flying. Hamlet had broken free of her grasp and was springing toward the steps that led down to Perky's, the star-spangled tether trailing after him. Serenity forgotten, Darla went bounding right after him. If he ran down the steps, she'd be able to corner him there, and—

Darla halted at the top of the steps, gripping the handrail as she stared down at the landing outside the Perky's door. The mango-painted door she'd previously admired was ajar, while one of the two wicker bistro chairs had been tumbled over. Hamlet leaped onto the glass-and-wicker bistro table, where he stared down at the crumpled figure who lay halfway inside the door.

All Darla could see from her vantage point was a pair of slim legs encased in black yoga pants topped by the hem of a bright red T-shirt. But it was enough for her to be certain of the identity of the woman who sprawled motionless on the ground.

Livvy King.

TEN

"I STILL CAN'T BELIEVE THAT LIVVY IS DEAD," DARLA declared the next morning as she clutched her oversized mug of black coffee and willed her eyelids to stay open.

She had been up well past midnight the previous night. Word had spread swiftly about Livvy, and Steve's restaurant had served as an unofficial gathering place as the locals had come together over the unexpected loss of one of their own. More prosaically, there had also been the rest of the block party decorations and booths to finish clearing away. Doug had been there, too, along with Hank and Hal.

Somewhat to Darla's surprise—or maybe not, given whatever past there was between her and the dead woman—Penelope had been a no-show. Although Darla did recall the dance instructor mentioning taking time off as soon as the Fourth of July event was over. Maybe she'd headed back to her studio directly after the final dance number, without ever realizing that tragedy had befallen the block party.

Even more surprising, George himself had briefly stopped by the impromptu assembly. If George's presence had been unwelcome at the establishment, given his past behavior toward Steve's offspring, Steve gave no sign of it. The fellow widower had been a gracious host. George, however, had waved away all offers of food and drink except for a glass of water, although even that he left untouched as he accepted his neighbors' condolences. He left a few minutes later, but not before he'd gestured Steve aside and the pair exchanged a few words. From her vantage point Darla hadn't been able to hear what was said, but neither man had appeared angry, which she took as a good sign.

Still, she'd worried about George going back to his apartment alone. While they'd been waiting for the police to finish up, she'd made a point of asking him if he had any local friends or relatives he wanted her to call. She had gathered from his silent headshake that there wasn't anyone; at least, not anyone that he cared to notify.

Darla shook her head as she dragged her foggy thoughts back to the present. "Livvy was, what, thirty-three? Only a couple of years younger than me. Someone her age shouldn't just keel over like that."

"You never know about these things, kid," Jake reassured her, stifling a yawn. "It didn't appear to be the result of a fall, since there were no visible scrapes, blood, or trauma, like she'd tripped going down the steps, but Livvy might have had some sort of medical condition none of us knew about. Just because she was young didn't mean she couldn't have had a bad heart. Or she could have had a brain aneurysm that suddenly ruptured."

"There was the whole thing with her rheumatoid arthritis," Darla replied, quickly relating to Jake what Livvy had explained to her. "She was self-medicating with herbs. Maybe she had some sort of bad reaction and her weakened system couldn't stand the shock."

Jake shrugged. "Maybe. But, don't worry. The medical examiner will figure it out."

Darla nodded, covering a yawn of her own. She, Robert, and Jake were upstairs in the bookstore, seated in the coffee lounge. It was only the three of them, since the store wouldn't open for another thirty minutes, and James wasn't scheduled until right after lunch.

Given their mutual lack of sleep, Robert's first assignment had been to brew up a pot of a dark specialty blend coffee supposedly guaranteed to wake up even the drowsiest of drinkers. Darla prayed the caffeine would kick in soon. Otherwise, she told herself, she'd be pulling a Hamlet and curling up in a quiet corner of the shop for a nap.

Robert had been behind the counter foaming up his cup of coffee with the steam wand. Now, clutching his mug in one hand and rubbing his eyes with the other, he sank in the free chair next to the seat where Hamlet sprawled. Looking rather like a raccoon with the remains of the previous day's black liner smudged around his eyes, he said, "I wonder how Hamlet, you know, figured out something was wrong."

"I don't know," Darla replied. "He'd acted kind of strange yesterday morning when we stopped by Perky's before the block party started. But he sure was Hammy-on-the-spot. I hate to think what would have happened if George had been the first one to find her."

Darla stared pensively into her coffee cup as she recalled what actually had gone down. After a single glance at his wife's motionless form, King George had lumbered back to his chair again, apparently deep in shock, and abdicated all responsibility. It had been Jake who'd confirmed what Darla had feared, that Livvy was beyond help. Hamlet, meanwhile, had slipped down off the table and trotted back up the steps to Darla's side, obviously satisfied that he'd done his part.

Jake's subsequent cell phone call brought a swift response from the various emergency personnel, who secured the area . . . a job made easier as the street was already blocked off. After taking Hamlet back to the bookstore where he'd be safely out of the way, Darla had given James a hurried explanation for all the commotion on the next block down, then had settled in to remain with Jake and a shell-shocked George for the next couple of hours.

What the police thought, Darla had no idea. She knew the cops would want to get formal statements from the three of them, since they were the ones who'd found Livvy, but she'd been surprised when the detective who'd finally showed up to take over the investigation had been none other than Reese.

And it was the cool, competent Detective Reese that she'd always known, rather than the sheepish fiancé Fiorello from earlier in the afternoon. After an offhanded, "So much for fireworks tonight," he'd been all business. While the uniformed officers maintained the scene, Reese had made the rounds of the nearby shops before returning to question the three of them.

Other than his halting responses to Reese—last he'd recalled seeing Livvy had been at the table before he fell asleep—George had stirred only when the time came to remove his wife from the scene. The dead woman's body was barely discernable under the covered gurney as the EMTs maneuvered her slight form up the concrete steps. It was then that the Coffee King had heaved himself up out of his chair and intercepted the wheeled stretcher.

"Wait," he grunted out. "I need to, well, make sure. Know what I mean?"

Darla had reflexively leaped up to join George, feeling obliged to make some show of support. But she'd promptly regretted the impulse when she caught a close-up glimpse of Livvy's preternaturally white, slack features as the EMT had obligingly flipped the blanket aside. And it had been the memory of that face that had kept her from readily falling asleep that night.

Now, Darla shoved her coffee cup away and reached for one of the leftover doughnuts that Robert had salvaged from Doug's pastry case.

"I have to say, Hank and Doug really stepped up to the plate," she said through a mouthful of stale, sugary dough. "As soon as the police gave us the okay, they notified all the retailers and shut down the block party without most people realizing anything was wrong."

"Right, and at least this all went down at the end of the day," Jake agreed. "Things were already winding down, so there were only a couple of dozen people still around.

Hardly anyone will know what happened until they read it in the paper today."

"Yeah, or until Facebook or the Twitter-verse explodes with the news." Darla sighed. "I know it's awful of me, but after all our hard work on the block party, I'd hate it if all people remember about it is Livvy's death."

"Awful, but understandable," Jake assured her with a faint smile. "And I'm pretty sure Livvy would forgive you for thinking that. She'd have wanted the event to be a success, if only for George's sake."

"I hope you're right."

Darla glanced at her watch, and then over at Robert. He was half snoozing over his cup, and a foam mustache trailed from his upper lip.

"Up and at 'em. Pat the pine," she said with a smile, echoing one of her father's favorite sayings he always used to roust her younger, sleepy self out of bed. When Robert stared at her in confusion, she explained, "That means feet hitting the floor, which used to be pine in the olden days before they invented wall-to-wall carpeting. Now, hurry. It's almost time to open."

"No one's going to be here this early the day after the Fourth," Robert grumbled, but he obligingly rose and headed back to the coffee bar to begin prepping.

Hamlet stretched and yawned, but remained firmly planted in his chair.

Jake smiled. "I think I'll take a page out of Hamlet's book and kick back awhile longer. All I've got on tap for the day so far is a stack of paperwork."

"Be my guest. But I've got to go power up the registers and do a bit of straightening, and then I'll unlock the doors. And, Robert, don't forget, you're only on for a half day, anyhow."

It was a couple of minutes before ten when Darla deemed the shop ready and headed for the front. She could see through the door's mottled glass window a shadowy figure waiting on the stoop, disproving Robert's prediction regarding the lack of early shoppers. Stifling another yawn, she unhooked the chain and turned the dead bolt.

"George," she exclaimed as she opened the door and saw the self-proclaimed King of Coffee—unshaven and looking unsettled—standing on the stoop.

He wandered into the bookstore wearing the same blue Perky's shirt he'd had on the day before, outlines of yesterday's sweat stains showing beneath the arms. He squinted at Darla for a moment, as if not certain who she was, and then said, "I needed a cuppa coffee, so I figured I could get one here."

"Of course!"

She knew without asking that he'd obviously not been able to face going back into his own shop alone, not even for a simple cup of coffee. From his puzzled expression, it seemed he still struggled to accept the fact of Livvy's death. While coffee wouldn't restore his world to what it had been a day ago, perhaps it would help clear his head enough that he could begin considering the steps to take next.

But Darla hesitated. When it came to literal steps, he looked more than a little unsteady on his feet. No way was she going to risk the stairs with him just to get him his coffee. Gesturing him instead to the bistro table near the dumbwaiter, she said, "Let's sit over here, and I'll send up an order."

Once she had him settled in a chair, she handed him the short list of their coffee offerings. George gave it an indifferent look and said, "Dark roast, two creams, no sugar."

"Got it."

She scribbled his order on the order pad and hit the "Call" button. George watched wordlessly as the dumbwaiter doors opened a few moments later, and Darla put his order on the vintage Blue Willow plate sitting there for that purpose. Then, as she punched the button again to send the dumbwaiter upstairs again, he grunted.

"Pretty clever," he admitted. Then, clearing his throat, he added, "I wanted to, uh, thank you and your friend for staying with me yesterday while . . . well, you know. It helped, having someone there."

"We were happy to do it. The whole neighborhood is so sorry for your loss. And I'm sorry that I didn't get a chance to know Livvy better." Then, choosing her words carefully, she added, "About the . . . situation the other day with the Kona Blue Party. Why don't we forget that happened?"

George gave a vague wave of one beefy hand. "Yeah, sure. Thanks. Like I said, that was all Livvy."

He dropped his gaze back down to the coffee menu. Wanting to fill the suddenly uncomfortable silence, Darla said, "I should mention that Livvy ordered an expensive herbal reference book before she . . . well, before. It's already paid for and should be here in the next few days, but if you want we can try to find another buyer for it."

"Nah, that's okay," was the morose response. "If she bought it, I should keep it."

"Sure. I'll let you know when it comes in." Then,

trying to keep the conversational ball rolling, she asked, "So, was Livvy a coffee connoisseur before the two of you opened Perky's?"

George shrugged. "Nah, nothing like that. She used to be a ballet dancer. She was with one of those—whaddaya call 'em—companies."

Livvy had been a ballerina?

Darla nodded to herself. It made sense; her sylphlike movements, even the bunned hair and leggings. She could readily picture Livvy practicing at a barre, could see her pirouetting across a stage.

"So what happened?" she ventured aloud.

"She quit because she couldn't do it no more, not professionally. She was tired all the time, started waking up stiff. When it turned into pain, she went to the doc and found out she had RA."

"Were you two already married then?"

George shook his head. "Nah, but that was around the time I met her. She was outta a job, and at loose ends, you know what I mean? Anyhows, I had some money back then, so we hooked up. You didn't think she married me for my looks, didya?"

Darla frowned a little. Surely something was missing from the man's account. She had a hard time picturing two such different people simply "hooking up," as George had put it. Maybe Livvy had found him amusing, or—though Darla shuddered to even think it!—maybe the man was exceptional in the bedroom. But now didn't seem the time to give George the third degree.

"I'm sure she found you attractive in many ways," was Darla's tactful response.

The sound of the dumbwaiter returning gave her an excuse to change the subject. "Here comes your coffee. I hope you'll find it up to your standards," she told him as she opened the doors and removed the steaming cup.

George took a perfunctory sip and then nodded.

"Not bad, for rookies. Anyhows, Livvy was doing okay for the most part, but every so often she'd have one of them flare-ups. That's when she needed me. She didn't like all them high-powered meds the doc gave her. She made up—whatcha call 'em?—these herbal tincture things, rubbed that herbal stuff on her joints. The problem was, no matter how much stuff she drank and rubbed on herself, she still couldn't do what she loved best."

George paused and tugged up one shirtsleeve, displaying high on his beefy left arm the tattoo of a stylized ballerina in midpirouette. Despite its simple lines, the image had an energy and grace that gave the inked image life. Below the figure was a tangle of flowered vines. Above the figure were curly letters spelling out the name *Livvy.*

"I did this for her, so she knew I always thought of her as my little ballerina. I always had a thing for them ballet girls."

Letting the sleeve fall back into place, he pulled a handkerchief from his pants pocket and honked loudly into it.

Darla felt hard-pressed not to do the same. Despite all the bluster, it was obvious that George had truly loved his wife. Discreetly wiping away a tear of her own, she asked, "Do you have any idea yet what you want to do as far as a service?"

He nodded.

"Yeah, she had it all written out, 'cause she figured she

might go before me. Yeah, yeah, I know," he added with a deprecating pat of his belly, "I'm not exactly the poster child for healthy living. But according to the doc, she has—had—a good chance of checking out early, you know what I mean?"

He honked again and stuffed the hankie back into his trouser pocket. "She said she didn't wanna be buried . . . said that wasn't green enough for her," he clarified with a snort that momentarily made him sound like the old George again. "So I'll arrange one of them memorial things for her, and then I'll go scatter her ashes around town like she wanted."

Darla raised a brow, picturing George in his Perky's shirt scattering cremains throughout the city. All she said was, "Let me know where and when for the memorial, and I'll be there." Then, as the bells on the front door jingled, indicating an incoming customer, she rose and added, "The coffee's on me, George. Feel free to sit here as long as you like."

"Yeah, well, it's kinda hard to get comfortable when you got someone staring at you."

He nodded in the direction of the bookshelves behind Darla. She turned to see that, unknown to her, Hamlet had decided to join them. He perched in a gap between books that normally held a blue, fat-bellied vintage vase but now also displayed an oversized black feline. He sat stiffly upright, tail wrapped around his paws, and his cold green gaze fixed firmly on George.

"Hamlet, it's rude to stare," she mildly rebuked him, even as she recalled that the cat had reason to distrust the coffee maven. On the bright side, at least Hamlet was confining his contempt to his patented glare of evil and wasn't batting things around with his paws again.

George shrugged. "Eh, I'd better go. Thanks for the cuppa. Maybe I'll come by again tomorrow."

"Sure, stop by whenever you want."

Not that she particularly looked forward to his morose company again, but it seemed like a kind offer to make. She could afford the daily cost of a cup of coffee while he worked to get back on his emotional, and professional, feet again.

While George saw himself out, Darla checked in with the newcomers, a young mom and her two grade-school-aged girls. "We'll look at books in a minute," the woman assured her. "What the kids really came for was to see that big black cat again, the one you had at the block party yesterday."

"His name is Hamlet," the older of the two girls piped up, "and he's a YouTube star."

"That he is," Darla agreed with a smile. "But he's pretty tuckered out from all the excitement yesterday. Let's see if he's up to meeting his public."

With their mom trailing behind, she walked the girls back over to the shelf where Hamlet had been scoping out George. With his nemesis gone, Hamlet had settled himself neatly in front of the books, paws tucked to his chest and tail lightly waving. He squinted at the girls as they approached, then gave the briefest purr of approval as they kept a respectful distance and merely oohed and aahed at him.

"We had such fun yesterday," the woman declared while her daughters debated the merits of cats of different colors. "The girls tried most of the games and crafts, and

I sampled all of the food. And we all thought the band was wonderful."

"So glad you liked them," Darla said, trying not to show her surprise at the Screaming Babies' apparently wide appeal. "They're a local group, but on their way up, so we were lucky to get them."

"They'd be wonderful entertainment at my nephew's Bar Mitzvah. Could you possibly give me their number?"

Nodding, Darla herded the trio to the register, where she looked up Pinky's contact information and wrote it on one of her store fliers. The woman tucked the page into her purse and then glanced at the tennis bracelet watch on her wrist.

"Oops, gotta run. We'll come back and look at books next week," she said, grasping a girl's arm in either hand and rushing them toward the door.

"At least someone got a boost from your block party," Jake said with a chuckle. She'd come down the stairs just in time to overhear the last exchange, and now she joined Darla at the register. "You never know, playing here might have been the Screaming Babies' big break."

"Well, if it was, Pinky better give us a shout-out when he and the boys are up on stage collecting their Grammy," Darla ruefully replied.

Jake's smile broadened. "Too bad they weren't listed by name on the flier as entertainment. You could have saved a handful then sold them off for big bucks in another few years on one of those auction sites." Then her smile faded. "So, I was looking over the railing and saw George leaving. How's he holding up after yesterday?"

"As well as can be expected, I guess."

Swiftly, Darla told her what she'd learned about Livvy's past and what George had said about Livvy's concern that she might die first. When she'd finished, Jake nodded.

"The fact she had rheumatoid arthritis might shed some light on why she died."

"But I didn't think RA could kill you."

"Not by itself, no—it's a chronic illness, not terminal one," Jake replied. "A cousin of mine has it, so I know a little about how it works. The problem is that sufferers are more prone to cardiovascular disease and serious infections . . . and *that's* what can kill them. And then there are some scary possible side effects from the medication, like gastrointestinal bleeding."

"Right, but, remember, Livvy pretty much treated herself."

Jake shrugged. "Like I said, it's just a possibility. No one will know anything for sure until the ME's report comes back. And speaking of reports, I'd better get that paperwork of mine finished. See you later, kid."

With the PI gone, that left Darla and Robert alone in the store. The latter came clattering down the stairs, though perhaps a little more slowly than usual. "Hey, Ms. P., pretty great that Mr. King thinks we make good coffee. You know since he's, like, the Coffee King and all."

"It *is* great, but how did you know he said that?"

"I heard him." He cocked his head, looking surprised. "Didn't you know? If the doors to the dumbwaiter are open on one end, and someone's talking next to it on the other end, you can hear everything they're saying . . . like they're, you know, standing right next to you."

"Good to know," Darla replied, hoping she hadn't had

any confidential conversations there at the bistro table. She added, "Since things are pretty quiet for the moment, why don't you go down to Doug's and pick up some doughnuts for the coffee bar for this afternoon? Half order only, and tell Doug to put it on our account."

While Robert went on his doughnut run, Darla made a round of the shop, stopping to scritch Hamlet under the chin as she passed him by. Normally, she didn't mind those occasional times when she had the place to herself. It gave her a chance to privately revel in being a business owner, to quietly savor the knowledge that she was her own boss . . . the captain of her own Darla ship. But today, she couldn't help thinking what it must be like for George, alone in his coffee shop and apartment.

She was still contemplating that a few minutes later when Robert returned from his errand empty-handed.

"The doughnut place was closed," he explained.

Darla frowned. "That's odd. Doug didn't say anything last night about not opening today. You mean that even the girl who helps him part-time wasn't there?"

Robert gave his head a vigorous shake. "Nope, no one. There wasn't a sign or anything on the door, but I tried it, and it was locked. Maybe he's, you know, sick."

Or maybe something has happened to Doug, as well.

The unexpected thought flashed through her mind, giving her pause. Darla considered that notion for a moment and then deliberately dismissed it. One untimely death in the neighborhood was enough. Even so, she reached for her cell phone.

"Maybe Livvy's death shook him up enough so that he wasn't up to opening. I'd better make sure he's okay."

She pulled Doug's number up in her contacts and dialed, only to get his voice mail. She hesitated and then hung up without leaving a message.

"He probably just needed a vacation day," she told Robert, though more to reassure herself than him. "Heck, we probably could use one, too. So let's not worry about it. Go ahead and finish unboxing the stock from the beginning of the week."

As Robert left to attend to the stock, her phone gave a little buzz, indicating an incoming text message. Maybe Doug had seen her call and was checking back.

But when she glanced at the message preview, she saw the sender was none other than Reese. Pulling up the full text, she read, *Lunch on me at Thai place. 1 p.m. OK? Need to talk.*

ELEVEN

***NEED TO TALK, MY BROOKLYN BUTT*, SHE THOUGHT, MOMEN-**
tarily channeling Penelope. He was a day too late for that! It would serve good old Fiorello right if she texted him back with a *Sorry, got to work thru lunch, maybe another time.*

She stewed for a good five seconds. Then adult Darla shoved sixteen-year-old Darla back into her mental closet and typed back a noncommittal *Fine, see you then.* James would be arriving for his shift by that time, so Robert wouldn't be alone.

The rest of the morning went by surprisingly fast despite the fact that business was slow. Another little family group stopped in for a little Hamlet meet and greet—this time, a dad and his two sons—but at least the father actually purchased each boy a classic chapter book that he'd no doubt read himself as a kid. The monetary transaction earned them a follow-up appearance from Hamlet, who allowed both boys to give him a tentative pat.

"You're quite the salesman, Hammy," Darla praised him, the compliment netting her the feline version of a derisive snort as he gave a small hiss in return and abruptly stalked back to the bestseller table from where he'd come.

Pinky paid a return visit, as well. To Darla's shock, he arrived dressed all in white, wearing cargo pants and what she recognized as a guayabera, or a Mexican wedding shirt: short-sleeved cotton, with a straight hem across the bottom, and rows of tiny vertical pleats in front. It would have been a far more practical ensemble in yesterday's heat than the all black he and his bandmates had worn at the block party, but Darla assumed they had a reputation to keep up, no matter how they suffered for it.

Robert was restocking the bestseller table when his friend walked in. "Hey, dude! Great ironic look," he said in approval. "And your sets yesterday . . . You guys really slayed."

Pinky ducked his head, seemingly embarrassed by what Darla assumed was high praise. "Yeah, well, it was kinda, you know, weird playing in the daytime, and for a bunch of normal people. But we sold, like, eleven CDs."

"You boys got lots of compliments," Darla added. "I even had a woman come in today looking for your number so they could hire you for a Bar Mitzvah."

Pinky shot her a look of alarm, but whether it was because she'd referred to the band as "boys," or because she'd suggested the Bar Mitzvah gig, she wasn't sure. She unlocked the drawer beneath the counter and pulled out her checkbook. "Here's the balance due," she told him as she signed with a flourish, having added in the extra amount for the promised CD that he'd brought with him. "I'm sorry you had to wait for it until today. Things got a little . . . hectic after you finished playing."

"Yeah, I heard about that." Pinky's twin chin braids momentarily quivered, the motion drawing Hamlet's attention from where he was sprawled on the counter. "Livvy, she was, like, okay."

Nodding, she handed him the check, though Darla wondered how the young goth musician knew the ballerina-turned-barista. "It was a shock, someone that young," she agreed, even as it occurred to her that Pinky likely considered someone in her thirties old. "But, like they say, you never know when your time is up."

Hamlet, meanwhile, apparently decided the chin braids weren't worth going after, and Darla left the two youths chatting as she locked away the checkbook again and went to assist a customer who'd just come in. Pinky departed a few minutes later, with a promise he'd be available for any and all future block party events. At quarter to one, Darla grabbed her purse.

"I'm headed over to Steve's place for lunch," she told Robert, who had returned to stocking the shelves. "I've got a couple of things to discuss with him about the block party. James should be here in a minute. You have things under control?"

"All good here, Ms. P.," he assured her with a cheeky salute.

She nodded and, with a final pat for Hamlet, headed out the door. Why she hadn't admitted that her lunch appointment was with Reese, she wasn't certain. Robert wasn't the type to crack jokes or gossip, particularly about his boss, so that wasn't the issue. But he might innocently mention something to Jake, who'd then jump on that morsel of information like a duck on a June bug, as they said back home in Texas.

Which wouldn't have mattered, she realized in wry amusement, since she'd probably end up discussing any dramatic revelations with Jake, anyhow.

The short walk to Thai Me Up was still long enough in the July heat for Darla to be glad that she'd opted for cropped yellow cotton pants and her favorite tropical print Pettistone's polo. She gave a sigh of relief when she ducked into the restaurant's cool interior. She'd left her sunglasses at the apartment, so it took a moment for her eyes to adjust to the dim light. A few tables were already filled near the front, but a quick scan of the place showed that Reese wasn't there yet. Probably running late due to some work-related crisis or another. Sure enough, just then her phone vibrated, and another text appeared on the screen: *On the way.*

"Hi, Darla," Steve's daughter Kayla Mookjai greeted her from behind the hostess counter. Today, the smiling teen was dressed in black capris and a white T-shirt topped by a cropped black vest. Her sleek black hair was twisted in some complicated knot and held in place with a red lacquered chopstick, giving her a casually professional look.

Steve must have laid down the law about the dress code, Darla thought with a smile. On most of her previous visits, Kayla had made do with cutoff blue jeans and logo T-shirts of various sorts.

"Is it just you today?" the girl asked, reaching behind the tranquil golden Buddha statue on the counter beside her for a menu and silverware.

Darla shook her head. "Actually, Detective Reese will be joining me in a bit." Keeping in mind the likely direction their conversation would take, she added, "Can we get a booth?"

Kayla obligingly led her to a booth directly beneath an ornately framed photograph of an elderly Asian gentleman in embroidered gold robes. The somber, kindly faced image was that of the Thai king, whom Darla had learned on a previous visit was the world's longest-reigning monarch. Taking a bit of comfort in his serene presence, she settled in and studied the menu for a few moments.

"Ah, Darla, it is good to see you. It has been so long."

She glanced up to see Steve, dressed in his usual crisp chef's jacket, standing beside the booth. Despite the late night—the restaurant had still been open when Darla had left after midnight—he looked relatively well rested and good-humored, smiling at his mild joke.

"It has been, hasn't it?" she greeted him with a matching smile, putting aside the menu. Then, sobering, she went on, "Thanks for hosting everyone last night. I know you've got good reason to dislike George, but that was kind of you to let us all gather here."

"Livvy was nice lady, so I thought it right. My children like her very much." He paused and made a show of glancing around. "So, you here alone today?"

"Actually, Detective Reese is joining me. He's just running a bit late." Then, recalling an earlier thought, she added, "Have you heard from Doug today? Now that I think about it, I don't remember seeing him here last night with everyone else. And when Robert went to pick up doughnuts for the coffee bar, his place was locked up."

"Did you call him?"

"Yes, but I only got his voice mail."

Steve shrugged. "Maybe he tired after yesterday and decide to take a day off. I do that, too, but I have two kids to send to college."

"That's what I was thinking, and I have to say I don't blame him. It's just that I was hoping that we could all get together sometime today or tomorrow for a postmortem."

Steve's eyes opened wide. "Postmortem? Like on *CSI*? I do not understand why we would do this."

Darla winced. "Sorry, bad choice of words, under the circumstances. I was throwing out a little business jargon from my old job. We always had a postmortem meeting after a project—you know, like our block party—finished, so we could figure out what worked and what didn't, and how to fix all the 'didn'ts' for next time."

"Ah, yes, a post-project evaluation," he said with a nod, earning a look of surprise from Darla. He smiled a little. "Remember, I go to business school, myself. Yes, a very good idea. If you call Penelope, I call Doug later."

"Perfect. And I'll call Hank, too. We can all meet at the bookstore as early tomorrow morning as you want. Send me a text after you get hold of Doug."

With a promise to send out some complimentary mango sorbet after her meal, Steve headed back to the kitchen. Darla, meanwhile, glanced at her watch. Quarter after one. Late for a civilian, but still in the ballpark of being on time for a cop. She wondered a bit uncharitably if Connie was with the program yet when it came to her future spouse's punctuality.

And then the restaurant door opened again, and Reese strode in.

He was dressed for work, wearing gray slacks and a summer-weight sport coat of pale blue and gray herringbone over a crisp white dress shirt. He'd definitely improved from a sartorial perspective since she'd first met him, Darla thought in approval, even though she knew it wasn't by choice. He had confided a while back that his superiors had strongly suggested the wardrobe upgrade if he wanted to be considered for promotion.

She watched as he stopped at the hostess stand. His gaze beneath his usual wraparound sunglasses swept the room and landed on her with a nod of acknowledgment. Despite herself, Darla couldn't help feeling the tiniest thrill of anticipation.

Just two friends having lunch, she reminded herself, trying to ignore the color she could feel rising in her cheeks. *Besides, he's an engaged man now, and off the market.*

Kayla, meanwhile, had been chatting with her brother, Jason, who was working this day as a busboy. Spying Reese waiting, however, the girl turned her back on the teen and practically ran to the front.

She added a distinctly saucy bounce to her walk as she gestured Reese to follow and led him over to the booth.

Without asking, Darla swiftly switched sides so that Reese could have his preferred seat, the one facing the door. *One of those "cop" things*, as he'd long ago explained to her. Jake did it, too, always sitting in a spot with a clear view of any entrances or exits so that she could keep an eye out for any potential trouble. By the time she was settled again, Reese had pulled off his sport coat and was sliding into her just-vacated spot.

"I'll be right back for your order," Kayla promised him as she provided another menu and set of silverware, seeming to forget that Darla was at the table as well.

Reese waited until the girl was out of earshot to say, "I appreciate you meeting on short notice, Darla. I really need to talk to you, without anyone else around."

She nodded, not certain which was more unsettling . . . the whole "needing to talk" thing, or the fact that he'd called her Darla, and not "Red." Irritating as she'd always found the nickname, it occurred to her now that she rather missed hearing it from him. Had he decided such kidding around was a bit too friendly under the current circumstances?

He'd slipped off his sunglasses as he spoke, and she could see fine lines and dark smudges beneath his blue eyes. No doubt he, too, had spent a very late Fourth.

"Was Connie disappointed to miss the fireworks?" she asked in an innocent tone.

Reese rolled his eyes. "Don't worry. She got to see them. We were headed back to her place when I got the call about Mrs. King, so I called in a favor with an off-duty street cop I know. I slipped him a few bucks to escort her out to the launch, and then put her in a cab back home afterward."

"Well, I'm sure she understood. It'll be like that a lot for her once you two tie the knot."

Reese shrugged. "Don't worry. Connie knows the drill. She's got an uncle and a couple of cousins who are cops."

He paused as Kayla came back to take their order.

Darla went with her usual shrimp fried rice—"and don't forget the bottle of chili sauce," she reminded the girl—while Reese went for basic pad Thai. Both of them opted for the traditional coconut milk soup flavored with lemongrass and chunks of chicken.

They chatted about inconsequential things until Kayla brought the soup; then, after a quick taste, Reese set down his patterned ceramic spoon. His voice lowered to a confidential tone now, he said, "Like I told you in my text, we need to talk. There's something I didn't have a chance to ask you about yesterday."

Darla set down her own spoon and nodded, her earlier nervousness returning. Was he going to demand to know if she had feelings for him, after all? Or, perhaps worse, did he want relationship advice?

"Ask away," she told him with more equanimity than she felt, and casually returned to her soup.

He glanced around as if to be sure they wouldn't be overheard, even though the only other diners were at tables along the front windows. Apparently satisfied, he leaned toward Darla and asked, "What do you know about vaping?"

"Vaping?"

She stared at him in confusion, trying to absorb what seemed to be a complete non sequitur. Weren't they there to discuss Reese's unexpected engagement? What did e-cigarettes have to do with that? Obviously, this wasn't the topic he'd wanted to discuss with her the other day in the bookstore, so she had been wrong about his motive for wanting to see her.

Unsure whether to be disappointed or relieved, she took another spoonful of soup to give herself a chance to regain her composure, and then replied, "I know what it is, if that's what you're asking."

"Go on."

Feeling like she was answering some sort of trivia quiz, Darla set down her spoon again.

"I'm not an expert, but from what Livvy told me about it, I know you put flavored nicotine oil into a reservoir in a battery-powered vapor pen that heats up. The oil—they call it "juice"—produces this warm steam that you inhale like you would cigarette smoke. Most people use vape pens to help quit the smoking habit, but a lot of people—particularly teenagers—vape for the sake of vaping."

"Go to the head of the class," he said with an approving nod. "So, anyone you know doing it?"

The detective's tone was casual, but all at once Darla was certain that he had a very specific reason for asking that question. Curious now herself—if she gave him some answers, maybe he'd share the true question?—she said, "Penelope Winston, the dance instructor, vapes, as they call it. And George King, too."

"Uh-huh," he muttered, reaching for his sport coat to pull out a small notebook, which he flipped open and scribbled in. "You said Mrs. King told you about vaping. So you're saying that she used a vapor pen, too?"

Darla considered that last question for a moment, a bit surprised he didn't already know this from George. "Yes, actually, she did . . . but not for nicotine. She had rheumatoid arthritis and said she used the vape pen with some concoctions she made to treat herself. Why do you ask?"

Reese's shrug seemed a bit too casual as he picked up his spoon again and dipped into his soup.

"Idle curiosity," he replied after a couple of swallows. "When we moved Mrs. King's body yesterday, we found one of those vape pens lying underneath her. I wondered if she'd dropped it when she collapsed."

Darla frowned, forgetting her earlier dismay. Maybe Livvy's death was connected to her vaping, just as she and Jake had theorized that morning. Could Livvy have accidentally overdosed on some potent herbal cure?

She was tempted to run her theory by Reese, but she knew from past experience that he'd likely dismiss her idea as the product of an overactive imagination. Besides, if there were any traces of herbs in Livvy's system, the ME would find them. It wasn't Darla's job.

She was saved from having to make any response when Kayla reappeared bearing a large plate of pad Thai in one hand and a condiment caddy in the other. She set Reese's plate before him and put the condiment caddy to one side.

"Here you go. Fish sauce, sugar, white vinegar with sliced chile, ground dried chile," she told him, pointing in quick succession to each lidded glass jar with its individual long metal spoon. "I had Pop toss on a few extra shrimp, on the house. Anything else I can get for you?"

"How about my shrimp fried rice?" Darla asked with a bland smile.

The girl had the good grace to look embarrassed.

"So sorry. I'll be right back," she exclaimed and scampered back to the kitchen. She reappeared a moment later with Darla's meal, along with a tiny foil packet shaped into a star.

"So sorry," she repeated, sounding legitimately contrite. Indicating the foil star, she added, "And I brought you some more shrimp to take back to Hamlet."

Well played, Darla thought in admiration. Aloud, she assured the girl, "Hamlet will be very pleased. Thanks for thinking of him."

Once Kayla retreated again, Darla and Reese settled in to eat, and for a few minutes the only sounds were those of clinking silverware and chewing. Then Reese set down his spoon and leaned back, swiping his mouth with his napkin.

"There's something else I need to talk to you about," he abruptly declared.

Darla set down her own utensils, sensing that the conversation she thought they'd avoided was going to happen, after all. Her first impulse was to cut him short and skip the drama, but Reese's expression was that of a man who had come to a decision and was prepared to see it through.

Might as well get all the awkwardness out of the way before it drags on too long, she thought with an inner sigh and nodded for him to proceed.

"Remember the other day in the bookstore when I stopped by?" he began. "I didn't just happen to be in the neighborhood. I came there specifically to explain about—"

The rhythmic beep from the vicinity of his sport coat cut him short. With an apologetic, "Sorry," he swiftly rummaged in his jacket pocket and pulled out his cell phone.

"Reese," he answered, tucking the phone between ear and shoulder as he reached for his notebook and pen. "Yeah. You sure? How long ago?" he went on, scribbling a few notes. Flipping the notebook closed again, he told the caller, "Got it. I'm on my way."

He hung up the call and slid out of the booth, gathering his jacket and cramming his gear into its pocket again.

"Sorry," he repeated. "Duty calls, gotta go." Waving Kayla over, he reached for his wallet, adding, "We'll catch up another time."

"Sure," Darla agreed aloud. *Bullet dodged*, she silently congratulated herself.

A few moments later, leaving the last bit of his pad Thai uneaten, Reese was out the door. *Connie had better know the drill, all right*, Darla thought with a snort.

She finished off her shrimp fried rice, and Kayla brought over the promised mango ice cream for dessert. Before digging in, however, Darla remembered her conversation with Steve about the post-project meeting, so she pulled out her phone and quickly dialed Hank. He answered on the first ring and, after she explained the plan, agreed he'd be available tomorrow morning. She also mentioned her concern over not having been able to reach Doug.

"Sorry, Darla, haven't heard from him," Hank said. "Call me back with a time as soon as you get hold of everyone else. If I hear from Doug, I'll tell him to call you pronto."

That task out of the way, she polished off the mango ice cream in a few bites; then, Hamlet's shrimp in hand, she headed out the door. But instead of heading directly to the store, she went a few stops the opposite way, to Penelope's dance studio. Might as well check in with the woman in person about the meeting tomorrow. Besides, maybe Penelope had heard from Doug.

As she reached the door, however, Darla found the dance studio was locked. A festive length of bunting still hung over the entry, though, and what appeared to be a hastily written sign in black marker on the blank side of a shoe box lid was taped to the front door.

"Closed for the holiday weekend," Darla read aloud.

Of course it made sense. Penelope had planned to be away, and with their block party obligation fulfilled, her students would all be with their families or traveling for the July Fourth weekend. Nodding to herself, she turned around and headed back to the bookstore.

Even so, something about the shuttered studio nagged at her. But it wasn't until she reached her own stoop that Darla realized what it was.

The sign.

TWELVE

DARLA GAVE A CONSIDERING FROWN AS SHE CLIMBED THE steps leading to the bookstore's front door. Penelope was nothing if not artistic. Darla had seen her handiwork in the signage and fliers for the block party. If she was going to be shutting her studio for the long weekend, surely she would have already had a notice made spelling that out, or, at minimum, she could have readily printed up something on her computer.

A hand-scrawled notice taped to the door just didn't seem Penelope's style.

Maybe she was overthinking it. Maybe Penelope had just been in a hurry, Darla decided. Or maybe she'd asked one of her students to put the notice up for her.

She stepped into the store only to practically stumble

over Hamlet, who came racing past her like he had a bottle rocket tied to his tail. Skittering after him with long pink tongue lolling and star-spangled leash trailing was Roma. Rushing right behind the dog was Robert.

"Uh, sorry, Ms. P.," he exclaimed over his shoulder as he continued the chase. "Since it's pretty dead here, we were working on 'sit' when Hamlet came over and hissed at her."

"And the race was on," James dryly finished for him from his spot at the collectible books locked case. He finished polishing the glass shelf front and then carried cleaner and rag to the counter.

"Perhaps we should rethink our 'pet-friendly' policy," he added as he tucked those items beneath the register.

Robert, meanwhile, had corralled Roma and returned her to the front. "Hamlet started it," he said a bit defensively, giving the small dog a consoling pat. "But, don't worry. I'll take her back to my apartment as soon as my shift is up."

"Go on ahead now. It's close enough," Darla said with a glance at her watch, smiling a little at the fact that, for once, Robert had taken Roma's side over Hamlet's.

As the teen left with his pup, Darla turned her attention to James and smiled as she took a good look at his vest du jour.

"Interesting sartorial touch," she said, indicating the mod paisley print he was wearing that shrieked 1960s and was a definite change from the traditional wool or tailored linen he favored. In fact, the vest looked like one of the funky thrift store finds that Robert often wore as a bit of friendly ribbing at the expense of the older man.

James gave the vest a straightening tug. “As a matter of fact, this was a gift from Martha,” he said with lofty dignity. “She found it in a vintage clothing shop. According to the vest’s provenance, it came from the Jimi Hendrix estate.”

“Impressive,” Darla agreed. But the mod vest reminded her of the story he’d told earlier. Changing the subject, she asked, “You know how people always start out stories by saying, ‘A friend of mine did such-and-such,’ when they really mean that they did it themselves, but they don’t want to admit it?”

“A common dissociative conversational tactic, yes.”

“Well, about that guy you said you knew back in the day who sold cat food lids. Was he by any chance you?”

“Certainly not.” James shot Darla an offended look, which Hamlet promptly echoed with an outraged meow. “And I assure you that, should I ever choose to engage in any such flimflam, my deception would not so easily be discovered.”

“You’re right, my apologies,” Darla said with a chagrined smile. Then she took a deep breath and said, “You know, I have a friend myself with a small dilemma that she told me about.”

“And what is your friend’s issue?”

“Well, she kind of had a thing going with this guy she liked, except that nothing really came of the relationship. She was okay with that, because she figured if it was meant to be, it would happen, and so she let things ride.”

“And the problem . . . ?”

Darla hesitated, wondering what had compelled her to begin making such a confession to her store manager, of all people. Finally, she finished in a rush, "The problem is that she found out that he's unexpectedly gotten engaged. Now she's thinking maybe she'll regret missing the boat, and she's not sure what to do about it."

"I see."

James considered the matter for a few moments, while Darla waited uncomfortably for him to share his opinion. When it came to personal relationships, James wasn't exactly the "Dear Abby" of booksellers. But when it came to cutting through the crap, Professor James T. James was definitely the champ.

Finally, he said, "As I see it, your friend has two options. She can choose to wish the man sincere felicitations and retain him as a friend, or she can choose to confess her true feelings to him and see where that takes them."

"Well, she's already tried option number one, and so far it's not working for her," Darla admitted. "But if she tries option number two, she might end up making a fool of herself if it turns out he doesn't have the same feelings and runs screaming into the night. And then, when all the dust settles, she's an idiot who's also lost a good friend."

"A difficult decision, indeed, and one where there is no right or wrong answer. But at the conclusion of the day, only you—pardon me, your friend—can make that choice. Everyone else's opinion is moot."

"Yeah, I—I mean, she—was afraid of that. I'll tell her to take that under consideration."

With the subject settled—at least, for the moment—James went upstairs to work on his special orders and troll his usual sources for any interesting deals. Darla, meanwhile, did a little inventory review and put the finishing touches on next week's orders. But when a couple of hours had passed and no other customers had dropped in, she summoned James from his rare book lair.

"No point in keeping the doors open until closing if we're not even going to cover the electric bill," she told him. "Why don't we call it a day a few hours early?"

"I have no objection to that."

"Perfect," she decreed. Then she frowned. "You know, as soon as I lock up, I might take Hamlet and wander down to Doug's shop. I tried to get him on the phone several times already today, and Robert said this morning that his shop was locked up, but maybe he's there now. I really want to meet with all the block party committee while things are fresh in our minds."

"I have no other plans, myself," James said. "Would you like me to accompany you there?"

"Sure, I'd rather like the company. Let me shut everything down and get Hamlet ready."

A quarter of an hour later, humans and feline were walking in the direction of Doug's doughnut shop. Perhaps it was the circumstances of the past day, along with the fact that Penelope was apparently MIA, too, but Darla couldn't help but wonder at her friend's seeming disappearance. She said as much to James, who gave her a reassuring nod.

"I suspect his cellular phone battery died and he did not realize it; that, or he turned the ringer down previously and forgot to turn it up again. I am certain there is nothing sinister surrounding his absence—or Ms. Winston's, for that matter."

Hamlet, padding briskly alongside them, meowed his agreement.

A block later, they crossed to the opposite sidewalk and halted outside Doug's DOUGhnuts. The neon sign in the window was on, falsely claiming that fresh doughnuts were ready for the eating, but the window display case that usually was filled with tempting offerings was empty. On the street-level door was taped a sign that looked familiar: black marker on the blank side of a shoe box lid.

"Closed for the holiday weekend," she read, and then glanced over at James. "Remember that I told you Penelope's studio was closed? Funny, this sign is identical to the one I saw on her door."

"Not so strange, if the same person made both notices," James pointed out.

Darla shook her head. "Maybe, but when Robert told me about checking out Doug's store this morning, he specifically said there wasn't a sign anywhere. And now there is."

"Really, Darla, you are making a mystery out of nothing. For all we know, Doug stopped by after Robert was here and posted his sign. And perhaps Penelope had asked him to place one on her door at the same time. Or maybe Doug asked Penelope to place a sign at his shop when she posted one on hers."

Darla considered that a moment. What James said made sense; still, something nagged at her. She peered into the shop window again, trying with little success to fight an unsettled feeling. Then a movement beside her caught her attention.

"Hamlet, what's the matter?"

Darla glanced down to where the cat had been sitting quietly at her feet. Now, he stretched on his hind legs to his full length so that he, too, could peer through the glass. With one oversized paw, he began tapping on the glass.

"James, try the door," she urged.

The man gave the knob a quick jiggle. "Locked," he confirmed. "Does Doug live above the shop?"

"No, he lives somewhere nearby, but I'm not sure exactly where."

"Me—OOW!"

Hamlet had increased his fervor from simply batting on the window to assaulting the glass. Darla shot James a worried look.

"Something's wrong, or Hamlet wouldn't be acting like this. We should call 9-1-1 for a welfare check."

"Darla, I find Hamlet's behavior concerning, as well," he said with a frown, peering into the window. "But you can hardly expect the police to break down Doug's door simply because a cat is meowing and pawing at the window of a food establishment. They would say—and rightly so—that there is probably some rodent within that has caught his attention."

"You mean, like the catnip?" Then her resolve stiffened again. "It wasn't just that he wanted the catnip. He was letting us know something was up with that coffee."

"Perhaps so, but others may take more convincing," he said, then with a sigh added, "Very well, I shall try the lock again. Perhaps there's a back way in, and we—"

"Hey, people," came a familiar voice from behind them, "if you need a doughnut that bad, there's a chain store down on West 63rd where you can get yourself one of those mass-produced lumps of lard."

"Doug!" Darla whipped around and nearly sobbed in relief at the sight of the grinning, burly baker.

She almost didn't recognize him, for he wasn't wearing his usual baker's whites. Rather, he was dressed in blue jeans that had been cut off below the knees and an untucked pale blue fishing shirt with the sleeves rolled to show his tanned forearms.

"We were worried because your store was locked up and no one could get you on your cell," she told him, feeling foolish now for panicking, and leaving off any mention of Hamlet's behavior.

He chuckled, the gold chains around his neck jingling. "Yeah, I couldn't find my phone, and I finally figured out I musta left it here, so I came back out to look for it."

He held up a set of keys and gave James, who still had a hand on the doorknob, a friendly nod. "Hey, pal, how about we go inside the traditional way?"

"Be my guest," James replied, stepping aside with a small sweep of his arm to usher Doug over.

The baker frowned, however, as he caught sight of the handwritten sign taped to his door.

"Where in the heck did this come from?" he muttered, his reaction drawing matching concern from Darla as she realized her previous suspicions were correct. "I just shut the place for the day, not the whole weekend."

Ripping down the sign, he tucked the cardboard under one beefy arm and stuck his key in the lock. He opened the door, and the familiar beeping of an alarm system greeted them. Doug stepped inside and punched a few numbers on the lighted panel next to the doorjamb, ending the beeps.

"Okay, we're good to go. C'mon in," he said, and then wrinkled his nose as he looked around. "Musta forgot to take the trash out last night."

Darla and James, accompanied by Hamlet, stepped inside the bakery. It was warm within, not much cooler than the outside temperature. Still, that made sense if Doug had planned to shut down the place for a day. But he was right, she thought, wrinkling her nose. The place held the faintest unpleasant aroma, though she couldn't identify what it might be.

While Doug headed back to the kitchen, Darla glanced around the store.

It was obvious that Doug had headed out in a hurry last night. Someone—presumably he—had tossed a couple of large red and blue striped cloth tarps over what Darla knew was a combination order counter and glass-fronted display case beneath. Darla recognized the coverings as the ones from Doug's booth at the block party. A couple of Penelope's giant red, white, and blue pinwheels—the ones she'd "gone Brooklyn" on to get in time—were propped against the counter's front, as well.

Hamlet made as if to paw at these, but Darla gently pulled him back by his leash and gave him a headshake, *no.*

Otherwise, the place looked its usual self: a few mismatched wooden tables and chairs meant for dining in, a pair of mixing bowl hanging lamps overhead, and oversized photos of elaborately iced doughnuts framed in salvaged barn lumber hung along one wall. *Food porn,* Darla always called it. Now, she stared at the photos a bit longingly. It was a while yet until supper, and she could use a snack.

Doug, meanwhile, came striding back from the rear. "Hey, James, you mind dialing my number? That phone's gotta be around here somewhere."

James obligingly pulled out his own cell and punched in the numbers Doug gave him. Almost immediately, the sound of an old-style telephone ringing filled the room.

"I believe the tone is coming from beneath those drop cloths," James said with a wave toward the covered counter.

Doug nodded his head. "I musta set the phone down while I was hauling in the decorations and didn't even realize it," he said, heading behind the counter and whipping off the tarps so that they pooled on the floor at his feet, revealing the glass display front.

"Look," he confirmed in triumph, grabbing up the still-ringing cell from the laminated countertop. "I feel like an idiot. It was here all along, and—what? What's wrong, Darla?"

Vaguely, Darla was aware that she'd taken a staggering step back and that Hamlet had pulled his leash free of her suddenly limp grasp and had trotted to the display counter. She heard Doug still speaking . . . registered James's shocked intake of breath as Doug's cell phone quit ringing.

Her attention, however, was fixed on what—or, rather, who—lay upon the cool white tile floor, wedged up against the glass display case.

Penelope Winston looked as if she were sleeping, gently curled on her right side, eyes closed and hands neatly folded beneath her cheek. She was wearing a flowing, lacy white sundress, and Darla was reminded of *Swan Lake*'s tragic Odette felled by an errant arrow.

But Darla knew that, just as with the swan princess, Penelope would never awaken to dance again.

THIRTEEN

"I MEAN, NO OFFENSE TO THE DEAD PEOPLE, BUT THIS IS really cutting into my time with my fiancé," Connie complained as she sat on the stoop near Doug's shop while fanning herself with a bridal magazine. "I can't believe this is happening twice in one weekend."

Darla shot the woman a sour look. Connie's outfit for today was a slight improvement over yesterday's wardrobe choice: a floral camp-style shirt, the top several buttons left undone, and a pair of white short shorts (all the better to show off her tanned legs). The oversized red canvas tote Connie had slung over her shoulder had more square inches of fabric to it than any article of clothing she wore on her body. As for her hair, it was still sky high, though today she'd accessorized with a perky headband that matched her shirt.

Catching Darla's disapproving expression, Connie shrugged. "Sorry, I was just sayin'," she huffed, opening her periodical and leafing through the pages.

Darla, meanwhile, settled in for the wait, wishing she had a magazine to fan herself with, too. She and James were waiting for their turns to be questioned by Reese. Two dead in two days . . . two ballerinas cut down in mid-pirouette. While she'd seen no immediate sign of trauma on Penelope's body to indicate anything other than a natural death, it was too strange—too coincidental—for the two women to have died within a day of each other.

Let Reese figure it all out, she told herself. She and Hamlet had done their part by discovering the body.

The body.

Shocking as Livvy's death had been, somehow the sight of Penelope's lifeless form lying there beside Doug's display case was even more unnerving. As for Doug, himself . . .

She shook her head at the grim memory. At the look on Darla's face, Doug had rushed around the counter to discover just what had stunned both her and James into silence. One look at the woman's lifeless body, and he'd dropped to his knees with a gasp. A moment later, however, he'd rallied and reached out to her, only to be held back by James.

"You cannot do anything for her," the older man had assured him as Doug attempted to break free again. "She is already beyond help. We must leave everything untouched and call the police right now."

Apparently, James's advice had sunk in, for he subsided, though Darla had been surprised to see tears trickling down Doug's plump cheeks, which were red now with emotion. *But, of course, it would have been a shock to find a body in one's place of business,* Darla had told herself, *let alone that of a friend.* She'd had a few tears running down her own face.

While James and Doug had waited outside the bakery for the authorities to arrive, Darla had hurried back to the bookstore with Hamlet. *No need to keep him there in the midst of what would very soon be a police investigation,* she'd told James. Having left the clever feline to his kibble, she'd headed back to the scene of the crime.

She had called Jake as she race-walked her way back to the bakery, needing a bit of moral support. She'd not worried about phoning Reese, certain that he'd be arriving soon enough in the wake of the 9-1-1 call.

The PI had been stunned, as well. Like Darla, Jake had only known Penelope casually, but the two women had enjoyed each other's company.

But that hadn't been Jake's only concern.

"I've got a bad feeling about this whole thing, kid," she'd said, echoing Darla's earlier unsettling thoughts. "First Livvy, and now Penelope? Not that there's any indication it's not just a weird coincidence, two people dropping dead like that. After all, Penelope was a smoker, and she might have had some health problems no one knew about. But the fact that she was underneath the drop cloth, not on top of it, seems to point to someone trying to conceal a body. And what was she doing in Doug's store, anyhow?"

"It doesn't make sense," Darla had agreed, and then hesitated. "Unless . . ."

Unless Doug had been the man that Penelope was

supposed to go off on a weekend holiday with, she'd thought with a sudden flash of insight.

The PI, however, was still talking. "With the holiday weekend and all, I doubt the coroner has come back with Livvy's cause of death yet, but until we know what—or who—killed her and Penelope, I think we all should watch our backs."

Jake had hung up after that unnerving bit of advice, leaving Darla to wish she'd never thought of a block party in the first place.

By the time she returned to the bakery, the police were already rolling in. Within minutes, a crime scene perimeter had been set, more yellow and black tape hung like grim party decorations from railing to streetlight to railing again. She, James, and Doug were shunted to one side with a street cop as chaperone while they waited to be questioned as material witnesses.

And not long after that, Reese had shown up, Connie again in tow.

Now, Doug walked over from where he'd been talking to Reese. He jerked a thumb in James's direction. "You're up next, boss, then Darla. They're done with me for now, so I'm gonna make a quick run down to the market."

James unfolded himself from where he'd been sitting on a small concrete bench outside the shuttered Child's Play shop—they, too, had a "Closed" sign on the door, albeit a more official-looking one than the shoe box lid—and stretched. As he walked past Darla, he murmured, "I fear I will have to tell Detective Reese about George's enterprise, if you know what I mean. I have a suspicion that there could be a connection between that and these recent deaths."

"Oh, right," she murmured back, surprised that she'd already forgotten about that incident. But how could the fake drug scam possibly link the two women's deaths?

Once James walked out of earshot, Connie lowered her magazine. Looking from side to side, in case she was overheard, she said, "I've been questioned by the cops before, Darla, so let me give you some advice. Don't volunteer nothing. They ask, you answer, the end."

"That even goes for when it's Reese, er, Fiorello asking the questions?" Darla wanted to know, smiling just a little.

Connie snorted. "It goes double for him. I swear, that man could pry a whole speech outta one of them street mimes."

Now, Darla grinned outright. "Well, it *is* his job."

"Yeah, his job." She gave an impatient tsk. "My uncle and two of my cousins are on the force, so I seen it all. I always swore I'd never fall for a cop, but there you go."

Connie gave a restless glance down at her magazine; then, abruptly, she looked up again, her expression brightening. "I have a great idea. You should be one of the bridesmaids at me and Fi's wedding!"

"Me? Bridesmaid?"

Darla stared at her in shock. Images of the ugly red dresses and crude photo ops that she and Jake had joked about at the block party flashed through her mind as she tried to decide whether or not Connie was truly serious. Finally, she managed, "That's a lovely offer, but to be honest, we don't really know each other. Don't you want your bridesmaids to be your close friends and relatives?"

"I got twelve bridesmaids already lined up, sisters and cousins," she replied with a dismissive wave. "The thing is, there's not anyone from Fi's side—girls, I mean—who's gonna be standing up with us. But he's talked to me about you. He says he thinks of you as an older sister. So I thought it might be fun if you were there. You know, kind of filling in, so he'd be represented. You can be lucky number thirteen!"

Darla barely heard that last bit, however. All that echoed in her mind was the realization that Reese apparently viewed her as a sibling . . . and an older one, at that! There was, what, a year's difference in age between them? Hardly enough to hang that "older sister" label on her. She could see him thinking of Jake that way, but her?

Connie stared at her expectantly, smile bright. Darla managed a matching smile, though inwardly she still fumed. For a few uncharitable moments, she actually considered agreeing to Connie's offer. How did that saying go? *Keep your friends close, and your enemies closer.* Then she shook her head. No way was she going to open this can of bridal party worms!

"Thanks, Connie," she told the other woman. "It's really sweet of you to offer, but I just wouldn't feel right being up there at the altar along with all your relatives and friends."

Connie shrugged. "Suit yourself. But you should know we've got some really cute groomsmen lined up. You should see my second cousin, Mario. He's a looker . . . and single, too!"

Before Darla could respond, she heard James calling her name, so she left Connie to her magazine and got to her feet. As he approached, James said, "Detective Reese is ready to take your statement now."

"What about you?" she asked. "Can you go now?"

"I am officially dismissed, though he may have more

questions for me later." James gave a lift of his brow, obviously quoting the detective verbatim. "But if you wish, I can wait here for you to finish and then walk you back home again."

"Thanks, that's okay. But maybe you could call Steve and Hank for me, and let them know what's going on."

James frowned. "It is possible that Detective Reese might want to speak with them, as well. He might prefer that we do not, shall we say, give them a heads-up regarding the current situation."

"Surely Steve and Hank wouldn't be considered suspects, would they?"

"I would postulate that anyone and everyone could be a suspect at this point . . . excluding you and me, of course."

She noticed that he didn't include Doug among the excluded number. And if her suspicion was correct, that he'd been the man Penelope had been seeing, that would definitely put Doug into the suspect category. Maybe James had already guessed as much, too. That, or he was simply being polite in including her in the "not a suspect" category.

"I tell you what," she decided, "I'll ask Reese if it's okay to talk to them. If he says no, I'll abide by that. But if he doesn't care, I'll give them both a call as soon as I can. I mean, if the situation were reversed, I'd be pretty ticked that no one let me know a friend of mine had been murdered."

"Agreed. And I shall see you again tomorrow at the store."

As James headed off and Darla mentally girded herself for the verbal battle to come, Connie lowered her magazine again. "Remember what I said. Don't volunteer nothing."

"He asks, I answer, the end," she replied with a slight smile, obediently finishing the official Connie mantra.

The woman nodded in approval. "Go get 'em."

Reese was talking to two of the responding beat cops when she approached. Excusing himself, he gestured Darla to follow him around the crime scene tape barrier to the far side of the building. Their route took them right past the open doorway to the doughnut shop.

Darla couldn't help but glance over. From her vantage point, she could see a portion of the counter. Half a dozen people—crime scene investigators, she guessed from their uniform of coveralls, booties, and gloves—were poking about, their activity thankfully blocking her view of the body near the display case. How quickly they would remove Penelope, she couldn't guess, but she prayed it would be soon.

The fallen swan should have long since exited stage right.

Reese motioned her to a nearby stoop. They both sat, and he pulled his familiar notebook from his jacket pocket. He hadn't removed his wraparound sunglasses—the better to frighten those mimes into speech, she wryly assumed—but his tone was off-the-clock Reese as he said, "Two days in a row, Darla? That's gotta be some kind of record."

To her mortification, she felt tears well up in her eyes. These were, after all, her neighbors—or, in the case of Penelope, her friend—that she had lost, and not some anonymous passersby.

Reese immediately dug into his other pocket for a clean handkerchief and handed it over. "Sorry, Red," he told her, sounding genuinely concerned. "Sometimes you have to keep the mood light, or everything goes to hell."

Welcome as those words were, it was hearing that familiar nickname again that made Darla's tears suddenly fall in earnest. She managed to compose herself again quickly, though, and asked instead, "Do you know yet how Livvy died?"

He shook his head. "We're putting a rush on it now because of Ms. Winston. Not to talk out of school, but if I was a betting man my money would be on something other than natural causes."

You think so? was Darla's reflexive thought. Visions flashed through her mind of a fleeced teenager seeking payback and taking advantage of Pinky's final, distracting number to smack the young woman over the head with a convenient crowbar when no one was looking. Aloud, however, she replied, "That's what Jake said."

Reese's headshake declared, *Yeah, I'll bet she did*, but all he said was, "Let's go over the timeline, when you last actually saw Ms. Winston, how you came to be at Doug Bates's store the same time he was. You know the drill."

Then he paused and looked over his sunglasses at her. "And please don't tell me that that cat of yours was involved again."

For the next several minutes, and with prompts from Reese, Darla went over the events of the past couple of days as they pertained to Penelope. Her last actual contact with the woman, she realized, had been waving to her after the flash mob dancers did their final routine.

"I did think something was off when I saw that sign on her door," Darla told him as she explained about stopping by Penelope's studio following her and Reese's abbreviated lunch.

Reese paused in his writing and held up his hand in a "wait one minute" gesture before waving over one of the street cops. "Bring me that evidence bag marked 'Sign.'"

The officer returned a moment later with a large paper bag that Darla saw had dates and numbers scribbled on it. Reese unfolded its top edge and carefully pulled out a familiar-looking shoe box top with writing on it. "You mean this one?"

"That one was on Doug's door, but one that looked just like it was on Penelope's studio door, too."

Reese nodded. "We're in the process of getting warrants to search her home and studio for evidence. While we're there, we'll grab the sign, assuming it's still hanging there. But how do you know that Ms. Winston didn't make both of them—the sign for her door and the one for Mr. Bates?"

"Because Penelope was, well, artistic. It seems unlike her to have just scribbled on a piece of cardboard like that."

Darla quickly explained how the woman had been the person who designed the fliers and other signs for the block party. She added, "And Doug acted pretty surprised to find a sign on his door. He didn't put it there, and he obviously didn't seem to have any idea who did."

"We'll get to that in a second. What about this?" he asked and flipped the box lid over, so that Darla saw the opposite side for the first time.

"Capezio," she read aloud, her eyes widening.

"What, is that an expensive brand?"

"It's a famous dance shoe brand . . . slippers, pointe shoes, and so on. Yeah, yeah, I took ballet for six months when I was ten years old," she added when he gave her another look over the sunglasses. "Wait. That must mean whoever wrote both the signs also had access to Penelope's studio. Where else would you find shoe box lids like these on short notice?"

Reese nodded approvingly as he repacked the lid into the evidence bag and made several more notes. Then he sat back a little and said, "So tell me about George and Livvy King's scam drug business."

Feeling a bit guilty for saying anything after she'd all but promised George she wouldn't, Darla explained how she had overheard two of Penelope's students praising the Kona Blue Party blend and, hoping to get a jump on her competition, had decided to try it for herself. Reese managed to keep a straight face as Darla related Hamlet's extreme interest in the coffee, which had prompted her and Jake to do their feline experiments to validate their guess as to what the baggie really held.

He frowned, however, when Darla told him how many customers Livvy and George were getting a day. "That's a nice little sideline . . . two, three grand a week, tax free. The trouble is, someone else besides Hamlet might have been smart enough to figure out it wasn't drugs that the Kings were selling. And they might not have been happy about getting burned like that."

"But how would Penelope fit into that scenario?"

The detective shrugged.

"You said the customer base was mostly kids. Maybe Ms. Winston was referring some of her kids to the Kings as customers, and she decided she should get a bigger piece of the action. You know what they say, 'no honor among thieves.'"

Then, when Darla made a sound of protest, he went on, "I'm not saying that's how it really went down. I'm not saying anything yet. And it might turn out that both women died of natural causes. Sometimes two separate deaths really are two separate deaths."

From there, they talked about Darla and James's original arrival at the doughnut shop. Darla made a point of explaining Hamlet's actions, from pawing on the front glass and meowing, to trying to check out the covered display counter. She was sure Reese was rolling his eyes behind his sunglasses, but he dutifully made notes all the same. Finally, he flipped the notebook closed again.

"I think that's all I need from you right now," he told her. "You know the drill. You think of anything else I should know, you give me a call. Oh, and I'd appreciate it if you'd keep quiet about this until I have a chance to talk to any other possible material witnesses first, like your friends Mr. Tomlinson and Mr. Mookjai."

Which answered her earlier question.

He rose from the stoop and held out a hand to her. Reflexively, she grasped his fingers to let him pull her up, and then caught her breath as she felt an undeniable tingle run through her at his touch. Whether or not he felt the same thing, she wasn't sure, though she noticed he continued to hold her hand even after she'd gained her footing.

"Connie asked me to be a bridesmaid in your wedding party," she blurted out, and then felt herself blush. Whatever had prompted her to say *that*?

Reese's expression behind his sunglasses was unreadable. "So, what did you say?"

"I told her thanks, but I didn't think it was a good idea."

"Yeah, you're probably right," he replied. "But I guess a gesture like that . . . well, that's Connie for you." Reese seemed to recall that he still held her hand, for he abruptly released her. "I'll let you know what I can on this later. Stick close to home, will you?"

"What? Do you think I'm going to flee town?" she asked, her laugh a bit shakier than she would have liked.

He shook his head. "Something's really off about this one, but I can't put my finger on it yet. Until we get a break in the case, make sure you always have someone working with you at the bookstore. And don't go out alone, not even to meet up with people you know . . . or think you know."

Darla was already feeling unsettled, but his last words made her shiver despite herself.

"You don't think I'm going to mysteriously drop dead, too, do you?" she asked, trying for a smile but failing miserably.

He pulled off his sunglasses and fixed her with an unshakable gaze. "Let's just say I'm worried that you and that cat of yours might know something about these two deaths that you don't know that you know."

And then, as she tried to untangle *that*, he added, "And sometimes, Red, not knowing can be the deadliest thing that can happen to you."

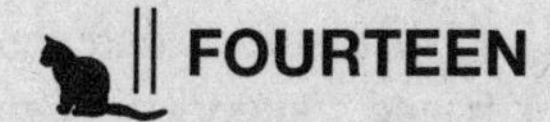

FOURTEEN

"REESE ACTUALLY SAID THAT TO YOU?" JAKE DEMANDED IN outrage the next morning over a cup of Robert's latte. She and Darla were downstairs seated at the bistro table near the dumbwaiter, since the crowd in the coffee lounge was larger than usual, most of the clientele being Perky's refugees. Darla had even done a brief stint behind the coffee bar to help Robert out until he caught up with all the orders.

Darla took a sip of her own coffee and nodded.

"If he was trying to scare me, he succeeded," she said, yawning. "I barely slept a wink last night, thinking about Livvy and Penelope. I made Hamlet stay in my bedroom with me, and when I did fall asleep I had my cell phone in my hand."

"Reese does have a point, though. Two deaths in two

days in this neighborhood is like something out of a bad movie. I have to say, kid, I'm kind of concerned."

Jake stared into her cup, her expression a thoughtful moue as she sat silent for a moment. Then she went on, "Consider me on call the next few days. You got a gap between shifts, I'll hang out here until James or Robert shows up. And no going out to lunch alone. And we do a full walk-through of the place at night when you're locking up."

"Got it," Darla agreed, giving her a mock salute, but still feeling reassured by her friend's support. Then, sobering, she went on, "When I met Reese for lunch yesterday, I thought we were going to talk about . . . well, never mind. But what he wanted to ask me was if I knew whether or not Livvy used one of those vapor pens. He said they'd found one under her body where she fell."

"You know, that's one thing I've been wondering about," Jake replied, only to stop short at the sound of a loud splat.

"Hamlet," Darla said, eagerly jumping up from her seat. "He must have snagged a book for us. Maybe he's got a suggestion about Penelope's killer."

More than once, Hamlet had knocked a pertinent title off of a shelf just when Darla needed a nudge. Others might scoff, but Darla was pretty sure her wily feline was usually trying to help her out.

"That'll put him ahead of Reese," Jake muttered as she dutifully got up to join Darla in the book search.

But a soft *meow-rumph* quickly had them both looking up. A yawning Hamlet was sprawled on a bookshelf above them, with no sign of a tumbled book below.

"Sorry," Robert called from over the stair railing. "That was me. I dropped a carton of coffee stirrers."

"That's okay," Darla called back in disappointment and slanted the feline a look. "Never mind," she told Jake. Glancing toward the register, where a potential customer appeared headed, she added, "Go ahead and finish your coffee. I need to take care of this gentleman."

Carrying her own cup with her, Darla made the sale, then did a quick round of the store, pausing to check the back door. It led out onto a small terraced garden behind the brownstone where she and her employees lunched in good weather. As a surprise for her friend a couple of months back, Darla had hired her contractor to restore the previously blocked access from Jake's lower level apartment up to that same enclosed terrace. Now, the PI had a garden apartment in all meanings of the word. But since the terrace also accessed a narrow alleyway behind, Darla planned to keep her door to it locked, just in case.

She was headed back to rejoin Jake, when she noticed something lying on the bookstore floor near the sports and hobby shelves. *Hamlet?* She glanced about but saw no sign of white whisker or black tail. Besides, Robert had claimed responsibility for the noise they'd heard, and Hamlet had been nowhere close to that shelf a few minutes earlier. Shaking her head, she went over to the wayward volume.

"*Introduction to Ballet*," she read aloud from the dust jacket, while a Degas ballerina stared back up at her from the front cover.

Picking up the book, she swiftly thumbed through it. It was a primer of sorts for the beginning dancer, covering everything from the basic five positions to popular ballet choreographies to famous performers to ballet as depicted in the other arts. Shaking her head, she hurried back to the table where Jake still sat and slid into the chair opposite her again.

"Look what I found. I wonder if Hamlet pulled this down sometime in the night."

"I thought you said he was locked in the room with you," Jake said as she took the book from Darla and studied the cover photo. Shrugging, she conceded, "Interesting, but not real helpful. We already know that Penelope and Livvy both were dancers."

"Yes, but maybe it's something else," Darla insisted with a glance in the feline's direction. He was asleep or else pretending to be, so she wasn't going to get any further help from him . . . at least, not for now.

She paused and took a deep breath. "Last night, while I was thinking about them both, I remembered my last real conversations with them. I mentioned Livvy's name to Penelope, and the claws came out. Same thing with Livvy, though she was a bit politer. Remember, both of them danced with the New York City Ballet at one time."

"You think they were some sort of dance rivals?" Jake asked.

Darla shrugged. "Could be. Penelope was, what, twenty years older than Livvy? I don't know if you've ever seen inside her studio, but there are a bunch of these fabulous old photos hanging on the walls of Penelope onstage. She was gorgeous . . . really ethereal."

She paused and swallowed back a sudden lump in her throat as she recalled her final glimpse of Penelope curled up on Doug's floor. Then, clearing her throat, she went on, "Who knows, maybe Penelope was the established star in the company, and Livvy was the newcomer who booted her out, and Penelope couldn't forgive being replaced by a younger dancer? That could definitely start a feud."

"True," the PI agreed, "but there's got to be more to it than that. So what else do women fight over besides career trajectories?"

"Men," Darla reflexively declared, and then felt herself blush when Connie's face flashed in her mind, and she realized she could possibly fall into that camp.

To her relief, however, Jake had slipped into one-track-mind mode as she worked on that angle. "The only known man in this equation is George, and somehow I don't see women fighting over him."

"Neither do . . . Wait!"

Brow knitted, Darla thought back to the last block party committee meeting, when a big point of discussion had been over George King not ponying up his share of the retailer's fee.

She repeated as much to Jake, adding, "Everyone started chiming in about what a jerk George was," she went on, "except for Penelope. She said something to the effect that he wasn't that bad a guy. That's when Steve jumped in and talked about how the man had insulted his son and daughter. Everyone else had something to say on that subject after that, except for her. I thought it was a bit odd at the time, but now it kind of makes sense."

"So it sounds like Penelope knew George, but she wasn't making that fact public for some reason." She paused, and her generous mouth quirked in a wry smile. "Maybe it was because she *knew* him according to all definitions of the word."

Darla gave her a look of mock horror. "Bad enough imagining Livvy knowing"—she gave the word finger quotes—"George, but now Penelope? My brain is officially boggled."

Then she sobered as another thought occurred to her. Snatching up the ballet primer again, she pointed to its cover.

"George has a tattoo on one of his arms of a ballerina with Livvy's name. It's more abstract than realistic—well, except for the flowers and vines around her feet—but the pose of the dancer in his tattoo looks an awful lot like this photo."

"So?"

"I'm not sure . . . but if Hamlet pulled down this book, I think there has to be a connection."

She paused, frowning into her coffee again. Then she shrugged.

"Who knows? Maybe King George was a real hottie back in his day. Shave off fifteen years and fifty pounds, dress him right and get him a decent haircut, and he'd be presentable. And George did say that he had money back when he and Livvy got married."

Something else niggled at the edges of her mind, however, just out of reach. Then, like Hamlet and his books, she snagged it.

"He said he had money, and he also said Livvy didn't marry him for his looks," she recalled. "And when he was showing me that tattoo, he said, and I quote, *I always had a thing for them ballet girls.*"

"A bit creepy," Jake decreed, "but you know how men always seem drawn to a type. Both of them were ballerinas.

And Penelope and Livvy did look somewhat alike . . . petite, and dark, with those gamine features."

Darla had been staring at the book cover again. Now, she nodded slowly at Jake's description of the two women.

"All right, so how's this for a theory, then? Years ago, back when she still was dancing, Penelope was seeing George. Maybe she takes him to one of those post-show parties with the rest of the company, and he gets a look at Livvy. She's the new and improved version, so George dumps Penelope and goes after her. But Penelope has this unrequited love thing still going on, which is why she moved into the same neighborhood when George and Livvy got married."

Jake shrugged. "Maybe, but I'll go you one better. This one's pure hunch, but you said something about his tattoo. Livvy's name was on it, but there was also this tangle of vines and flowers?"

"Here," Darla said, reaching for the order pad and pen on the bistro table. "Let me show you."

Swiftly, she did a crude if serviceable sketch from memory. "This is the ballerina, and here's Livvy's name in cursive," she said, pointing. "And right beneath the ballerina's feet, there are all these plants that really don't belong."

"Cover-up," Jake flatly said. "I would almost bet that if you looked real close at the plants, you'd be able to see another name underneath—maybe Penelope's. He had those letters tattooed over and Livvy's name added when he got married. Happens all the time, according to a buddy of mine who's a tattoo artist."

"Not bad," Darla agreed. "So, should we call Reese and tell him our theory?"

They smiled a moment at their mutual cleverness. Then Jake said, "Not to burst your bubble after all this brainstorming, kid, but chances are Reese chatted with your buddy George again and has already figured out pretty much the same thing as we did. So as far as he's concerned, we'd be talking old news."

"Oh."

Her bubble didn't burst so much as all the air in it oozed out, like a balloon that had been untied. She checked her watch and picked up the ballet primer again for later. It would make an interesting bedtime read.

"That's okay," she said, standing. "I think all my brainstorms have pretty well dried up, which is probably a good thing since I need to get back to work."

Jake rose, too. "Yeah, I probably should get to work myself. I actually got a client from that ten-minute speed PI dating thing I had going at the block party. Seems like a nice guy, but he's gotten himself into a jam. I hope I—"

She broke off all at once and slapped her palm against her forehead in the universal "what an idiot I am" gesture. Then, staring at Darla in seeming disbelief, she said, "I can't believe I forgot this. She stopped by my booth at the block party and wanted to find out what it would take to hire a PI. She had a hunch her man was fooling around on her, but she wanted to be sure before she took any action."

"Wait," Darla said. "Are you talking about Livvy?"

"No," Jake replied. "I'm talking about Penelope."

"WE ARE ON TELEVISION," JAMES INTONED AS HE ARRIVED PROMPTLY for his shift at 2 p.m., "and not in a good way. The national news channels are calling us the Brooklyn neighborhood where tragedy has struck twice in two days. And there is now speculation that not one but both of the deaths are murder, and that we have a serial killer in our midst."

"A serial killer?" Darla groaned. "That must be what all those voice mails from my mother are about. And that's probably why we haven't had a single customer since the morning coffee rush."

And during that extended lull, she'd had plenty of time to stew over her earlier chat with Jake. The PI had left her hanging with that bombshell about Penelope but had promised to get with her for supper that night to give her the full scoop. Her impatience to learn more about that potentially important conversation about the dance instructor's private life had made the time pass even more slowly.

Now, Robert looked up from the beanbag chair in the children's section, where he and Roma had been quietly napping for much of the shift. His black kohled eyes were wide in concern. "Is that, like, for real, what they said on the news?" he asked James. "Maybe we should, you know, get a gun or something."

"I am certain you are aware of the firearms laws in this city," James reproved him. "Besides which, neither you nor I have any experience with handguns. I would assume that expertise would lie with Darla, given that she is from a state that promotes public shoot-outs."

Darla, however, didn't react to that dig at her Texas birthplace, occupied as she now was with pulling up news stories on the store computer. The two women's deaths topped the headlines for all the major Internet news pages, she saw in dismay.

"Oh great," she said with a moan. "Here's a clip from that same blond barracuda from the local channel who did a hatchet job on us during that whole Valerie Baylor incident last year."

Knowing she'd regret it, Darla clicked on the "Play" arrow. The clip took a few moments to download, during which time James and Robert—clutching Roma to his chest—crowded around the computer with her. Then the blond newswoman popped up on the screen, microphone in hand as she stood outside of Doug's closed doughnut shop. The video started a few seconds past the beginning, with the blonde gesturing with a manicured hand at the crime scene tape that still blocked off the area.

"*. . . that the body of fifty-six-year-old Penelope Winston, a local dance instructor, was found inside a local doughnut shop by bakery owner Doug Bates and two of his neighbors. Winston's cause of death has not yet been released, though sources close to the investigation tell us the case is being treated as a murder.*"

"Poor Doug," Darla choked out. "Why did the news station have to film the front of his building? Who's going to want to buy doughnuts somewhere someone died?"

"*As our viewers may recall, this is the second death in this same Brooklyn neighborhood in as many days,*" the newscaster continued. "*This past Friday afternoon, during a July Fourth block party event, thirty-three-year-old Olivia "Livvy" King was found deceased on the steps of the local coffeehouse she owned with her husband. King's death is still under investigation, with no determination yet if foul play was involved. But rumors are surfacing that a serial killer might be targeting local women with connections to the world of dance. Like Ms. Winston, Ms. King was a former soloist with the New York City Ballet.*"

Darla hit the "Stop" button, not wanting to hear more. So much for all the time and expense the local retailers had put into the block party. All the positive feedback they'd garnered was being overshadowed—heck, trampled into the dirt—by Livvy's and Penelope's deaths.

No offense to the dead people, she thought, momentarily echoing Connie.

Feeling more than a little panic, she reached under the counter for her cell phone. "I'm going to call Reese. If the police don't hurry and find whoever did this, the whole neighborhood is going to go down like a line of dominos."

FIFTEEN

DARLA PULLED UP REESE'S NAME IN HER CONTACTS AND HIT "Dial," and then mentally counted the rings. Just when she feared the call would roll over to voice mail, he answered.

"It's Darla," she told him in a rush . . . though, of course, he would have seen her name on caller ID. "Reese, we're dying over here . . . no pun intended. I haven't had a single customer since the story about Livvy's and Penelope's deaths hit the news. Now the local television station is trying to boost their ratings by starting the rumor we have a serial killer. Please tell me you've got some good news for me."

"That depends on your definition. We have the autopsy results on Livvy King."

"Good," was her reflexive reply, and then she added,

"but I'm not liking the sound of that. Someone killed her, didn't they?"

The silence on the other end stretched out a moment, and then she heard Reese's reluctant, "We're not exactly sure. All we have at this point is a cause of death. I told you we found one of those vaping pens underneath her body, right? The lab analyzed the oil in it, and they found it contained a fatally strong concentration of"—she heard the rattle of paper as he consulted his notes—"oleandrin."

"Oleandrin?" she echoed, drawing a look of surprise from James, who was listening intently to her side of the conversation. "You mean, like oleander, as in the flowering bush that will kill you if you roast hot dogs with its branches?"

"The same. The ME told me that was pretty much an urban legend. But eating the leaves or inhaling smoke from burning the branches *can* be very deadly. They found oleandrin residue present in her lungs, and according to the autopsy she died from an increasingly irregular heartbeat consistent with oleander poisoning."

"But where would she even get hold of . . . Wait! The little bushes outside Perky's. They're oleander," Darla exclaimed.

"Right. I did a little image search online and confirmed it. Plenty of leaves for the taking."

Darla considered this a moment and then asked him, "Any chance it was an accident? You know that Livvy used herbs and such to help control her RA. Maybe the oleander got mixed in by mistake, or maybe it was a homeopathic treatment gone wrong."

"That would be the best outcome. I mean, it would make life a heck of a lot simpler for me. Not that simple's the most important thing."

He halted, and she heard his sigh through the phone . . . or was that the sound of him taking his foot out of his mouth? He finished with, "You know what I'm trying to say."

"Sure, I get it. Are you going to search inside Perky's for oleander leaves?"

"Just waiting on the warrant, though Mr. King has been quite cooperative so far. The thing is, concentrated as the oleandrin was, I'm thinking it's not very likely Mrs. King cooked that up accidentally."

Which led back to someone purposely spiking Livvy's vaping pen with the fatal substance. Which wouldn't be that difficult, she realized. So far, the vaping pens she'd seen were all the same brand and color, courtesy of Porn Shop Bill. The killer could have spiked his own pen and then swapped it out with Livvy's, with the woman being none the wiser.

Then, tentatively, she asked, "Any word on Penelope?"

"Not yet. But you've got to keep in mind that it's a holiday. We've got the usual three-day-weekend backlog of auto fatalities, floaters, shooting victims . . . you name it. According to Tina at the coroner's office, they've got dead bodies practically stacked to the rafters like cordwood."

And thanks for that nice visual, Detective Reese, she thought with a shudder.

Then, recalling her and Jake's theory, Darla asked in as casual tone as she could muster, "How about Penelope's family? Was there anyone you were able to contact on her behalf? Parents? Siblings?"

Boyfriends, past and present?

"Next of kin have been notified," was his noncommittal response before he added, "Look, Darla, I've told you all I can so far. You don't need to be jumping at every shadow, but try to use some common sense until we figure this thing out. No hanging out by yourself in dark parking lots, don't meet anyone alone in an empty building. That sort of thing. Last thing we need is another body to add to the count."

"Don't worry. I should be fine," she protested, doing her best to keep her tone light. "Remember, I'm not a dancer."

"What about those six months of ballet when you were ten years old?" he countered, and then rang off before she could reply.

James gave her a quizzical look as she stuck her phone back under the register again. "Was Detective Reese enlightening on any fronts besides horticulture?"

Recalling that he'd heard only one side of the conversation, Darla summed it up as, "He says Livvy's death might have been accidental, but more likely it was murder. And poor Penelope is with all the other cordwood stacked up at the medical examiner's office until they can figure out how she died. Oh, and since I took ballet when I was ten, I could end up dead, too."

"Like, that is really bad," Robert said, cradling Roma and gently scratching her behind her ears. "This is the worst Fourth of July ever, and not just because we missed the fireworks."

"I concur," James said.

Darla nodded. "Me, too. Why don't we salvage what we can of the weekend? I'm going to close early, so at least we can save a little on the electric bill. You two enjoy the rest of the day off on me, and we'll try again on Tuesday."

Since, of course, they were closed on Mondays.

Robert didn't have to be told twice. "Thanks, Ms. P.!" he called over his shoulder as he and a happily barking Roma raced for the front door.

James's departure, while more sedate, was no less enthusiastic.

"Martha is back early from her visit with her family in Georgia. I would appreciate the opportunity to spend some additional quality time with her." Then, as Darla gave him a knowing smile, he added, "In certain circles, Darla, quality time is equated with lively conversation and enthusiastic interaction with one's peers."

"I'm all for enthusiastic interaction," Darla said, her smile broadening. "Tell Martha I said hi."

With James out the door, Darla locked up after him and did a quick closedown of the register. Then, reaching for her cell phone and purse, she turned to Hamlet. "Looks like it's just you and me, Hammy. You wanna go upstairs and watch movies the rest of the day until I go meet Jake?"

The cat needed no further encouragement and rushed to the side door with her, the one that led out into the narrow foyer of her building. This was her short commute. She could either head out the front door to her private stoop, or else take the stairway two flights up to her apartment. After setting the store alarm, she headed for the stairs.

Hamlet was far ahead of her. By the time she reached

her front door, he was already seated before it, green eyes fixed in concentration on its wood paneling as he seemingly willed it to open. Which it did once she turned the key.

She turned on her television and, swiftly scanning past the news outlets, tuned in to her favorite retro movie channel. "All right, Hammy," she said as he nudged her in the shin with his big head, "I'll get you some early supper."

It wasn't until she finished in the kitchen attending to His Catness—fresh bowl of kibble, fresh water in cut-glass water dish, with just a sprinkling of crushed ice floating on top—and headed back to the living room that she realized what old-time movie was playing.

"Bad choice," she muttered as she saw a frightened Audrey Hepburn on the screen, cane in hand and stumbling through a darkened apartment. She grabbed the remote and checked the channel listing. Next up after *Wait Until Dark* was *The Maltese Falcon*. It was obviously a thriller-themed lineup, when she'd been hoping for a mood-lightening comedy.

She sighed and instead flipped over to Hamlet's favorite nature channel.

"Ah, much better," she wryly noted as a giant anaconda flashed on the screen, silently swimming its way toward a hapless baby hippo. The sound of crunching kibble in the kitchen ceased, and Hamlet came rushing in, leaping onto the back of her horsehair sofa and settling in to watch some heavy-duty hunting. She sat in companionable silence with him until the anaconda show ended, and a crocodile special began, then rose.

"You hold down the couch," she told the cat, "and I'll be back in a minute. I've got a call to make."

With an indulgent smile, she left Hamlet to his viewing and reached for the old-style turquoise princess phone hanging in the kitchen (she'd never bothered to get rid of Great-Aunt Dee's ages-old landline). She dialed Jake and, reminding the PI of how she'd been left hanging, made plans to meet at Thai Me Up for dinner for the rest of the Penelope story,

An hour later, she and Jake were sitting at their favorite window table in Steve's restaurant.

"At least someone's got customers," Darla observed as she glanced around the place, which was filled almost to capacity. "I guess sometimes bad publicity equals good publicity."

"That, or everyone's July Fourth BBQ'd out and in the mood for good old-fashioned Asian cuisine," Jake said with a shrug. "But you're probably right about the publicity. I swear, every news channel on the tube was leading off with the story about the quote, unquote ballerina murders. The way they're playing this up, you'd think the gutters were flowing with blood, or something."

Darla suppressed a shudder and, vowing not to order anything with red sauce, picked up her menu to see what was on special that night. She wasn't even really in the mood right now for Thai food, not after that uncomfortable lunch with Reese yesterday, but it was the closest open restaurant, and after Reese's warnings, she felt better being out in a familiar place where she knew the staff.

Steve passed by their table, giving them a sober nod but not stopping since he was carrying a tray overflowing with various Thai delicacies. He was already aware of the Penelope situation, for Darla had made an executive decision and called him once she'd hung up with Reese the previous night. As far as Darla was concerned, Reese's moratorium on her talking to her friends was now a moot point, given the suspicious death on their hands. Steve hadn't said much when she'd broken the news, but the few words he'd spoken had been thick with grief.

She'd called Hank, too. He had been equally shocked, but to Darla's surprise he had swiftly moved on to another subject . . . his concern for Penelope's students.

I hope someone breaks it to them all nice like, he'd told her. *You know how kids are, especially the younger ones. They look up to their teachers. How do you explain something like this to a ten-year-old?*

Darla hadn't been able to answer that last question. And, as far as she knew, Penelope had no local relatives, and no second-in-command at her studio. The nearest thing to that would be her accompanist and a few of her senior students who Darla knew helped with the beginner classes. Presumably, most, if not all, of the students' parents would have heard of Penelope's death from some news source or another. But given that it was a holiday weekend, some of the students might still be in the dark.

She'd decided after hanging up with Hank that she would discuss the matter with Doug as soon as she could track him down. Perhaps he could help settle things with notifying students and shuttering the studio; he was the closest thing at the moment to a next of kin.

But, for the moment, she wanted to hear just what Jake knew about Penelope's love life.

Darla waited until Kayla—still in crisp black and white but far more subdued this time around—took their orders before leaning toward Jake and demanding, "Okay, spill. Why did Penelope want to hire a PI? You said she told you that she thought some man was cheating on her. Did she name names?"

Jake shook her head. "It was all pretty vague. She seemed kind of embarrassed to be bringing it up at all. According to her, she didn't have much to go on except a hotel receipt and a gut feeling. But I'm a big fan of guts. They usually know what they're talking about. But that's all I was able to get out of her. She said she'd call for a consultation after the weekend."

"What about Reese?" Darla wanted to know. "Did you call him and tell him about your conversation with her?"

"Yeah, I called him this morning, right after I finished with my client, and he read me the riot act," Jake remembered with a shake of her curly head. "Not that I blame him, but excuse me for having a lot of other stuff on my mind. This just temporarily slipped through the cracks."

She broke off as Kayla brought them their usual coconut milk soup. Darla gave her bowl a considering stir and then reluctantly asked the obvious. "Do you think it's possible that the guy she was worried about was the person who killed her?"

"Yeah, the thought crossed my mind maybe twenty or thirty times since it happened. But I didn't get that kind of vibe off of her. She was . . . I guess you'd say . . . disappointed. And maybe sad. But she wasn't afraid. So *my* gut says the two things aren't related."

"I hope not. Because my gut has a theory that her mystery man is none other than Doug Bates."

"Doug? Well, tell your gut that's an interesting theory,"

Jake said in approval. "Is it just a guess, or do you have anything concrete?"

A certain butt swat came to mind, along with Doug's referring to her as Penny during the block party. Little things, Darla conceded, but possibly part of a bigger pattern.

Aloud, she said, "Mostly guess, but now that I think about it, Doug's reaction when he found her body seemed more . . . well, extreme than simply shock at stumbling over a dead person. It looked like there was some real emotional investment."

"Well, I'm sure Doug confessed that relationship to Reese, since it would look pretty bad after the fact if the police found out he'd kept that tidbit from them," Jake assured her. "So let's let Reese do his job, and we can enjoy our dinner."

They finished their soup in companionable if a bit uncomfortable silence. Kayla's brother, Jason, swung by to clear their empty bowls. As he leaned past her, Darla noticed what looked like a vaping pen tucked into the breast pocket of his busboy's jacket.

She gave him a considering frown as he left, recalling that George had mentioned it was an Asian youth who'd first approached Livvy about so-called drugs. It was quite the stretch to assume Steve's son was the same teenage boy. On the other hand, according to their father, Jason and Kayla had words with George, which definitely put the two kids at the scene of the sting, so to speak. Impulsively, she gestured him over again.

"Excuse me—Jason, right? I'm Darla, a friend of your dad's."

"Yes, how may I help you?" he asked, his tone far more formal than any of the teens she knew.

She gave him a bright smile. "I couldn't help noticing you have one of those vapor pens in your pocket," she began. Then, jumping straight into outright fiction, she went on, "I'm trying to give up smoking, and I heard those vape pens were the way to go. Do they really work?"

"I don't know. I don't smoke."

"Oh." Momentarily thrown, Darla tried again, going for a conspiratorial tone. "I understand you can put stuff other than nicotine in them, if you know what I mean."

Shrugging, he dropped the formality and replied, "Yeah, I guess. Uh, I really need to get back to work now."

"Sure, thanks for your time."

As the busboy hurried off, no doubt questioning the sanity of anyone over thirty, Jake gave her a look. "You're trying to quit smoking? That's funny, because I had no idea you'd taken up the habit. You want to 'splain, Lucy?"

"Someone's been watching the retro channel again," Darla replied to Jake's use of the old *I Love Lucy* catchphrase. Then, after first making sure no one else was listening, she went on to "'splain" about her and James's talk with George.

"You do know there's a pretty good-sized teenage population around here," the PI pointed out when she'd finished. "The chances that Steve's kid is the same one who set the Kings on their path to pseudo drug dealing are pretty slim."

"But what about proximity?" Darla argued. Lowering her voice, she went on, "He works just a couple of blocks from Perky's, and I know he and his sister have been there at least once before. If he's like all the other kids who like to hang out around coffee shops because they're too young for bars, it makes sense. He could have been there and seen all of Livvy's herbal offerings. What can I say, it's a gut feeling."

Jake rolled her eyes. "Fine, but I'm not going to play unless you can come up with a little more of a case than just your gut. At least Penelope had a receipt. So how about we put this in the 'to be reviewed again later' pile, okay?"

Kayla brought their meals just then, putting a temporary halt to the conversation. While Jake had gone the full pad Thai route, Darla had decided to try one of Steve's salad specialties. As soon as she took her first bite of the chopped salad—replete with edamame, baby kale, bell peppers, and other veggies, and topped with cashews and a sesame garlic dressing—she knew she'd made the right choice. Even Jake, normally a confirmed carnivore, gave a longing little look at Darla's salad bowl before she started chewing on a mouthful of chicken-topped spicy noodles.

Darla had made good progress on her meal when her cell phone rang. She glanced at the caller ID and then gave Jake a look of surprise.

"It's Mary Ann," she said and pushed the "Talk" button.

"Oh, Darla, I don't know what to do," the old woman exclaimed almost before Darla could manage a "hello." "With all these rumors about serial killers in our neighborhood, Brother is beside himself. He managed to get upstairs onto the roof, and now he's sitting by the ledge with a pair of binoculars keeping an eye out for suspicious people."

The Plinski neighborhood watch, Darla thought with a smile, hoping the old man didn't have an antique rifle up there, too.

"Mary Ann, I'm sure Mr. Plinski isn't hurting anyone being up there, as long as it's not too hot out there on the tar for him."

"There's a bit of a breeze up there with the sun going down," Mary Ann replied, "so it shouldn't be too warm. But, Darla, what if he actually does spot the serial killer?"

"Tell him to call Jake"—she grinned a little as her friend, having heard enough of the one-sided conversation to get the gist, began waving, *no!*—"and I'm sure she'll be happy enough to check things out. And if he really does see the killer, she'll take charge of calling the police."

"Well, I suppose that would work." The old woman gave a tsk, and Darla could practically see her shaking her head. "I vow, I don't know what this world is coming to. Serial killers on every block. All right, Darla, I'll take your advice and leave Brother to keep watch."

Darla was smiling as she hung up. "Sorry to throw you under the bus, Jake, but you really don't want Mr. Plinski calling 9-1-1 every time he sees some guy in a hoodie wander past."

"I don't want him calling me, either," she grumbled, but her expression was amused as she, too, doubtless pictured the frail old man as stern sentinel.

Making a game of casting the octogenarian in various Clint Eastwood movies, the two of them snickered their way through the remainder of their supper. Jason had silently cleared away that course, and Kayla had brought them more mango ice cream, when Jake's cell phone buzzed that she had an incoming text.

"Whoops, me, too," Darla said when her phone abruptly

let loose with the typewriter key sound that indicated a message. "I wonder if it's Mr. Plinski?"

Though she doubted the old man even knew how to operate your basic cell phone, let alone find the messaging icon and type out a text.

"No," Jake said, "it's Reese."

"Me, too," Darla replied with a frown as she opened the message.

The older woman, however, was already reading aloud, *"Cause of death 4 Ms Winston = oleandrin poisoning."*

"Oh no," Darla breathed, her stomach clenching into a knot. Two women dying within two days of the same rare cause could not be coincidence.

"Wait, I've got a second text," Jake exclaimed, just as Darla's phone snapped out the typewriter cadence a second time, as well.

Darla opened the second text and read it; then, gripped by disbelief, read it again. Finally, she lifted her gaze to meet Jake's.

"I guess Mr. Plinski doesn't need to search for serial killers anymore," was the PI's grim comment as she sent a quick text back to Reese.

Darla could only shake her head as she read the message once more: *Preliminary ruling on Winston & King deaths is murder-suicide.*

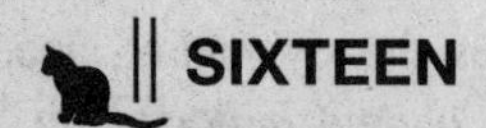

SIXTEEN

"YOU SURE YOU WANT TO DO THIS?" JAKE ASKED AS SHE and Darla left the brownstone the next morning, headed on foot toward Doug's doughnut shop. "The man pretty well hung up on you when you called to see if he was going to be there."

"Doug said he was in the middle of receiving a delivery. There's a difference."

"He was putting you off. That's what you say to someone when you don't want them to think you're hanging up on them."

Darla sighed. "Fine, he doesn't want to see me . . . but that doesn't mean I don't want to see him. The worst he can do is toss me out of his shop. If he doesn't want to discuss his personal life with us, fine, but I'm darn sure going to do what I can to get him to open up."

After the first shock of Reese's text from the previous evening had passed, Jake had dialed up the detective for more answers. Though sympathetic, Reese hadn't been much help, citing departmental policy in discussing details at that stage of the investigation.

Until we release a public statement, you'll just have to take my word for it that for the moment, we've got enough circumstantial evidence to be pretty sure that's how it went down.

He *had* let them know two critical pieces of information. A brief note in Penelope's handwriting had been found with her body, indicating the probable suicide. He'd also confirmed Darla's theory by telling Jake that Doug had readily admitted to both an ongoing relationship with Penelope, and—a bit more reluctantly—a one-time, recent fling with none other than Livvy. All this had given her even more reason to want to see Doug face-to-face.

Now, Darla considered what she knew to this point, feeling vindicated that at least her theory about Doug and Penelope had proven correct. But while she could accept the hot-tempered ex-ballerina possibly murdering a rival in the heat of the moment, she couldn't picture her doing it in such a clandestine way . . . nor could she picture Penelope then killing herself from guilt. It didn't make sense.

Now, Jake broke the momentary silence that had fallen between them as they walked.

"I understand where your head is, kid. All these bits and pieces Reese is feeding us is raising a lot of questions for me, too. If it were my case, I'd be looking at that whole suicide scenario a bit harder. But Reese said she left a note behind."

Darla reluctantly nodded. "I know, but I still can't believe she'd kill herself over a man. I need to hear what Doug knows, and if this whole thing about the affair is true. I just can't accept that a nice guy like him would be in the middle of something so, well, unsavory."

"Believe me, the nice guys are the ones you have to watch out for. And I've got a filing cabinet drawer full of case files to prove it."

"I suppose so."

They lapsed into silence again as they reached the street corner and prepared to cross to the next block. Already the midsummer heat had begun to build, though it was barely nine a.m. Traffic, however, was light . . . doubtless because a good number of nine-to-fivers had decided to extend their three-day weekend to four days.

"Well, kid, I stand corrected," came Jake's wry voice as they neared Doug's place. "It looks like Doug really *is* getting a delivery."

A box truck with liftgate was parked on the street outside the doughnut shop, the vehicle blocking traffic as a four-man crew wrestled an open-crated, full-sized, glass-fronted counter off the back of the truck. As Darla and Jake watched from a short distance, the men lowered the fixture to the ground. After some lively debate, when it became obvious the counter couldn't fit through the door as it was, they crowbarred off the wooden slats and shoved it through the front door with inches to spare.

By the time Darla and Jake reached the shop, Doug was signing off the trucking company paperwork. The doors were still propped open, so they slipped inside before he could protest. To Darla's relief, however, he didn't seem inclined to toss them back out onto the street.

The baker waited until the deliverymen had trudged back out to their truck to nod toward the new display case sitting where the old counter had been.

"My insurance agent is a buddy of mine," he explained. "I got him to agree that the other display counter was, you know . . . I mean, I couldn't look at it anymore because . . ."

He trailed off, expression haunted, and then finally finished, "Anyhow, he got it declared damaged and rushed my claim through."

Darla nodded, suddenly uncertain just quite what to say. She'd last seen the baker as he'd wandered from his store after being questioned by Reese. Then, after an initial frantic reaction, he had been in seeming shock at seeing Penelope curled up against the glass display.

Today, the distant look had begun to fade from his eyes, but he wasn't quite the same Doug. True, he was wearing much the same outfit as he'd been sporting the other day, cutoff jeans and an untucked fishing shirt, but even though only two days had passed, he appeared to have lost weight. But what most struck her was the fact that his gold chains were missing from around his neck.

A symbol of mourning? A nod to a newly ascetic lifestyle?

He settled heavily into one of the wooden chairs at the window table and struggled for a smile. "Sorry, ladies," he said in a voice that cracked, "no doughnuts today. Maybe tomorrow."

Abruptly he began to sob . . . harsh, gasping chokes

that wracked his whole body. Darla shot a helpless look at Jake, who gave a fleeting shrug and shake of her head.

What to do?

A pat on the shoulder seemed far too inadequate, while an attempt at a hug felt intrusive. But even as Darla hesitated, Doug managed to regain his composure. Wiping his eyes and nose on a handful of paper napkins from the metal table dispenser, he gave her and Jake a helpless look.

"She left a note for me. That detective fellow, Reese, showed me so I could identify her handwriting."

"Do you remember what the note said?" Darla gently asked him.

He choked out a laugh. "It was only a few words. I memorized it." Gazing at the far wall, as if the photographs of doughnuts spelled it out for him, he recited, *"Sorry. It should never have happened."*

Darla frowned. Not much of a note, under the circumstances. What was Penelope trying to say should never have happened? Their relationship? His cheating? Livvy's death? Her own? It was too vague to pinpoint. And as for the note itself . . .

Her frown deepened. Doug had sounded sincere in his assertion that the note had been penned by her. But surely the police were giving it a more thorough look than simply taking Doug's word that the writing was hers.

The baker, meanwhile, shook his head and heaved a sigh. "I don't understand any of this. Why would she kill Livvy over my stupidity? And why kill herself . . . and in my shop? How am I ever supposed to get that picture outta my head?"

Darla and Jake took chairs on either side of Doug, and this time Darla opted for a simple clasp of his hand. "I know it's hard, but I've always found that the more times you repeat a painful story, the less hold it starts to have on you."

"And maybe it would help if we told you a couple of things," Jake spoke up. "At the block party, Penelope asked about hiring me to check up on the man she was seeing. She told me she'd found a receipt from a local hotel for a day the guy had claimed to be out of town. Between that and the gut feeling she had, she was pretty sure he was having an affair. Sound familiar?"

"It was just one stupid time," he blustered. "It wasn't until afterward I figured out Livvy was just using me to get back at Penelope and George, both."

"Wait," Jake protested. "How did Livvy know about you two, when as far as the rest of us were concerned, the fact you and Penelope were dating was such a state secret?"

"Uh, maybe I told her?"

Despite her dismay, Darla couldn't help but roll her eyes at this.

Doug caught her look.

"I didn't mean I was bragging or nothing," he quickly explained. "But I was talking to her over at Perky's one time—I buy a sack of coffee there every couple of weeks—and outta nowhere she asks me how serious me and Penny are. I wasn't thinking. I just told her we were taking it a day at a time."

Then he frowned. "You know, Livvy always seemed to know things about the neighborhood. I don't know how she figured out about me and Penny. Heck, maybe she had some sort of spy thing going on with those kids that would hang around her place."

Jake, meanwhile, persisted, "Back to what you said before, about Livvy wanting to get back at Penelope and George. Get back at them for what?"

He shrugged. "Search me. Anyhow, Livvy kept coming on to me, and I finally decided, what the heck? I mean, it's not like me and Penelope was engaged or anything."

"Maybe, but Livvy was married," Darla pointed out.

Doug had the good grace to look embarrassed at the observation. "Yeah, I kinda forgot about that until afterward. So I told Livvy that we'd had a few laughs, but the one time was it. She seemed good with that, and I made sure to toss the receipt in the trash. I dunno, maybe Livvy dug it out and put it somewhere Penelope would find it."

While Darla considered this, Doug gave his new counter a sorrowful look. "I wonder if maybe I should just close up and be done with it. Who's gonna want to buy doughnuts here again? I'd better tell Emma she needs to start looking for another job."

"Emma?" Darla recognized the name as one of the girls from her coffee shop. "Short, dark hair, thin?"

"Yeah, one of Penny's students. She works part-time for me. Good kid, hard worker, but I might need to lay her off now . . . you know, if things don't work out."

"Nuthin's working out!" came a boozy declaration from the open doorway. "You made sure of that!"

George King had staggered his way inside the shop. His stained Perky's shirt looked like it had been dragged through the gutters . . . though from the look of the man,

Darla wouldn't have been surprised had George been dragged along with it.

Clutching the doorjamb, the Coffee King pointed a beefy finger at Doug and blustered, "My Livvy's gone, an' it's all your fault. You need t'pay for it!"

"Hang on, George," Jake interjected, sliding back her chair before Doug could respond. Stepping into the gap between the two men, she went on, "We all know you've suffered a shock, but so has Doug. Coming in here and making threats won't bring either woman back."

"Yeah, but it'll make me feel better," George puffed out, swaying as he gathered himself to move closer. "I think it's time me and Dougie-boy had it out."

Doug, meanwhile, had shoved back his own chair and risen, a spark of his usual swagger returning. "I'm not going to fight you, George. Why don't you go back home and sober up?"

The Coffee King's face abruptly crumpled. "I can't go home. I can't stay there alone."

He slid in slow motion down the length of the doorjamb, until he was seated splay-legged across the transom, head lolling. Alarmed, Darla exchanged looks with Jake and Doug. "What do we do with him?"

"We need to get him sobered up, first," was Jake's practical advice. "If he won't stay in his own place, maybe we can set him up someplace."

"Don't look at me," Darla said in alarm, holding up both hands in a "stop" gesture. "I feel sorry for the guy, but no way is he camping out on my sofa."

"Don't worry, kid. I'm not volunteering my place, either. Maybe we can get him settled in a hotel somewhere."

"Eh, he can bunk with me," Doug spoke up.

Darla stared at him in surprise, but it was Jake who put into words what they both were thinking.

"Are you serious? George just came in here looking for a fight. Somehow, I don't think he's going to be too thrilled when he sobers up and finds out you're his new roomie."

Doug gave a sheepish shrug. "Yeah, yeah, I get it. Drunk or sober, my face is the last one he wants to see. But look at him. He's all bluster and no action. Least I can do is give him a place to lay his head until he's ready to go back to his own place. If things go south when he sobers up, well, I'll deal with it then."

Jake raised a brow. "You sure?"

"No, but I feel like it's the right thing to do." Bypassing Jake, Doug walked over to George and reached down to give the man's shoulder a shake. "C'mon, pal, let's get you up."

"Wha . . . ?"

"Heads up, Georgie. We're gonna take a hike over to my place and get you a shower and a nap."

"And a change of shirt," Darla suggested sotto voce to Jake, who smiled a little.

Between the three of them, they managed to hoist a nonprotesting George to his feet. While Darla and Jake kept him balanced out on the sidewalk, Doug went back inside to shut off the lights and lock his shop. By the time the baker was ready to go, George had begun to rally.

"Darla? Wha-whaddaya doing here?" he asked, squinting at her. "Didja bring me coffee?"

"No coffee this morning," she brightly told him. "The

bookstore's closed today. You'll have to suffer with whatever Doug can brew you up."

"Doug? He's here? Why, that low-down—"

"Yeah, pal, it's me," the baker exclaimed, giving him a slap on the back that sent the other man stumbling. "Remember, we already talked about it. You're coming to stay with me for a couple of days."

George looked confused but nodded. "Yeah, I can do that."

After promising Darla he'd update her on George's condition, Doug gripped the man's arm and steered him somewhat unsteadily down the street. Darla watched the pair go, and then turned to Jake.

"For some reason, I keep thinking *blind leading the blind*," she said with a shake of her head as she and Jake set off in the opposite direction from the men. "I wonder how things will go when George sobers up a bit more?"

"I imagine they'll work it out," was Jake's dry response.

They walked in silence for a few more minutes, but as they crossed to the next block, her attention was on the shops across the street from them. Penelope's dance studio was among them. The place was, of course, closed, but as she'd seen before following other tragedies, a shrine of sorts had begun to build at the studio door.

"I want to take a look," she told Jake and, waiting for a break in traffic, hurried across the street.

Jake followed after her. Together they silently surveyed the broad scattering of flowers—mostly pale pink roses—that lay against the step. From bouquets to single blooms, the roses offered a mute tribute to Penelope's influence. Tucked in with the floral offerings were several crayoned drawings of roses as well: some mere scribblings of pink and green, and others almost botanical in their petaled accuracy. No doubt these had been left by the youngest of her students who also wanted to share their grief in some tangible way.

"I'll bet that's how it looked onstage after Penelope performed in her heyday," the PI observed after a few silent moments. "Admirers tossing flowers onto the stage as she took her bows. Pink roses must have been her favorite."

"I saw her dance just a few days ago, here in the studio," Darla said, fighting back a quaver in her voice. "I was here to talk to her about the block party, but her lesson ran late, so I stayed to watch. When the girls couldn't get this new combination right, she stepped out onto the floor and demonstrated it herself."

Darla smiled a little in remembrance. "It was just a little thing, a couple of turns and a jump, but I swear it took my breath away. Suddenly she was transformed from good old potty-mouthed Penelope into this incredible, graceful being. The students felt it, too. She really was a star."

Which was why Darla still couldn't understand how Penelope could do what she'd done . . . and why Reese's claim of murder-suicide was so hard to accept, at least until she saw some better proof.

"We'd better get back," she told Jake, suddenly unable to stand there among the roses any longer. "Hamlet's probably cranky because we haven't taken our walk yet, and—"

She broke off abruptly, puzzled, as the faintest of vaguely familiar notes, oboe mixed with violin, drifted to her. "Jake, am I going crazy? I swear I hear music playing. It sounds like something out of Tchaikovsky's *Swan Lake*."

Jake frowned and tilted her curly head, listening. Then she shrugged. "I don't hear anything, kid. Maybe someone drove past with their radio on the classical station."

"No, I still hear it. And I think it's coming from inside the studio."

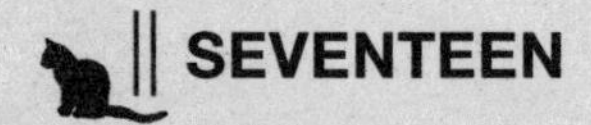

SEVENTEEN

A SMALL, SUPERSTITIOUS CHILL WENT THROUGH DARLA AS she made her cautious way to the studio's curtained windows. The sheer lace drapes were pulled closed, but a gap between them allowed a tantalizing glimpse into the darkness. She squinted, trying to see what could be the source of the piece she heard playing.

Enough morning light seeped in that she could see most of the room reflected in the mirrored walls. She glimpsed a human-sized shape near the barre and gasped, until a second look proved that the shape was actually a coatrack draped with someone's forgotten wispy fringed shawl.

Jake joined her, leaning closer to the glass.

"All right, I hear the music now. Probably one of Reese's guys accidentally left something on." She stepped back and gave Darla an amused look. "Don't worry, kid. I promise it's not Penelope's ghost in there playing the top ten classical ballet hits."

"I hope not," Darla muttered, only to gasp a second time. A shadow, reflected in the mirrors, had flitted by as she'd spoken . . . and this was no coatrack.

"Someone's in there, Jake," she softly exclaimed. "Watch the mirrors. You can see a shadow moving about, like someone dancing."

"You're sure?"

Jake was all business now as she leaned in for her own look. Sure enough, a moment later, the shadow flitted past again.

"Yeah, I saw it, too," she said, reaching for her cell phone. "No ghost. Definitely human."

"You mean, someone's broken into Penelope's studio?"

"It happens, kid. People read about a death in the papers and figure the house—or, in this case, the studio—that's left behind is ripe for the picking. I'll call the precinct and have them check the place."

"Wait!" Darla cut her short as she again glimpsed the person moving within. "I don't think it's a burglar. Whoever it is, they're dancing. It must be one of Penelope's students."

"Yeah?" Jake pressed her face to the glass again for a better look. "Student or not, that doesn't mean they can just waltz in like that . . . no pun intended. It's not a crime scene or anything, but legally, the studio is part of an estate now, and Penelope's heirs are the only ones with any right to be there. I'm going to run whoever it is off."

"Do you have to?" Darla asked as Jake raised a fist to knock on the window glass.

The PI nodded. "Better we do it than someone else calls the cops."

And then an unexpected if familiar male voice behind her made both her and Jake jump.

"Whaddaya doing, looking for ghosts?"

"Hank!" Darla exclaimed as she swung about to see the beefy martial arts instructor standing behind them. As usual he was dressed in his baggy white gi pants and black gi jacket with the sleeves cut off, the better to show off his tattooed, muscled arms.

He was grinning, obviously pleased to have startled them. Despite herself, Darla smiled a little, too. "That was a rotten trick."

"What can I say, rotten tricks is my middle name. So what are you doing?"

"One of Penelope's students is in there," Jake told him. "Guess she decided to get in a little private practice. We were just wondering if we should run her off."

Hank's amused expression vanished. "Don't worry. I'll take care of that. Hey, you, kid!" he shouted through the glass before Darla could stop him, pounding on the window with a big fist. "Get outta there now, before we call the cops!"

"Wow, pretty harsh," Darla told him. "We were thinking about something a little more low-key, like talking to her."

As she spoke, the faint music inside abruptly ceased. A moment later, the door opened and a familiar face complete with pink-dyed chin braids warily peeked out.

"Pinky?" was Darla's astonished cry as she and the young musician stared at each other.

He blinked and then nodded, opening the studio door

wider. Like the male dance students Darla had seen the other week, Pinky was wearing black dance tights, though his T-shirt was black instead of white. "Hey, uh, Ms. Pettistone?"

"Yes, it's me. What in the world are you doing in there?"

"Uh, dancing? I'm a student."

Then, at Darla's disbelieving look, his expression became defensive.

"I really am, and Madame Penelope said it was okay," he declared. "She gave me a key so I could practice after hours, since I couldn't come to class much. You know, with gigs and stuff. I have an audition coming up, and she said . . ."

He trailed off abruptly, the chin braids suddenly quivering, and Darla gave him a swift, impulsive hug.

"It's okay, we understand," she assured him. "But you probably shouldn't be in there now. The police are still investigating the case, and it might not look good if they found you."

"Yeah, I guess," he agreed, looking embarrassed to have been the recipient of Darla's display of emotion. "Let me get my stuff."

A few minutes later, black backpack slung over his shoulder, he was headed down the street, having first left his key in Darla's care once she'd assured him she'd turn it over to Reese.

As the youth turned the corner, Jake spoke up for the first time since the trespasser's identity had been discovered. "I have to say, I wasn't expecting that," she said, lips quirking. "No way would I have guessed Pinky was a . . . What do you call a male ballerina, anyhow?"

"Technically, he'd be a danseur or a *ballerino*," Darla told her, flashing back to those ballet lessons, "but I think these days you'd just call him a male ballet dancer."

She was waiting for a sarcastic comment from Hank, but to her surprise he gave an approving nod. "Yeah, we send some of our black belts for dance lessons or yoga lessons sometimes. It improves their body awareness and uses some different muscles. Though we've had to have that argument with a few of the parents."

"The gender stereotype one?" Jake asked. "Yeah, I know that one."

"Speaking of stereotypes," Darla broke in, "are you carrying around those flowers for a reason, Hank?"

The man glanced down at the small bundle of pastel carnations he held in one hand, as if only just remembering what he carried. His expression a bit sheepish, he said, "Yeah, I thought I'd leave them here. You know, for Penelope."

He bent to carefully add them to the other blooms and then took a step back. "I remember it meant a lot to me and my brother to see all the flowers and stuff people left at the dojo for our stepdad. So I thought I'd, you know, do the same for her. She was a good broad."

And then, as Darla and Jake nodded their appreciation of that sentiment, he added, "Say, how about I walk you ladies back to the bookstore? I was headed that way, anyhow. I was kinda in the mood for coffee, and what with Perky's being shut down . . ."

"Actually, we're closed on Mondays," Darla reminded him. Then, at his disappointed expression, she added,

"But I could go for a nice latte, myself. How about I open up the coffee bar just for us?"

They walked in companionable silence the rest of the way back to Pettistone's, where they found Robert sitting on the stoop outside the Plinskis' shop, Bygone Days, enjoying the relatively mild morning. He was reading a paperback novel—something fantasy or horror, from what Darla could see of its black and purple cover—and Roma, once again wearing her patriotic harness and leash, was seated prettily beside him.

"Hey, Ms. P. . . . Jake . . . Sensei," he said as he looked up from his novel.

"Hey, kid," Hank answered with a friendly smile, adding with a nod toward Roma, "So, how's the little rat doin'?"

Robert and his sensei had long since made their peace on the subject of the little canine, who'd once been a subject of contention between them, so Darla knew the insult was just a joke on Hank's part.

Roma, however, had not quite learned to forgive and forget.

As Hank drew even with the stoop, the little dog flattened her ears and bared tiny white teeth. Her initial growl morphed into a surprisingly low-pitched bark, and Robert promptly put a comforting arm around her.

"That's okay, girl," he murmured in her silky, folded ear. "Sensei is very sorry he ever said anything mean to you before."

Darla shook her head. "Hank, you should do something—dogs have almost as long a memory as cats do," she told him, thinking of how Hamlet held a grudge.

Hank puffed up his cheeks a moment and then blew out a resigned sigh. "Yeah, yeah, I'm sorry. Robert, how about you tell your little doggie I'll send a donation to your animal rescue friends to make up for being a jerk, okay?"

"Really? That would be, like, awesome! I'll bring the address to my next class." He addressed the pup, "Roma, did you hear that? Do you think you can forgive him now?"

The tiny greyhound appeared to consider the question, her luminous brown eyes fixed unblinkingly on the man. Then she gave a little yip, and her white-tipped tail wagged just a bit.

"She forgives you," Robert said in delight. "Thanks, Sensei."

Hank gave a rueful shake of his head but moved on toward Darla's stoop without further comment, while Jake grinned back at them both. As for Darla, she stopped to give Roma a quick pat. Then she told Robert, "I'm going to go inside to play barista and make lattes for Jake and Hank. Do you want me to bring you one, too?"

She smiled at his swift look of alarm—the hapless boss taking over his well-run station!—before he schooled his features back to neutral. "Thanks, Ms. P., I'm good. But do you want me to, you know, come over and help you out or anything?"

"I need the practice," she assured him. "Besides, it's your day off. But, don't worry. I promise I'll clean up when we're finished."

Robert didn't look reassured, but he nodded. "Okay, but maybe don't use the roaster. It's a little, you know, tricky."

Darla assured him she'd leave it alone. She left the

youth to his book and let the three of them inside the bookstore through her private entrance. A few minutes later, Jake and Hank were lounging in the upstairs coffee bar watching with interest while Darla attempted to duplicate Robert's effortless mastery of all things brewed and steamed. After a false start when she set the foaming temperature a notch too high and overboiled the milk, she finally produced what she considered three acceptable lattes and brought them over to the table.

Jake took a sip of hers and promptly gave Darla a thumbs-up. "Great job, kid. Almost as good as Robert."

"Not bad," Darla agreed as she tried hers. "Except for the lack of cute cat faces in the foam like he does. You'll have to make do with the real thing."

She was speaking, of course, of Hamlet. The clever feline had migrated down into the store from the apartment above through one of the many secret passages he had discovered over the years. Now, he sat atop one of the bistro tables (Darla made a quick mental note that all the tabletops should get a thorough wipe down before they opened the next morning) and was fixing his green gaze on the human interlopers.

Actually, on just one interloper, Darla realized. Hamlet's attention was focused entirely on the martial arts instructor.

"Hey, what?" Hank exclaimed as he noticed the cat's scrutiny. "I already said I was going to make a donation."

"I don't think Hamlet is worried about that," Darla said with a smile. "He and Roma are not exactly BFFs. Maybe you made him mad last time you were here."

"Well, all I did was what I always do, which was ignore him. So you can tell that cat of yours that I don't have anything to feel guilty about."

But a moment later, Hank blurted, "Okay, I wasn't going to say anything, but she tried to hit on me a few weeks back."

It took Darla a moment to realize his confession had nothing to do with cats or dogs. Then she stared at him, wide-eyed.

"Hit on you? Who, Livvy?" she exclaimed, mildly scandalized. *Had Livvy cheated on George with the whole neighborhood?*

Hank shook his head. "No, actually, I meant Penelope."

There was a moment of stunned silence, and then Jake grinned a little. "So, spill. Did you do the dirty with her?"

"No way," Hank shot back, looking slightly scandalized, himself. "She had to be, what, thirty years older than me."

"What's wrong with that?" Jake, herself about the same age as Penelope, asked in mock-disapproval. "Get with the program. The whole cougar thing is pretty popular these days."

"Yeah, well, not for me. I mean, I didn't want to be rude, but she was coming on strong. She started talking about mutton and lamb and Fonteyn and Nur-y-something."

"Rudolf Nureyev," Darla clarified for him.

Then, when Hank and Jake both glanced at her uncomprehendingly, she went on, "Nureyev was a world-famous Russian ballet dancer who defected to the West in the 1960s. Margot Fonteyn was a world-famous English dancer. When they met, she was in her forties, and he was almost twenty years younger. In the beginning, she refused to dance with him and called their pairing mutton and lamb. But they still supposedly had a long-lasting love affair along with their professional relationship."

"Wow, they taught you that in ballet class?" Jake exclaimed.

Darla shook her head, smiling. "No, I read that in the book Hamlet pulled down the other day."

Hank shrugged. "Well, it sounded kind of pervy to me, so I lied and told her I was seeing someone. She was a good sport about getting turned down, though." Then he frowned. "I don't know. Maybe I really dodged a bullet there. I still can't believe Penelope would kill Livvy like that. The whole murder and suicide bit doesn't seem her kinda thing, you know what I mean?"

No, it didn't seem like her, Darla silently agreed. And yet from what Reese had said, the evidence pointed to murder-suicide . . . unless maybe that was the story the police were putting out to lull the actual murderer into complacency?

But Darla barely had time to consider this unsettling possibility when Jake spoke up again, all traces of amusement gone.

"I know it's tough, guys," she told them, hands wrapped around her latte as if for warmth. "I liked Penelope, too. But when I was a cop, I don't know how many times all the friends and relatives swore at the beginning that so-and-so couldn't have possibly done the crime. But then when you checked back with them later, a lot of them eventually decided that it really did fit the pattern."

"Wait," Darla countered, setting down her own latte as the obvious hit her. "We know that Penelope was seeing

Doug at the same time she was putting the moves on Hank. So why would she then go ballistic over Doug doing the same thing with Livvy? It doesn't make sense."

Jake nodded. "Yeah, sounds to me like she didn't really consider that she and Doug were exclusive, so I don't get why she went to the trouble of talking to me at the street fair about being two-timed. Or for that matter, why she'd be angry enough to kill Livvy and herself over it."

Hank, meanwhile, tilted his mug high, finishing the last bit of foam and coffee. "You ladies figure that out. I've gotta get going. Thanks for the coffee," he said and shoved his chair back.

Jake rose with him, her expression preoccupied. Darla wondered if the PI had some additional theories on the whole Livvy-Penelope-Hank situation, but she wasn't going to ask with the latter still there. Whatever Jake was mulling over, they could discuss that later, out of Hank's hearing. Aloud, Darla merely asked her friend, "You want to take that cup with you?"

"Yeah, thanks. I've got a little pro bono job I need to get going on, so I need all the caffeine I can get."

Carrying her own coffee with her, Darla escorted the pair to the shop's front door. Robert and Roma had apparently retreated to their apartment, for the steps outside Mary Ann's place were empty now. Jake waited with Darla on their stoop until the martial arts instructor headed off along the sidewalk in the direction of the dojo; then the PI turned to Darla. But rather than bringing up her theories about Penelope and Livvy, as Darla expected, Jake moved to an entirely different subject.

"I didn't want to say it in front of Hank, but that pro

bono I'm doing is for this one woman who stopped by my block party booth. Her teenage daughter got sick after vaping a few weeks back."

"That's terrible!" Darla exclaimed. "Is the girl going to be okay?"

"She's fine now, but the daughter's not talking about where she got the stuff she smoked. I'm guessing maybe she got hold of Livvy's Kona Blue Party and had an allergic reaction to it. I'm going to poke around and see if I can trace anything back to Perky's."

"All right. Be careful. I'm just going to hang out for a bit and get a few chores done, and then kick back with a book."

While Jake headed down the street, Darla settled on her own stoop with her coffee cup. It occurred to her that she didn't do this often enough, the basic "stop and smell the roses" routine.

Heck, I'm lucky to see the darn roses in the distance, she told herself with a shake of her head. She'd had one not-so-relaxing vacation earlier this year. Maybe it was time to take some more time off while things were slow.

She spent a good twenty minutes simply sipping coffee, and weighing the virtues of vacationing in Colorado versus Seattle versus a quick run over to the Jersey Shore. So deep was she in thought that it took a moment for her to even register it when a familiar voice was calling her name.

"Earth to Darla," Reese said, smiling down at her.

The sun was behind him, enveloping him in a yellow glow that, had she been in a whimsical mood, she might have deemed celestial. Since she was feeling far from fanciful at the moment—or maybe she still was suffering from a bad case of dog in the manger—Darla simply squinted up at him, raising a hand to block the worst of the light.

"Hi, Reese. Sorry, if you're here for coffee, I already shut the bar down," she told him.

He shook his head. "Don't worry. I've had my quota of caffeine for the day. Actually, I'm here to see Mary Ann. She called me all upset about Mr. Plinski."

As if on cue, the old woman's reedy voice hailed them.

"Detective Reese! Oh, thank heaven you're here," Mary Ann called from the open door of her antiques shop. She stepped out onto the stoop; then, with a furtive look upward, she hurried over to join Reese and Darla.

"Oh dear," she said, hand over her heart as she tried to catch her breath. "I hope I'm not taking too much advantage. I tried phoning Jake a bit ago, but she said she was out on a case."

"What's wrong?" Darla asked in concern.

Mary Ann wrung her wrinkled hands. "It's Brother. I told him that there wasn't a serial killer in the neighborhood, after all, but he won't listen. And now he's gone back up to the roof to stand guard, and I can't get him to come down again!"

EIGHTEEN

REESE GAVE THE OLD WOMAN A COMFORTING PAT ON THE shoulder. "Mary Ann, you want me to go talk to your brother, see if I can get him to give it up?"

The old woman gave him a grateful nod. "Oh, Detective Reese, thank you! Maybe he'll listen to another man. He certainly isn't listening to me, and I'm a bit worried that he . . ."

She paused, her lips trembling; then, determinedly smoothing the skirt of her belted coral shirtdress, she went on. "Well, I don't want to borrow trouble. Let me show you the way."

They followed Mary Ann into the antique store. Then, while the woman led Reese upstairs—to Darla's relief, the elderly pair had recently installed one of those stairway lift chairs, so Mary Ann rode—Darla browsed about the shop. Unlike other similar establishments with their emphasis on European antiquities, Bygone Days Antiques specialized in eighteenth- and nineteenth-century Americana. Over the past year, however, the brother and sister had been concentrating more on collectibles dating from the early twentieth century.

The faintly musty scents of old wooden furniture and vintage clothing and linens always made Darla feel at home in the crowded shop despite the fact that the place never looked quite the same any time she stopped in for a visit. For the month of July, Mary Ann had gathered all manner of examples of Americana and displayed them up front near the cash register. From brass eagle andirons to vintage bunting to an exquisite Chippendale walnut chest of drawers, the collection was a cheerful tribute to the Founding Fathers.

The soft sound of a motor that was the lift chair descending heralded Mary Ann's return. Once it reached bottom, she hopped off the seat and made her brisk way over to where Darla stood.

"Well, I certainly hope Detective Reese gets through to my brother," she said with a sigh. "I've worn myself out trying to explain things to him."

"Don't worry. Reese is pretty good at that." Then, running a longing hand along the Chippendale chest, Darla added, "This dresser is simply beautiful. Where did you find it?"

Mary Ann entertained her with the story of that particular piece while Darla tried to convince herself that she really didn't have room for it in her apartment. Fortunately, Reese returned downstairs just as she was weakening enough to consider asking Mary Ann about payment plans.

"Don't worry," he told the old woman. "Mr. Plinski and I talked for a while, and he understands that there's no serial killer wandering around. But he's still concerned about the neighborhood. Sitting up there with his binoculars is his way of helping."

"But I *do* worry about him," Mary Ann replied, voice quavering. "What if he gets confused, or he gets too warm up there?"

"He's got a big glass of ice water and his walkie-talkie, so he can call you if he needs any help."

And Darla hurried to add, "Robert and I can come by to check on him every so often, if you'd like."

The old woman smiled, visibly relieved.

"That would be wonderful, my dear. I try not to fuss, but there's no two ways around it. Brother and I are getting old, and you know what that means. We're frail . . . forgetful . . . and we certainly have no business being guardians of the neighborhood. That's a job for young people."

Reese gave her an encouraging smile. "Don't sell Mr. Plinski short. Surveillance takes patience, and that's something he's got that most young guys don't. And he knows the neighborhood . . . what should and shouldn't be going on. I say if he wants to keep watch, let him. We cops can use all the extra eyes we can get these days."

"Very well. If he can do it, so can I."

With that, Mary Ann reached across the counter for what presumably was the other half of the walkie-talkie set her brother carried. She clipped it to the belt of her shirtdress. "I'm set. Thank you, both of you."

"Another day, another good deed," Reese quipped as, leaving the old woman to her shop, they walked down the concrete steps to the sidewalk. "I wish all my cases were this easy to solve. Now, how about I take you to lunch to make up for bailing on you the other day?"

Darla considered the offer for a moment. On the one hand, this would be an opportunity for her to quiz him on the whole Penelope situation. Even if he gave her no answers, she might be able to read between the lines of what he *did* say. On the other, she had a good suspicion that "lunch" was code for *I'm going to try again to bring up some awkwardness about our relationship that'll just embarrass us both.* Unsettled as she was feeling over the whole Penelope situation, the last thing she needed was more drama to sort through.

She smiled and shook her head. "How about I take a rain check on the rain check? Today's my day off, and now that the block party is behind me, I have lots of stuff to do around my place."

"All right, scratch the lunch. But give me five minutes to talk, okay?"

By now, they'd reached her stoop. The detective halted and stretched one arm to grasp the opposite balustrade, so that he was blocking her way up to her door. Whether or not the gesture was deliberate, Reese's body language was that of a man who wasn't prepared to take "no" for an answer.

Great. Darla gave the offending limb a pointed look and purposefully crossed her own arms.

"Mr. Plinski is three stories up and watching your every move," she reminded Reese, only half kidding as she added, "He might call the cops if he sees you're trying to keep me from my home."

It took him a moment to register what she meant.

"Oh, sorry," he muttered, swiftly lowering his arm and stepping to one side. "So, you gonna give me that five minutes?"

"I'll give you two," she said with a bright smile. *Might as well get this over with.* "What's on your mind?"

"I wanted to explain about Connie and this whole engagement business. I mean, since you and me . . . that is, because we once . . ."

"Reese, you don't owe me any explanations," she cut him short as he stumbled over his words. "It's not like we were dating. We went out, what, twice? We didn't click that way, so that was the end of it. You were certainly free to do your own thing without my approval—up to, and including, getting engaged."

Even if you had to go and settle on Miss Jersey Shore, she silently added.

Reese, meanwhile, gave a relieved nod. "Right. That's what I thought, but you never know with women."

When Darla shot him a look that said, *You're wandering into dangerous territory, bub*, he shrugged and added, "You know what I mean. Sometimes, they get these ideas in their heads that've got nothing to do with reality. You and me, we're friends, nothing more. So we're all good?"

"All good," she agreed. "And I think it's great you're getting married. It was just a big surprise to everyone."

"You want the truth? It was a surprise to me, too."

He hesitated, and Darla stared at him. Had the engagement been Connie's idea? Before she had time to consider that possibility more fully, however, he went on, "But, bottom line, I had to do it."

"No, not that kind of *had to*," he clarified with a snort when Darla widened her eyes. "Not that my Ma would mind at this point. Look, I'll be thirty-five years old in a couple of months. You know how long I've been listening to Ma ask when she's gonna get some grandkids? Besides, I'm tired of coming home to an empty apartment every night. I hate cooking my own dinner and doing my own wash. Connie might not be perfect, but she gets me. She's not one of those liberated broads, not like—"

He broke off, apparently realizing that "dangerous territory" was about to be his permanent address, but Darla mentally filled in the blanks for him.

She's not one of those liberated broads, not like you.

Telling herself she wasn't insulted by that sentiment—at least, not too much—she shook her head and smiled a little.

"Don't worry. I get it," she assured him. "Anyhow, congratulations again. Connie's a great catch. Now, I need to go clean up the coffee bar. I promised Robert I'd tidy up after playing barista."

"Yeah, well, thanks for understanding. You're a good broad, Darla Pettistone."

She leaned closer to him. "Word to the wise," she softly said. "Where I come from, the term 'broad' is *not* a compliment."

Still, she was smiling as she gave Reese's hand a swift, impulsive squeeze as she passed him on the steps and headed back inside. She waited, however, until she'd relocked the door behind her before she drew a deep breath and sagged against the foyer wall.

Liar, liar, she thought with a shake of her head, checking to make sure that her khakis weren't by chance on fire. Because despite all her protestations to the contrary, she realized that she didn't think Reese's getting married was the least bit great.

"*Me-OOW!*" came a protesting yowl at her feet that made her jump.

Satisfied that he had her attention, Hamlet strode over to the door leading to the store. As soon as Darla opened it, he flew past her into the bookstore and headed up the stairway to the second floor.

"Right, Hamlet," she muttered. "Let's keep things in perspective. We all know what's important around here, and that's you."

Still, Darla smiled as she watched him go. By the time she made it upstairs, Hamlet was already perched on the coffee bar counter with his nose deep in the tiny stainless steel pitcher that she'd used to steam the milk for the lattes earlier.

Darla rolled her eyes. "Shoo, Hammy," she told him. "You're lucky we're closed. A customer sees you doing that, and the health department will shut us down so fast it'll make your whiskers spin."

Hamlet raised his fuzzy black snout from the small jug and shot her a disapproving green look. Darla could almost read his mind. *What do you mean? Can't you see that I am assisting with the washing up?*

"Seriously, Hamlet, scoot," she told him and gave a little clap of her hands as emphasis.

Foam clinging to his whiskers, the feline stalked off in a huff. He found a spot on the floor beneath one of the tables and began his après-steamed-milk bath. Darla, meanwhile, gathered the cups and containers from earlier and scrubbed them clean. A few minutes later, she had just put the last item on a clean towel to dry, when a rhythmic noise nearby caught her attention.

Roll-clack; roll-clack.

"Hamlet, is that you?"

Shaking her head, Darla abandoned her post behind the bar and went looking for the cat, assuming that this would also bring her to the source of the sound. Sure enough, she found Hamlet facing the far corner and batting something back and forth into the wall. On closer inspection, the object of his interest proved to be something familiar looking.

"Where did you get this?" she demanded as she reached down to retrieve a red vapor pen. No doubt a customer had dropped it . . . but how long ago?

"You're a better janitor than Robert," she told the cat. "I'll stick this in our lost-and-found and see if anyone claims it."

Hamlet on her heels, Darla went downstairs again. The store's lost-and-found was nothing more than an open cardboard box tucked under the register. Darla pulled it out and took a quick inventory of its current contents: a Yankees ball cap; a flashlight key chain minus any keys; and a crumpled ten-dollar bill that, if not claimed by week's end, Darla planned to donate to the animal rescue group where Robert volunteered.

She added the vapor pen to the lot. It was by far the most expensive item in the box, so chances were its owner might come looking for it. But if it remained unclaimed for too long, she would toss it in the trash. *Last thing we need floating around here*, she told herself. She was returning the box to its spot, when the sudden smack of a book hitting the wooden floor made her jump.

"Hamlet!" she called in exasperation. "Quit playing around and let's go back upstairs."

But when she looked, the cat was already sitting quietly at the door waiting on her. Shaking her head, she told him, "Stay there. I'll be right back."

She made a quick round of the shelves, looking for the book that had gone flying. Why was Hamlet doing his book snagging thing now, when the matter of Penelope and Livvy's deaths had supposedly been resolved? Did the crafty feline have his doubts, too? Or was he simply ticked that she'd taken away his new toy and so had decided to punish her by making her work a little on her day off?

It wasn't until she reached the fine arts section that she found the fallen volume. Curious, she picked it up to return it to the shelf.

"*A Short History of Body Art*," she read aloud, frowning a little at the cover photo of a woman's hand embellished with intricate henna designs.

What mehndi had to do with anything, she couldn't guess. Curious, she flipped through the pages and then turned to the back cover. The photo on the reverse was a close-up of a muscular male arm totally covered in bright ink, the images of fish and water and blooms definitely Asian inspired. The copy listed the author's name and background and then went on to briefly extol the international cultural influence of various body arts . . . primarily tattoos.

Tattoos?

Darla studied the back cover photo more closely, a sick feeling rapidly building in her stomach. The brightly scaled koi erupting from a stylized splash of blue waves resembled the one tattooed on Hank's arm more than she cared to admit.

Was Hamlet trying to tell her that Reese had come to the wrong conclusion regarding Penelope and Livvy's deaths? And, even more chilling, was the clever feline trying to say that Hank Tomlinson had had something to do with them?

"No way," Darla exclaimed as she swiftly reshelved the book and rushed to the door. Hamlet was still waiting, green gaze fixed on the exit. At Darla's approach, however, he swiveled his fluffy black head and gave her an emerald blink.

"All right, spill," she told him as she reached for the knob. "What do tattoos have to do with anything? Are you trying to pin something on Hank just because he made fun of Roma?"

But as her hand closed on the cool metal, she mentally replayed that get-together with Jake and Hank. Hamlet had done his feline best to stare down the latter, perhaps even being responsible for Hank's confessing to an uncomfortable encounter with Penelope. The tale that Hank had told seemed to indicate that Penelope had been the aggressor, and that he'd been happy to keep his distance.

But what if Hank had lied about the whole cougar scenario, and *he'd* actually been the one to put the moves on Penelope? And what if he'd been rebuffed by her . . . and hadn't taken that rejection well, at all?

But even as the notion flashed through her mind, she dismissed it.

"No way, Hammy," she said aloud as they climbed the stairs to the third floor. "You've got your whiskers crossed on this one. For one thing, you're forgetting about Livvy. Both deaths have to be connected because of the whole oleander thing. And for another, if Hank ever did decide to off someone, don't you think he'd use some kind of martial arts trick instead of poison?"

But as she let herself and Hamlet into the apartment, it occurred to her that maybe the cat's tattoo clue was supposed to be generic.

Abruptly, her thoughts turned to George and his ballerina tattoo. If there was one thing she'd learned from both Reese and Jake, it was that you could never dismiss a victim's "significant other." It wasn't hard to imagine the explosive-tempered George having turned against both Livvy and Penelope.

Certain she was onto something, Darla wrestled with the issue of George's theoretical guilt for the rest of the afternoon as she went about her typical day-off chores. She could picture him killing Livvy in a fit of rage, no question of that. Unfortunately, just as with Hank, what she simply couldn't see was George distilling up a poisonous batch of oleandrin-tainted "juice" with which to spike her vapor pen.

On the other hand, George was meticulous when it came to roasting coffee, so maybe he would have also had the patience necessary to concoct a deadly tincture. Moreover, he had ready access to the necessary plant. And she couldn't forget that George did have a powerful motive . . . at least, in Livvy's case.

"But what about Penelope?" she wondered aloud midway through sorting a pile of laundry, the question drawing a keen look from Hamlet. What reason would the coffee shop owner have had to kill her, too? Even if they'd once been an item, that was old history.

"Come on, Hammy," she urged the feline in question. "What else do you know?"

Unfortunately, Hamlet proved of no further help in the matter. Rather than snagging more books whose titles might clarify the matter, he settled onto the back of her horsehair sofa while she labored. There, he spent the afternoon napping in between watching repeat episodes of his favorite cable television shows on the nature channel. As for Darla, by six o'clock she finally called a halt to chores and treated herself to a quick supper of homemade Cobb salad. Then, still mulling over the issue of oleanders, she fired up her trusty laptop for an Internet search on that plant.

The images she found were of a bushy shrub, the dark green, spiky foliage bearing five-petal blooms that she learned could be pink or yellow or red or white, depending on the species. She studied the pink oleander photo more closely. No doubt about it, this was the same bushy, flowering plant that was tucked away on the landing behind the bistro table at Perky's.

Then, hoping that Reese never had cause to seize her computer for evidence, she did a search for oleander poisoning.

In a short time, she knew more about that toxic shrub than she'd ever hoped to learn: how all parts of it—seeds, leaves, sap—were extremely poisonous, although some preliminary studies were being done on its use in treating cancer.

That last stopped her for a moment. Maybe Livvy had found some literature touting oleandrin as a cure for rheumatoid arthritis and had decided to experiment, with fatal results.

Then she shook her head. That might explain Livvy's death, but not Penelope's. Apparently, it was quite a bitter plant, so that it would be rare for anyone to ingest it accidentally without noticing. She frowned over that for a bit, wondering if perhaps the taste could be camouflaged. From what little she knew about vapor pens, the oil that was "smoked" often contained sweet fruit flavors that might well mask the bitterness, the same way one added cream and sugar to coffee.

More compelling, however, was the laundry list of symptoms that oleander poisoning caused. Nausea, blurred vision, dizziness, disorientation . . . and that was but a sampling. Depending on how and how much was ingested, and how quickly medical treatment was given, she read that it wasn't always fatal. But with a high enough concentration, and no immediate intervention, death was usually swift and inevitable. Shuddering a little, Darla closed the browser window and rose from her computer desk.

"What do you want me to do, Hamlet? Reese is the detective, not me."

The cat was still in his favorite spot, having moved only to grab a quick bite of kibble while Darla was eating. Now, he was avidly watching the television screen again, his green gaze fixed on a python devouring what looked like a feral hog. Deliberately moving between him and that gruesome scene—he'd watched enough of that sort of thing the other night!—Darla went on, "Sorry, I tried, but I don't think I'm going to bring Reese over to our side with only your word—um, your book snagging—that George might have been involved."

Obviously irritated that she'd dared block his view, Hamlet gave a muttered *yow* and leaped over to the sofa arm, where his sight line of the television was no longer impeded. He did, however, shoot her a look that said, *You're on your own, human . . . I've done my part.*

"Fine," she muttered back at him. "You started it, I'll finish it. Tomorrow, I'm going to have another little chat with the King of Coffee, and we're going to talk murder."

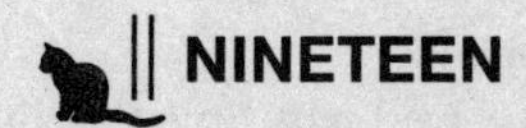

NINETEEN

YEP, DEFINITELY OLEANDER, DARLA THOUGHT IN GRIM SATISfaction the next morning as she gave the two potted bushes on the Perky's landing a closer examination.

Now that she knew what to look for, she could see that the long, narrow leaves and five-petaled pink flowers were textbook examples of the genus. *An attractive little shrub,* she told herself as she gave one fragrant bloom a sniff. *One would never suspect it had a more sinister side.* Remembering that Hamlet had been sitting out there under the bistro table the day she'd bought the "coffee" from Livvy, she gave a quick thanks that the usually nosy feline hadn't munched on any of the fallen leaves there.

Reviewing her mental clipboard with its "to-investigate" checklist, she thought, *Oleander confirmed, one item down . . .*

Then she glanced at her watch. Next up would be confronting George. The problem was that, last she knew, he was staying with Doug. (Unless, of course, he'd stormed out of his rival's place as soon as he'd sobered up . . . certainly, an outcome well within the realm of possibility.) Since Doug hadn't picked up his phone when she'd tried calling him earlier to confirm George's whereabouts, she had decided to gamble that the King of Coffee might've decided to return to his own domain.

It was a little after ten thirty, well past time that the coffeehouse would have been open on a normal day. Since the wrought iron gate to the steps was open, she assumed she'd been right about George being there; the sign on the locked door, however, insisted that Perky's was closed.

She peered in the window glass to see if George was inside. As far as she could tell, the front room was empty of people, though a light or two appeared to be on within. Maybe he was in the back room puttering away at something, or maybe he always left a light on for security purposes. Either way, she was there, so might as well give it a shot. Steeling herself, she stepped to the door—to the spot where Livvy had lain dead—and firmly knocked.

Somewhat to her surprise, she heard George's raspy voice beyond the door call out, "Whaddaya want? We're closed."

"George, it's me, Darla. I wanted to see how you were."

When he made no reply, she knocked again. "George, we're all concerned about you," she went on, lying just a little. "Do you want to come over to the bookstore for another—?"

The door abruptly pulled open before she could finish

her question. George stuck his big head out and squinted bloodshot eyes at her.

"Darla? Whaddaya doing here? The coffee so bad at your place you need to go running to the competition?"

If anything, he looked worse than he had the day before, still unshaven and with his snowy hair sticking out at all angles, the dark bags under his eyes almost large enough to take on vacation. At least he was wearing a different Perky's shirt today—this one a soothing mint shade that would have gone nicely with Darla's red hair, but only accentuated George's pallor.

"Hi, George," she replied, ignoring the insult even as she began to regret her decision to confront him.

The King of Coffee might be doughy looking, but she suspected there still was some muscle beneath the fat. She knew that wholesale sacks of raw coffee beans easily weighed a hundred pounds each, and he doubtless wrestled those around on a regular basis. If her questions made him feel threatened enough that he wanted to keep her from leaving, she might well have difficulty escaping his grasp.

"Look, I know you're probably not in the mood for company," she began, suddenly hoping he'd agree and send her on her way, "but I wanted to check on you. Last I saw you was when Doug was taking you over to his place. Are you still staying there?"

"Stay with that lying, cheating skunk of an SOB?" he replied with an angry snort. "I'd rather sleep in the gutter. Besides, I figured I needed to come back here. You stay away too long, you get the riffraff trying to break in and steal you blind."

Then, jerking a thumb over his shoulder, he asked, "You wanna come in? I can brew you up a cup."

So much for being sent on her way. Darla hesitated. If she begged off now, only to come checking up on him later when she was feeling a little braver, he might get suspicious. This would likely be her only real chance to question him.

"Uh, okay . . . that is, if you're sure you don't want to come over to the bookstore, instead?"

"Nah, I got some ground coffee I need to use up, so we might as well drink here."

He opened the door wider, and Darla went on in, putting a reflexive hand to her jeans pocket to make sure her cell phone was there. Of course, she had been sure to let James know where she was headed when she left the store—*If I'm not back in an hour, send the cops*, she'd only half jokingly told him—but she felt safer knowing her phone was in quick reach.

The place had a stale smell to it from having been closed up for a few days, but at least the air conditioner was working. George flipped on the lights, dispelling the shadows if not the mustiness. He lumbered around the counter while Darla took a seat on one of the tall barstools.

"Whatcha want? Espresso, latte, or just a plain old cup of joe?"

"Plain old joe is fine. With cream, if you have any fresh," she clarified. Then, casually, she asked, "I know it's soon to be making plans, but have you given any thought to what you want to do going forward?"

George shrugged as he opened a sealed bag of coffee,

the enticing smell promptly dispelling much of the staleness in the air. "I dunno," he said as he measured out the ground beans and put them in the brewer. "It's hard to run a place like this alone. I guess I could hire a kid to help out."

"Steve's son and daughter both work part-time for him, and that seems to work out okay," she said before recalling that George had had his own interaction with the Mookjai siblings and not come out looking particularly good.

But to her surprise, he said, "Well, that Steve might be okay, but you oughta watch out for his kids. They were in here the other week, an' I finally figured out his boy was the same one who got Livvy started on that whole stupid Kona Blue Party nonsense. The pair of 'em was acting all smart-ass like, like they thought they was some kinda gang."

"Wait, what?"

George snorted as he reached beneath the counter for a couple of Perky's mugs.

"Yeah, they started threatening Livvy, telling her she had to give them a cut of the action, or she'd be sorry. I was in the back unpacking stuff, but I heard the whole thing. I ran their sorry butts off and told them never to come back again, or I was gonna tell their dad what they was up to. Livvy was scared they'd try something, but they never came back. You just gotta know how to call someone's bluff," he finished, puffing out his chest.

"Wow," was the only response Darla could summon.

According to Steve, Jason and Kayla had claimed that George had refused to wait on them and called them racist names. But maybe that had been a little CYA action on their part, in case George made good on his threat to tell their dad. Maybe the coffee shop owner wasn't the bigot they'd made him out to be. She'd have to let Steve know about this conversation and let him take it from there.

"Yeah, well, not all kids are like that," George was saying with a shrug as he went to check the coffee's progress. "That one that works for you—"

"Robert?" she supplied.

He nodded. "Yeah, he seems like a good worker even with all that dumb makeup. You tell him he ever gets tired of working for you, he can come work at a real coffee shop with me."

"I'll do that," she said with a wry smile. Then, as a thought occurred to her, she added, "Actually, I know someone who might need a job—Emma, the girl who works for Doug at the doughnut shop. Doug said he might have to lay her off if his business doesn't come back."

George had been reaching for the coffeepot, which was almost full. He paused and gave Darla an unreadable look.

"You're talking about the girl who's a student of Penelope's." At her nod, he went on, "I dunno if you heard by now, but Penny and me, we go back. We dated awhile before I hooked up with Livvy. I was good with staying friends, but she wasn't so much. You know how broads are. They get funny about stuff like that."

Darla mentally rolled her eyes as she heard echoes of her conversation with Reese. On the other hand, did that portend that she and Connie would spend the next twenty years secretly plotting each other's downfall?

"Actually, Jake figured out the Penelope situation

already, but I have to admit we were surprised. I mean, since Livvy was so quiet and polite. Usually, divorced men marry the same type of woman again. Except for being dancers, she and Penelope didn't seem much alike."

"Yeah, well, that's what you think."

Pouring out two cups of coffee, he set one in front of her and turned to open a small refrigerator built into the counter behind him. Pulling out a carton of cream, he placed it beside her coffee.

"You wouldn't think it to listen to her," he went on with a snort, "but Livvy can—could—be a real piece of work. You think what's coming out of her mouth is all sweetness and light, and then you figure out a minute later she just ripped you a new one."

Then his expression softened. "But Penny, she had this nice side. Soft, you know. I met her at a ballet party, believe it or not. The lady I was dating at the time, she drug me to see *The Nutcracker*, of all things. But it was Christmas, so I decided to be a good sport."

He waited for Darla to finish with the cream, and then poured a good dollop for himself and took a swig from his mug.

"That's a cuppa coffee," he said with pride. "Now, where was I?"

"At *The Nutcracker*," she reminded him, intrigued despite herself.

"Oh, yeah. Anyhow, my date, she knew the director, so we got to go backstage," he went on and swirled his forefinger in a "whoopee" gesture. "While she was hobnobbing with the dancers, I snuck out to the alley to grab a quick smoke. Who do you think was out there already, dressed up like the Sugar Plum Fairy in her pink and white tutu, and dragging on a cigarette? I tell you, she got me going," he went on, hand lightly slapping back and forth over his burly chest as he pantomimed a heartbeat.

Darla took a sip of her coffee and then asked, "Don't tell me, that was the last date you ever had with the other woman?"

"Yeah, it was," he admitted with an odd little smile that made her draw back a bit. "I got Penelope's phone number, and that was all she wrote. We was happy as clams for about five years, even talked about getting married. I was making good bucks back then—did I tell ya, I used to be a stockbroker?—so I kept her in real good style. But then she started losing out on roles to the younger dancers, and things started to go downhill for us, too. I guess I didn't understand what that meant to her . . . I mean, I was just some schlub who liked pretty ladies. We was fighting all the time."

He paused and took another drink from his mug, as well.

"Turns out there was this one dancer in particular that she was butting heads with . . . some new girl in the company. Anyhow, I was curious, so I went to the theater one night to pick her up. And there was this young broad dressed in that same pink and white tutu. She was only eighteen, but she knew where she was going . . ."

George trailed off, staring into his coffee cup, and Darla didn't have to ask who the young dancer was. She could pretty well fill in the blanks of how it all went down over the next few months, as well.

Then he snorted again. "I don't want you to think I'm

some kinda pervert or nothing. I mean, Livvy was just a kid then. I was just looking, know what I mean? But things got worse between me and Penny, and a couple of years later we broke it off for good. And then one night, I was at this bar uptown, and who do you think I run into? And, like I said, I had the bucks, so that was good enough for her."

To Darla's relief, he didn't do the pitty-pat heart routine again. Curious, though, she ventured, "If you were a stockbroker, how did you end up in the coffee business?"

"It was after we got married. I had a streak of bad luck, lost some big accounts . . . you know the drill. So I decided to cut my losses and get outta the rat race. One of my clients had this coffee bar that he wanted to unload. I always liked coffee, so I figured, why the heck not?"

He frowned a little. "Livvy, she wasn't too happy when the big money train rolled off the tracks, but she stuck with me, I guess 'cause she knew I'd take care of her no matter what. So we ended up here, in this fine establishment."

Darla smiled a little at the posh accent he gave to that last word. Still, she had one more question. "But what about Penelope? How coincidental was it that you bought a place in the same neighborhood as her dance studio?"

George shook his head. "It wasn't no coincidence. That space where her studio is was empty when Livvy and I got here. A few months later, I seen a sign go up. I didn't think nothing about it until I turned around one day and, bam, there she was ordering a cuppa coffee like nothing ever happened. Livvy said she was stalking me, but Penny never came back after that."

His expression grew pensive . . . pensive, that was, for George. "It was just that one time to let me know she was nearby . . . I guess kinda like a dog peeing to mark its territory, or something."

Darla did roll her eyes at that last, but all she said was, "I guess Livvy was still jealous, though, wasn't she?"

"Well, she didn't hafta be. Me, I'm the one that had to worry. After Livvy got sick, she kind of put a halt to things between us in the bedroom, if you know what I mean."

He paused at that and frowned, as if a thought had just occurred to him. "I dunno, maybe being sick was just an excuse. You know how women fake it the other way."

Trying not to wince at his caveman stereotypes, Darla gave him an encouraging nod to continue.

"Anyhow, it wasn't that long ago I tell her I'm thinking about finding myself wife number two so I can start getting some action again. I was pretty much joking, but she goes ballistic and tells me I'm stuck with her until she dies, because no judge is gonna let me divorce a sick wife. Next thing I know, she goes off for a good time with old Doug the baker."

His beefy fingers abruptly tightened on the mug, like he had Doug—or Livvy—in his grasp. "I found a copy of the hotel receipt stuck behind a mug on the counter. Not much of a hiding place, huh? Anyhow, I had it out with her. So Livvy acts all sad and says she's sorry, and I tell her I forgive her. Except I guess I really didn't."

He looked up at Darla then, the pensive look hardening into a sneer as he added, "You know, I had the sneaking suspicion that Penelope put her up to it somehow. You know, to get back at me. Well, no one outsmarts old Georgie King."

He did it, Darla thought with a sudden shiver of dread realization that she prayed he didn't notice. *He killed them both, and made it look like Penelope did it.* The only thing that seemed out of place was the suicide note, which, as far as Darla knew, had only Doug's confirmation that it was Penelope's handwriting. But an ex might have enough old samples of her handwriting stashed away somewhere to be able to forge a believable note . . .

Carefully, she set down her mug and stood, casually slipping her hand into her pocket to palm her cell phone.

"Thanks for the coffee, George, but I've got to get back to the bookstore. I told James I wouldn't be gone long."

For a fleeting moment, she feared he was going to protest. The image flashed through her mind of him holding her down and shoving oleander leaves into her mouth, holding his beefy hand over her lips until she was forced to swallow. Deliberately, she squelched that image and managed a smile.

To her relief, he nodded. "Yeah, well, go ahead and go," he said, making an impatient shooing gesture toward the door. "You got better things to do than hang around Georgie King."

She managed to walk unconcernedly to the door, but once she reached the door she fairly flew up the steps and was halfway down the block before she slowed again to a walk. By then, she had her cell phone in hand and was dialing Jake's number.

"Hey, kid, what's up?" she heard the PI's voice on the second ring.

Trying not to gasp for breath, Darla said, “Can you come by the bookstore later? I really need to talk to you.”

“Sure. What’s wrong? You sound like you just ran a marathon.”

“I’m on my way back from Perky’s,” she managed. “Jake, I talked to George about Livvy and Penelope. I think Reese was wrong about what happened. I-I’m pretty sure George was the one who killed them both.”

TWENTY

HAMLET LAY WITH HIS FUZZY HEAD PROPPED ON A SHORT stack of mass-market paperbacks, paws dangling off the counter, apparently asleep. His twitching tail, however, told another story. His eyes might be closed, but he was definitely keeping a feline ear out for anything out of the ordinary around the shop.

Darla gave him a grateful scratch behind the ears as she passed him on the way to the register. After her unsettling conversation with George that morning, she appreciated the cat having her back. She rang up the celebrity bio for an elderly gentleman and then turned, only to give a little start as she found James behind her, a packaged special order in hand.

Her store manager frowned down in concern at her as

he set the package in the outgoing mail box beneath the register.

"Darla, you have been as jumpy as Hamlet ever since you returned from Perky's. Would you care to share what is troubling you?"

She hesitated, tempted to confide in him, but reluctant to do so until she'd run her theory past Jake. So for now, all she told him—truthfully—was, "I'm just concerned about George. I'm not sure how well he's coping with everything."

To her relief, James nodded. "I agree. The man has no emotional support system, which any good therapist will confirm is necessary to get through a tragedy. It is probably the neighborly thing to do, checking up on—"

"Me-OOOW!"

The unexpected yowl from Hamlet made them both start this time. The cat was on full alert, fur bristling as he stood on all fours staring over Darla's shoulder. She whipped about to see what was wrong.

James, meanwhile, smiled at the newcomer. "So sorry. Hamlet is letting us know that we are neglecting our customer," he apologized to the gamine-featured teen with short, spiked dark hair standing on the other side of the counter.

Emma! She was by herself today, and moved with a dancer's quiet grace, not even jostling the string of bells on the door as she'd entered the store. She was dressed in black dance tights topped by a long-sleeved, loose-weave sweater in pale blue that came almost to her knees and was belted low on her waist.

Before Darla could ask what brought the girl there, James went on, "Good afternoon, miss. May we assist you?"

"Uh, yeah. I was in here last week and I think I lost something. Did you maybe find a vape pen? It's red. I might have, you know, dropped it while I was up in the lounge."

"Vape pen?" James turned a helpless look on Darla, who was already reaching beneath the counter for the lost-and-found box.

"I think she means this," Darla explained and pulled the red metal cylinder from it.

"Me-OOOW!"

Darla shot the cat a questioning look. His green gaze was fixed on Emma, who seemed quite oblivious to his scrutiny.

"It's okay, Hammy, we've got this," she assured him and held up the pen, even as she wondered why the cat was so concerned. "This the one?"

Emma all but snatched it from Darla's hand. "Thanks. These aren't cheap, you know. Is the coffee bar open?"

"Sure. A couple of other customers are up there already, and it's open until six, so you've got plenty of time."

Emma scampered toward the stairway,

Darla's cell phone chimed to indicate an incoming text. Checking the screen, she gave a relieved sigh at the message.

"Jake is heading over in a few minutes," she told her manager. "Could you watch the shop while I talk to her for a minute? It's kind of important."

"Of course. If we are fortunate, you will have finished up by the time my shift ends at four o'clock." Since, Darla knew, the ever-punctual James always liked to depart his shift on time.

Two more customers walked in just then, diverting

James's attention while Darla psyched herself up for the conversation to come with her friend. The phone conversation with Jake on her way back from Perky's that morning had left her on edge; this, despite the fact her friend had tried to talk her down, as the PI had put it, following her dramatic declaration regarding George's likely role in Penelope and Livvy's murders.

Unless he's chasing after you right now with a gun or knife, take a deep breath and put it out of your head until I can stop by this afternoon, Jake had instructed. *Otherwise, you're just going to make yourself crazy.*

Since Darla had no indication that George knew of her suspicions, she'd agreed to take the suggested deep-breath/out-of-mind route . . . even though, as James had observed, she had been as jumpy as Hamlet all afternoon.

A few minutes later, the bells on the shop door jangled, and Jake strode in. She was dressed in her usual "kick butt and take names" attire that she wore while on investigations: black jeans, man-tailored white shirt, and stacked black Doc Martens boots that added a good three inches to her height. As a bonus, she sported dark-tinted aviator sunglasses that gave her a vaguely menacing Lady Terminator look. All that was missing was her usual tailored black leather jacket . . . an obvious concession to the July heat.

"Hey, kid," she greeted Darla, sliding up the sunglasses so they perched on top of her head. "Shall we go up to the lounge for a bit of privacy?"

"We'd better not. Robert's up there along with a few customers."

She looked around and saw James standing a few

shelves away with one of the women who'd just walked in. Another customer had settled into one of the nearby armchairs and was leafing through the latest release in a popular dystopian fantasy series.

"Looks like we're stuck with the bistro table," she decided, leading the way over.

Jake took the chair opposite her, sliding aside the coffee menu and order pad to make room on the table for the black leather portfolio she carried. With a quick glance about to make sure none of the customers had drifted in their direction, she said in a low tone, "I've got some intel about my pro bono case that's pretty interesting. Do you want to hear about that first, or do you want to start off by telling me about your visit with good old Georgie?"

"Let me get George off my chest, please," was Darla's fervent reply as she launched into a swift but detailed recounting of Hamlet's latest book snagging of the body art book the afternoon before, and then her visit that morning to Perky's.

Jake listened with obvious interest, waiting until Darla had ended with George's comment about not being outsmarted to give her a considering nod.

"Good job, kid, but I can tell you Reese is going to shoot this one right down. No, wait." She held up a hand as Darla opened her mouth to protest. "Let me explain."

"First off, practically everybody and their dog"—the PI paused for a quick look at Hamlet, lounging now on a shelf nearby—"and probably their cat, has got a tattoo these days. Remember when we went over to Doug's shop and he was with the delivery guys bringing in the new display case? I saw he had an eagle or something tattooed on his right calf. So that's not narrowing down your suspect base by much."

Doug was tattooed, too? Darla frowned. But she didn't have time to mull over the possibility of Doug being a killer, for Jake was still talking.

"Second," the PI went on, "when a hothead like our George decides to kill a woman, chances are he strangles her or bludgeons her over the head . . . that is, if he doesn't shoot her with an illegal gun."

"Talk about sexist," Darla softly exclaimed. "Are you telling me what Sherlock Holmes said about poison being a woman's weapon is true?"

Jake shook her head.

"Actually, old Sherlock was wrong, for once. Statistically, it's about fifty-fifty as to whether the person who slipped you a nice cup of arsenic was a man or a woman. But when it comes to the choice of weapons, yes, women are more likely to go with poison when it's a premeditated crime. And there was premeditation written all over this one . . . at least, the Livvy portion of it. So, much as I hate to say it, I think we're back to the murder-suicide thing."

"But the oleander," Darla persisted. "George had easy access to the oleander. He could have doctored his vapor pen with oleander juice then swapped it out with Livvy, and then done the same with Penelope, just as easily as Penelope could have done it with Livvy."

If any of that tangled explanation made sense.

Jake, however, apparently got her drift, for she nodded. "I'm not debating that, kid. All I'm saying is that the evidence and timeline all point to Penelope. And don't forget the note."

"Maybe George forged it."

Jake shook her head. "I had a message about that from Reese. Apparently, the department's forensic document expert compared it with other samples of her writing they got from her studio, and she said it was legit. Although," Jake paused, "come to think of it, Reese did say that the note was written on a scrap of paper, so it's not much to go on."

She sighed. "Look, kid, I understand why you're trying so hard. It'd hurt less if it turned out Penelope was a victim, too."

"That's part of it, yes, but you should have seen George's face while we were talking." Darla suppressed a small shiver at the memory. "I saw something pretty awful in his eyes."

"I get you. How about I mention all this to Reese, just so we can say we covered all our bases. And if he thinks George needs a second look, he'll be on it. Deal?"

"Deal," Darla agreed, feeling a bit lighter in spirit. Whatever the outcome, she'd done her best here. Then, curious, she asked, "Now, what's this about your pro bono case?"

"It seems like there was some nasty little drama going on at the Brooklyn Modern Dance Institute."

"What do you mean?"

"The goal for all of Penelope's top students is to land a spot in the New York City Ballet, of course. But you just don't go knocking on the NYCB's door and ask to audition. Apparently, they harvest their dancers from an apprentice program. That means all the girls—and boys—who might have a shot all take part in a summer dance intensive that's a step toward getting into the apprentice program."

Just like Pinky, Darla thought with a nod.

"I've seen *Dance Moms*," Darla told her. "It's all pretty much dog-eat-dog for the ones who hope to go pro . . . and I'm talking the ten-year-olds. I can't even imagine how bad it can get for the older kids."

"Exactly. Anyhow, a few weeks ago my client's daughter had a big audition connected with one of those programs. Apparently, Allison is a heck of a dancer and had a pretty good shot at winning a slot to become an apprentice."

"Allison?" Darla echoed, recalling how Penelope had scolded two of her students for drinking whipped cream–covered lattes the day of their last committee meeting. One had been the rebellious Emma, and the other had been named Allison. She described the latter girl to Jake, who nodded.

"That matches the picture her mom showed me. Unfortunately, Allison got deathly ill—I'm talking "crawling on the floor" kind of sick—the night before the audition. She had to drop out, which means she has to wait another whole year to try again. Her mom is pretty steamed, because she's convinced that one of Allison's dance friends had something to do with it. But if Allison knows who slipped her a mickey, she isn't admitting it, so that's what her mother wanted me to look into."

"So did you find out who did it?"

"I've got a couple of ideas. But in the meantime I found an interesting connection. You know Steve's son, Jason? Apparently, you were onto something when you tried to get him talking about vaping. Allison's mom said he's the one who started the vaping fad with the local kids . . .

plus, he's the one who went to Livvy and got that whole Kona Blue Party thing going."

"Yeah, I just found that out, too," Darla told her, recalling George's mention of the shakedown involving Steve's offspring. "But there's more to it than that."

She went on to relate the story she'd heard from the coffee maven, along with Steve's version according to his children.

When Darla had finished, Jake shook her head. "George might not be on my favorites list, but I'm glad he gave the kids what for. And I'm glad George isn't the racist pig everyone thought he was. We probably need to pay Steve a visit and let him know what's going on with his kids . . . Jason, in particular."

Darla nodded her agreement.

"In the meantime"—Jake slid back her chair and picked up the portfolio—"I still need to check a few theories of my own. But, don't worry. I'll chat with Reese tonight about the George situation."

"I appreciate that. And I'll let you know if Hamlet pulls down any other book titles."

"You do that. If nothing else pops up that can't wait, I'll drop by tomorrow with an update."

The PI rose and strode to the door, departing in a jangle of bells. James had finished up with the two customers from before, and was now gathering his things in preparation to leave as Darla—Hamlet on her heels—made her way back to the register.

"Ah, perfect timing," her manager said with a glance at his watch. "I shall leave you and Robert to it."

With a final farewell, he followed Jake out. It wasn't until the door closed after him that Darla recalled wanting to ask Jake about one other thing: the two handwritten "Closed" signs. Had the forensic document examiner determined whether or not Penelope had written both those notices? It seemed likely that she had, given that they were scrawled on dance shoe box lids, and that Penelope would have had good reason to keep people away from both establishments.

Curious as she was about this detail, Darla figured it probably didn't fall under the "popped up/couldn't wait" category. She'd make a mental note and simply mention it to Jake in the morning.

That decided, she took a quick look to make sure no other customers had come in while she was occupied with Jake. Then she headed upstairs to the café, Hamlet still doing escort duty.

She noted immediately that the two original coffee bar customers were still there, each leafing through books despite the prominently displayed sign that said, "Sorry, only purchased reading material allowed in coffee lounge." Channeling Mary Ann and tsk-ing a little, she looked around for Emma. The young dancer was nowhere to be seen.

Darla was disappointed; she'd wanted to question the girl a bit about George to see what she knew. And given the fact Emma was one of the first people Darla had heard mention Kona Blue Party, she had obviously been a customer of Livvy's at some point. And, if nothing else, Emma might have an idea for Jake about who had tried to sabotage her friend Allison's dance chances.

Robert was at the bistro table near the dumbwaiter

wiping down the glass top, an empty latte mug in hand. Darla went over to join him. "Did the girl who was sitting here leave already?"

"Yeah, but she just left."

Hamlet, meanwhile, was playing crazy kitty, zipping around the lounge to the amusement of the customers.

"Hammy, simmer down," she scolded him. "You might run into someone and hurt them."

The cat shot her a look but obediently halted, though the look in his green eyes said, *I'm only listening to you because we have customers in the house.* And, to Darla's relief, each of the customers in question went on to purchase their respective books once they'd finished their coffees.

The remainder of the afternoon was busier than usual for a weekday, which buoyed her spirits. Luckily, the "serial killer" Sunday afternoon appeared to have been an aberration. She was beginning to feel that all their hard work on the block party was paying off. Maybe they'd make the July Fourth block party an annual event!

A few minutes before six, Robert came rushing down the stairs to the main shop floor. "All cleaned up and ready for tomorrow," he told her. "I was pretty busy today. I even, you know, sold two of our coffee mugs."

The logoed coffee mugs with Hamlet's silhouette on them had been a particular favorite touch of Darla's, and she smiled. "You and Roma have a good evening. I'll see you in the morning."

She followed him to the door and locked it behind him, and then did her usual quick run-through of the store. More than once she'd surprised someone lounging in one of the armchairs, so caught up in their reading that they hadn't realized it was closing time. Her final stop was the restroom, where she flipped on the lights, looked beneath the wicker privacy divider for feet, and closed the door again.

"All set, Hammy," she called to the cat, who was crouched on the counter, long black tail whipping just a bit. "Why don't we run upstairs to the apartment for a moment and freshen up, and then we can go for a walk before supper?"

By way of answer, Hamlet all but flung himself from the counter and went bounding toward her . . . and then passed her by, halting in front of the restroom door.

"Me-OOOW! Me-OOOW!"

"Hamlet! What in the heck—?"

Shooting the cat an uncertain look, Darla started toward the restroom, where Hamlet was now pawing insistently at the door. She frowned. She'd already looked inside but hadn't seen anyone.

Hadn't seen any feet, she corrected herself. But what if there was a mouse in there that had set the cat off like this?

Her first impulse was to call Robert and ask him to come check for critters, but she didn't want to be the stereotypical female afraid of creepy-crawlies. Jake, she knew, would dispatch any unwanted fauna without blinking.

Determinedly, Darla went over to the far wall, where a fireplace once graced the place back when the room had still been a parlor. The firebox itself had long since been bricked in, but her great-aunt had left the elaborately carved walnut mantelpiece and surround in place, as well as a set of decorative brass fireplace tools. Inside what remained of the original hearth, Darla had placed a large arrangement of red silk flowers in a basket, representing a cheery fire.

Darla reached for the poker and went back over to the

restroom door. Hamlet had stepped aside, apparently content to let her take the lead now.

"All right, Hammy," she muttered, reaching for the knob, poker held high. "On *three. One, two—*"

Before she could finish the count, the knob turned beneath her hand, and the door opened inward.

Darla leaped back with a reflexive shriek when a girl's familiar voice cried, "Wait! It's me. Emma."

TWENTY-ONE

"EMMA! WHAT IN THE HECK ARE YOU DOING, TRYING TO scare me like that? Surely you knew the store was closed," Darla demanded, lowering the poker and grabbing the girl by the arm to drag her out into the light.

Emma ducked her head, the neckline of her oversized sweater slipping down to bare one shoulder. "I'm sorry. Honest, I wasn't trying to scare anyone."

"Well, you sure frightened my cat!" Darla shot back, turning a concerned look on Hamlet, who had bristled to double his size and was hissing like a steam engine. "Look how upset he is."

Emma stared back at her, eyes wide and mouth opened in a frightened little O.

"Seriously, Ms. Pettistone, I'm really, really sorry. I know this was totally stupid, but can you let me explain?"

"Make it fast," Darla clipped out, wishing she hadn't left her cell phone under the counter.

Emma, meanwhile, was nodding eagerly.

"I know this was stupid," she repeated, "but I needed to talk to you, and I couldn't figure out another way. I didn't want Robert to see me."

"Robert? What does he have to do with anything?"

The girl heaved a breath, and then said in a rush, "I work part-time for Mr. Bates at the doughnut shop, but he's going to have to lay me off because no one wants to buy doughnuts there anymore. I filled in part-time at a coffee bar once and learned how to do all the drinks, so I'm pretty good. But I was afraid Robert might think I was trying to steal his job, and so—"

"Hang on." Darla stared at the girl in disbelief. "Let me get this straight. Are you trying to say that all this hiding and sneaking is your way of trying to apply for a job as a barista?"

Emma ducked her head again, her almost inaudible answer more of a question. "Yes?"

Darla sighed and leaned the poker against the wall, then glanced over at Hamlet. The hissing had subsided, but he was still on full feline alert.

"It's okay, Hammy," she reassured him. Then, addressing the young dancer, Darla went on, "I don't suppose it ever occurred to you that this kind of stunt would make for a really bad first impression?"

"I know. You're right," the girl replied, dragging an oversized sleeve across her eyes. "It's just that I really need the extra money. I got accepted into the ballet apprentice program that starts this fall, but I'll still need to pay for dance shoes and clothes, and all those other expenses. My parents are divorced, so my mom really can't afford it. Madame Penelope was going to help me out, but she's gone now, and I don't know what to do."

At that, Emma burst into noisy sobs. Darla shook her head and sighed again. On the one hand, the girl's drive was admirable; on the other, her common sense quotient left much to be desired. And it wasn't like they needed another barista at this point. But she couldn't quite make herself turn down the girl outright.

"Look, Emma," she said as the dancer's tears began to subside. "I'm not hiring at the moment, but I can give you an application to take home with you. Robert's been talking about going back to school part-time, so maybe at some point I'll need someone to fill in for him on occasion."

Emma swiped her face again and looked up, smiling a little.

"You mean it?" Then, eyes widening, she went on, "Please, Ms. Pettistone, let me make you a café mocha or something so I can show you how good I am."

"I don't think so, Emma." Darla frowned a little. "Robert has already cleaned all the equipment for tomorrow, and—"

"Please, Ms. Pettistone! I can write anything down on that application, but you won't know if I'm any good unless you try one of my drinks. And café mocha is my favorite."

Darla hesitated. The girl's argument made sense. And, on the off chance she did need a spur-of-the-moment barista if Robert couldn't come in for some reason, she wouldn't have time to do a test run.

Besides, she couldn't help feeling a little sorry for the girl, losing her teacher and likely her job.

"All right," she agreed, "but it better be the best you've ever made."

She led a smiling Emma upstairs to the coffee bar. Hamlet trailed behind them. His fur had flattened back to normal, but she could hear his faint, pantherlike rumble deep in his throat. Obviously, he did not approve of this unorthodox job interview.

Once behind the coffee bar, Emma was all business. She grabbed an apron and put that on, then rolled her sleeves up and out of the way. While Darla took a seat at one of the bistro tables, the girl spent a moment orienting herself, opening cabinets and drawers. Finally, with a bright smile, she said, "You asked for a café mocha, ma'am?"

"Large, and with plenty of whipped cream on top," Darla agreed with a smile, playing along.

She watched as the girl pulled out a pitcher and added chilled milk, then deftly pumped chocolate sauce into it. She steamed the milk, and Darla could see her keeping an eye on the temperature, just as Robert always did.

So far, so good, Darla thought as the girl set aside the pitcher of steamed milk to clean the steam wand.

The next part involved making the espresso, which mostly happened behind the espresso machine. The girl seemed to stumble over the process a little, and Darla noted to herself that Robert was faster at filling and properly tamping the ground beans. Still, in short order Emma had pulled the espresso shot, the familiar aroma wafting through the lounge. The girl expertly poured the steamed, chocolate-laced milk into a large mug, using a big spoon to hold back most of the foam. Then, slowly adding the espresso to the milk, she reached for a couple of small jars from behind the counter.

"My secret ingredients," she said, giving the mug a generous sprinkle and a stir. She finished with a big dollop of whipped cream on top, adding a dash of mocha powder and a bit of shaved chocolate.

Carrying the mug out on a tray, Emma walked to the bistro table where Darla sat and with a proud smile set the drink before her.

"One café mocha," she proclaimed.

Darla eyed the drink and nodded. "Looks very professional. So let me give it a taste."

"ME-ROOOW!"

With an angry scream, Hamlet leaped onto the bistro table. Luckily, Darla's reflexes were swift enough so that she grabbed the mug and pulled it out of reach before the cat could send latte, whipped cream, and pottery flying.

"Hamlet!" she scolded him, standing and carrying the mug to the counter for safekeeping. "You almost made a heck of a mess here. Now get off the table right now!"

To Emma, she said, "Sorry, I don't know what's gotten into him. I guess he's just cranky because he wanted to go upstairs for his supper."

With a hiss, Hamlet leaped from the table again, tail twitching as he stared at Darla. Shaking her head, she reached for a long metal coffee spoon sitting on the bar top. Scooping a little dollop of whipped cream with her coffee, she took a taste. "Not bad," she determined, "but it's a little different."

Emma's smile slipped. "Oh no. That's my own recipe. I add nutmeg and cinnamon along with the chocolate. You had some here, so I figured I'd use it."

Darla shrugged and smiled. "It's just a little more bitter than I'm used to, but then I'm kind of a coffee wimp. I like mine really sweet."

Emma ran back to the bar and grabbed the whipped cream can, then came back to the table. "Just stir in the whipped cream, and that should counteract it," Emma advised. "Here, I'll add some more."

Darla did as suggested and took another sip.

"Better," she agreed. "You do seem to know your way around a coffee bar. Where did you work before?"

While Darla drank her coffee, Emma gave an enthusiastic account of an independent coffee bar where she'd worked previously.

"Not a Starbucks or anything," she conceded, "but they roasted all their own. And we used to have contests to see who could come up with the best new drink. It was fun."

"So why did you leave?"

Emma shrugged. "I think the owner's wife didn't like me much." Then, brightening, she asked, "Do you want me to make you something else? Maybe a plain latte?"

"No, I don't think so," Darla replied as she set down her empty mug. She winced a little as a sudden cramp wracked her. "I probably shouldn't have had that café mocha on an empty stomach. Way too much acid."

"Okay. Why don't you wait there while I clean up, and then I'll get out of your hair?"

The girl reached for Darla's cup, and Darla noticed something she hadn't seen before. On the inside of

Emma's wrist was a tattoo of two small pink toe shoes: one facing up and one facing down, their pink ribbon laces curling around them.

"Cute," Darla said, "but I can't believe Penelope would let one of her dancers have a tattoo. Did she know about it?"

Emma rolled her eyes.

"There's a lot of things Madame Penelope wouldn't let us do," she said, reaching for the whipped cream can and, with a grin, squirting a sizable blob directly into her mouth.

Darla blinked at her inappropriate action but decided it wasn't worth calling the girl on it. Still, she made a mental X against the girl's employment worthiness when it came to good sense.

Then Emma laughed. "You should have seen how mad Madame was when I won that pie-eating contest at the block party."

"Right, that was you." Darla frowned, recalling seeing a distracted-looking Penelope not long after that contest. No doubt the woman had just finished giving her student a dressing-down. Feeling a bit guilty that she'd been responsible for that little conflict, since the block party had sponsored the pie-eating contest, she asked, "So when did you get the tattoo?"

"The day after she died," Emma said, her eyes filling with tears. "It was in memory of Madame Penelope."

Darla studied the girl as Emma carried Darla's empty mug back to the bar. The girl was definitely moody, going from laughter to tears in seconds. Part of it, Darla was sure, could be attributed to the shock of Penelope's death . . . that, and stereotypical teenage girl flightiness. But though Darla sympathized with her, it didn't seem like she'd be a good fit at Pettistone's. Maybe she'd suggest the girl talk to George once things settled down a bit.

And then Darla shut her eyes, feeling suddenly faint. Maybe it wasn't the coffee, she decided, gritting her teeth against another cramp. The stress of the block party and then its tragic aftermath was probably getting to her. *With my luck, I'm getting some sort of summer flu.*

The sudden bump of something fuzzy against her arm made her open her eyes again. Hamlet was sitting on the table, green eyes wide as he stared at her.

"Don't worry, Hammy," she told him, giving him a weak scritch under the chin. "As soon as Emma is finished, we'll go upstairs and get your supper."

But the girl seemed to be taking an extraordinarily long time to wash up . . . or maybe it was just the fact she was feeling queasy that made her impatient.

"Emma," she called, "I'm feeling a little under the weather. Go ahead and leave it. I'll clean up in the morning."

"Just another minute," the girl called in a singsongy voice.

Darla shook her head, and immediately regretted it, for a wave of dizziness swept her. She tried to get up, but the dizziness grew worse, and she felt her stomach roil as she came dangerously close to throwing up.

"Emma," she faintly called, shutting her eyes, "I need to toss you out of here so I can go home. I really feel sick."

Crawling on the floor kind of sick.

Darla put a hand to her forehead. Wasn't that how Jake had described Allison's illness? She pried open her eyelids again to see Hamlet almost nose-to-nose with her, his green eyes narrowed to slits.

Oleander.

The symptoms of oleander poisoning that she'd read about on the Internet the night before drifted through her head again. *Nausea, check. Dizziness, check. Blurred vision, check.* Among that laundry list of symptoms had been the big one: death. And under prognosis: *The faster you get medical help, the better the chance for recovery.*

She had to get out of there, call for help . . .

"What's the matter, Darla?" Emma asked in the same singsongy voice as she left the sink and plopped into the chair across from her. She'd rolled down her sleeves again, so that her tattoo was covered. Hamlet growled low in his throat, sounding like something off the veldt.

"What did you put in my coffee?" Darla choked out, squinting when the girl's image seemed to blur before her.

Emma shrugged. "You're the smart one . . . You figure it out. I was sitting by the dumbwaiter this afternoon, and I could hear you and your friend—the tall lady—talking about Madame Penelope." She shrugged, her sweater slipping again. Idly, she played with one sleeve, poking a finger through the loose weave. "Then you started talking about Allison, and how she got sick before her audition. I figured it wouldn't be too long before you figured out it was me."

Darla swallowed hard against the bile that was rising in her throat. "I-I don't understand. Why would you poison us all?"

"It was all Livvy's fault," the girl said with a pout, jumping up from her chair while Darla tried to stay upright in hers. "She stole George from Madame Penelope all those years ago, and then she was trying to take Doug away, too.

Madame pretended she didn't care, but I saw her crying. I knew if I fixed things, made Livvy go away, Madame would be grateful to me. She'd make sure I got the dance scholarship instead of Allison."

She smirked. "I found the hotel receipt in Doug's trash at the doughnut shop, so I took it. I left a copy in Madame's office and one at Perky's, so everyone would know what was going on. I thought it worked. I heard Doug on the phone telling Madame he was sorry, that he wouldn't do it again."

Then the smirk morphed into a scowl. "But Livvy wouldn't quit, so I had to try something else."

Emma paused and abruptly seemed to blink back tears.

"I tried it out on Allison first to see how it worked . . . The oleander leaves, I mean. I went to summer camp once, and the counselors told us they were poison, so I figured they would work. And it was so easy. All I had to do was swap out my vape pen with the oleander juice in it for hers. The vape pens all look alike—she never noticed the one she was smoking wasn't hers."

"But . . . your friend . . . she almost died," Darla managed.

Emma shrugged. "It just made her sick enough to miss her audition, so that was good. And I got a top spot for tryouts next month. But I couldn't be sure I'd be accepted . . . not without Madame Penelope's recommendation. So I waited for the block party, when it was crowded and everyone was busy so I could take care of Livvy. I thought Madame would be so happy when I told her what I did, she'd give me the best recommendation ever."

Then, abruptly, the girl sagged back onto her chair.

"But she wasn't happy. She was mad. She was going to tell . . . and then I'd never be a professional dancer. So I had to take care of her, too."

With an effort, Darla shoved away another bout of dizziness. She didn't need to hear how Emma must have lured her teacher to Doug's shop, and she didn't ask how Penelope's body came to be hidden beneath the drop cloths. Oddly, the only thing she could focus on was—

"The suicide note," she gasped out. "You wrote it?"

"Madame Penelope wrote it," Emma said, anger abruptly lacing her tone as she sat up straight. "It was my dance critique. She wrote some really mean things about me."

Assuming a raspy, nasal tone in credible imitation of the dance instructor, she parroted, "*Your skill does not excuse your behavior toward your fellow dancers. I've seen those little 'accidents' on the floor and at the barre, especially when you deliberately let Allison fall last week. It doesn't matter that you said you're sorry. It should never have happened. If another incident like this occurs, I won't be giving you my recommendation to the apprentice program.*"

She paused and scrambled to her feet again as she gave Darla a preening smile. "I'm going to be a soloist with the New York City Ballet, and nothing's going to stop me. I'm better than any of them. You'll see. Well, maybe *you* won't, but the rest of the world will."

Darla wondered how Emma would explain things when it occurred to Jake or Reese that she'd killed Darla as well, but another spasm wracked her. When she opened her eyes again, the girl was gone.

Vaguely, she was aware that Hamlet was gone, too. *Gone for help?* But, clever as he was, the cat couldn't dial the emergency number. She thought she heard the bells at the front door jangling, but that could have been in her head.

The faster you get medical help, the better the chance for recovery.

She took a deep breath and tried to stand. Her cell phone—where was it? Beneath the front counter, where the main phone was. She'd meant to add an extension upstairs, but she'd never gotten around to it, because one or the other of them always had a cell phone on them. She had to get downstairs, call for help.

"Hammy," she croaked out, but no familiar flash of black fur appeared. She let go of the table edge and took a faltering step, only to drop to her knees. *Crawl, then,* she told herself. *Get down the stairs and get to the phone, and everything will be fine.*

But it was like one of those nightmares where the road ahead kept stretching and stretching out of reach. Luckily, she hadn't turned off any of the overhead lights, since she needed every lumen to see where she was going. And then, finally, she found the stairway.

How to get down it? Crawl down backward without being able to see where she was going, or try it headfirst, and risk tumbling head over heels to the bottom.

Backward.

After a bit it became almost mechanical, sliding one knee down and then the other. *How many stairs were there?* She'd counted them once, after Robert had read a

Sherlock Holmes story where Holmes had asked that very question of Watson to illustrate his powers of observation, and he'd challenged her and James to guess. The answer had been twenty . . . yet it seemed she'd descended that many already, and still she hadn't reached bottom.

And then she heard a voice calling to her. "Darla! Darla, are you in there?"

Jake! she shouted back . . . or, rather, she tried to. Her mouth opened, but she heard nothing come from her lips. She realized then that she had made it down the stairs after all and was lying near the register. Hands were on her shoulders, lifting her up against the counter. Jake's voice was in her ear. "Darla, what's wrong? What happened? How long have you been lying here?"

"Oleander . . . Emma," she choked out, but whether Jake understood her or not, she wasn't certain.

"Hang in there, kid. I'm calling an ambulance," Jake told her.

Vaguely, she was aware of her friend's tightly frantic voice as she told the 9-1-1 operator, "I think she's been poisoned. Oleandrin."

She blinked again and saw Mary Ann and Robert both there as well, their features drawn in fear and concern. But what about—?

"Hamlet," she managed, trying to hold back a sudden sense of panic on his behalf.

She had no doubt that he'd be able to get away from Emma, but his feline curiosity could well have done him in. Had the oleander been in the milk, she wondered, or in the espresso? If the former, he might been lured by any leftover foam and been poisoned, too.

Jake grasped her hand.

"The ambulance will be here any second. And don't worry. Hamlet's fine. He's down in my apartment right now. He's the one who let us know you needed help . . . Well, Hamlet and Mr. Plinski."

TWENTY-TWO

IT WAS, DARLA DECIDED, QUITE THE MOST UNPLEASANT night of her life. The EMTs had already started an IV and had her on oxygen as they monitored her vital signs on the way to the ER . . . the trip made worse by the fact she began throwing up at that point. The next step in the ER had been what they'd called a gastric lavage, which sounded civilized enough until she realized they were talking about pumping her stomach. Which they proceeded to do, even though she still had the presence of mind at that point to explain that it probably wasn't necessary now.

By the time she woke up in a hospital bed the next morning, she felt almost human again, save that her throat was raw from the tube that had been slid down it. But the worst of the dizziness and blurred vision was gone, as was the nausea. And her emergency room doctor, the cheerful Dr. Gables, had assured her that the fact she'd been treated within an hour of her poisoning meant they'd been able to flush the greatest portion of the oleander's poisonous chemicals from her system, so that they'd be discharging her by the end of the day if all her vitals remained good.

Which was all quite fine by Darla. But first she needed to make sure that Hamlet had escaped the store unscathed.

"Seriously, kid, he's fine," Jake assured her, having used her PI credentials and Reese's name to slip into her room before standard visiting hours. "I swear that cat is half human. He managed to get out of the store and started yowling on the stoop, trying to summon help. It was Mr. Plinski who spotted him first. He was up there on his roof with his binoculars and spied Hamlet doing his mad-cat routine. So Mr. Plinski called down to Mary Ann on his walkie-talkie, and Mary Ann called me. You know the rest."

Darla smiled, pride and a bit of awed disbelief filling her at the thought of Hamlet's heroics. As soon as she was home again, she would call for a nice order of take-out shrimp just for him.

"He spent the night at my place," Jake went on, "and now he's back up in your apartment, all fed and watered. James came over to give him a little moral support. He's also fending off the media, since it's turned into a real feeding frenzy over there. I had to run a gauntlet just to get out of my apartment."

As Darla stared at her in alarm—What if the news reached Texas? What would happen if her mother and father flipped on the news over breakfast and saw their daughter's bookstore?—Jake gave her a reassuring smile. "No need to panic. James called your parents already and let them know you were going to be fine."

"Thank goodness for that." Darla sank back against the thin hospital pillows. "I know I was complaining about needing another vacation, but this really wasn't the way I wanted to get my time off. Do you know when we'll be able to reopen the store?"

Before Jake could answer that, another more disturbing thought occurred to her. She shot Jake an alarmed look. "What about my coffee bar, and all the equipment? How can we ever use it again?"

"Don't worry, kid. James and I already talked to Reese about that. He has someone who can handle it for you. When they're finished, you'll get an official sign-off from the health department and you'll be good to go again."

"Good to go" was good, Darla told herself. Then she sobered. "Have they found Emma yet?"

Jake nodded, looking pained. "They picked her up last night, and last I heard she's being held without bail. There's going to be a mental health evaluation, and then a decision will be made whether to charge her or institutionalize her. Either way, she's probably going to spend the rest of her life locked up."

"She admitted to me that she did it . . . and she also was the one who made Allison sick the night before her tryout." Darla shuddered. "She seemed to have everything all justified in her head to where it just wasn't any big deal. The only thing that seems to mean anything at all to her is being a prima ballerina."

"Tragic all around."

Jake looked at her watch and then rose. "I've got to meet with Allison's parents and finalize things with them."

Client paperwork, Darla guessed.

"As soon as you know when the hospital's going to let you out," Jake went on, "give me a call, and I'll come get you."

With Jake gone, and no roommate to contend with, Darla spent the rest of the morning flipping through the television channels and waiting impatiently for her doctor to spring her. The one bit of excitement was when a nurses' aide walked in grinning and bearing a huge glass vase overflowing with a hothouse's worth of roses.

Her first reflexive thought was that Reese had sent them, and a small shiver of delight swept her. Then she took a look at the accompanying card and gave a rueful smile.

"*To one tough broad. Feel better soon. Respectfully. George King,*" she read aloud, shaking her head. She could only hope that the King of Coffee didn't have an underlying motive in sending her flowers. No way was she lining up to be wife number two!

It was late in the afternoon when Darla finally made her escape. Eager as she was to leave, she was still shaky enough on her feet to feel grateful for the mandatory wheelchair ride. Jake, Robert, and Roma were waiting for her. Jake was at the wheel of Maybelle, the older model Mercedes sedan that Darla's great-aunt had also left her, and which was garaged a few blocks from the bookstore.

"Who's the admirer?" Jake asked with a grin as she caught sight of the veritable rose garden in Darla's lap.

"Don't ask," Darla warned with a roll of her eyes as

Robert helped her into the front seat of the Merc and Roma gave her a welcoming lick.

The roses came in handy, however, when they arrived back at the bookstore only to find that a news crew was still camped outside.

"Get ready to tuck and roll," Jake said, only half kiddingly, as she pulled up behind the news van. Darla ducked her face behind the proliferation of blooms as, flanked by Robert—Roma remained in the Mercedes with Jake—they made a rush for her door.

With Robert's help, Darla got up the stairs and inside her apartment, where Hamlet was waiting impatiently for her return.

"*Me-OOW!*" he exclaimed.

But when Darla greeted him with an enthusiastic, "Hammy!" he brushed past her and made a beeline for his food bowl.

Darla exchanged wry glances with Robert. "I guess he figures his work here is done," she told the youth. "Time for more important things. Do you mind topping off his kibble?"

By the time Darla was settled comfortably on her sofa—and Hamlet had satisfied the worst of his hunger pangs—Jake had re-parked the car and walked back from the garage with Roma.

"I'm just a phone call away if you need anything," Jake reminded Darla, while the little greyhound trotted over to shove a narrow snout at Hamlet. "Robert's there if I'm not, and James will come by first thing in the morning to run off the press. Oh, and Mary Ann already sent up soup and a veggie casserole. They're in your fridge."

"I'll be fine," Darla assured them. "The doctor said I'd just be weak for a couple of days, but nothing critical. And, after all, I've got Hamlet to look after me, and y'all for backup. Now, shoo," she finished, giving them the "bad kitty" treatment.

Once they'd left, Hamlet deigned to settle on the couch beside her. Darla smiled and gave him a scritch under the chin. "I know you're not going to take credit for it, Hammy," she told him, "but you really did save my life."

Barely had she said this when the intercom buzzer sounded. Darla jumped, and then shot the offending device an irritated look. "It better not be someone from the local news," she muttered as she got up to answer. "Who is it?"

"It's Reese," came a familiar voice made tinny by the old technology. "Jake said you were back home again. Are you up to having a visitor?"

"Sure, come on up," she said and buzzed him up, leaving her apartment door ajar.

As she unlocked the door and settled back on the couch to wait for him, it occurred to her that once she would have been concerned about the fact she'd not had a chance to put on fresh makeup or even brush her hair. But now . . .

A quick knock sounded and Reese walked in.

"Hey, Darla," he said, his smile warm. "You're looking a heck of a lot better than you did last night."

"Last night?"

"As soon as I heard I headed up to the hospital, though by the time I got there they'd already pumped your stomach, and you were pretty out of it."

"Great," she muttered, not even daring to picture how she must have looked at that point. *Something that Hamlet dragged in* would probably be complimentary.

Reese, meanwhile, walked over to the dining table, where Robert had put the oversized vase of roses for her. "From your family?" he asked with a nod toward the arrangement.

"No, they're from a . . . friend."

She hadn't deliberately meant to hesitate over that last word; rather, she'd simply been a bit reluctant to admit George was the sender. Still, she could see from the subtle shift of Reese's expression that he took that word to mean something more. He looked a little surprised but nodded.

"Good," he said, settling on one of her ladder-back chairs. "Oh, I ran the news van off for you, but don't be surprised if they're back in the morning."

Then, after an awkward pause, he asked, "So, how are you feeling?"

Like I've had a tube shoved down my throat, was what she planned to say, deliberately wanting to keep the mood casual. But the word she was surprised to hear come out of her mouth was, "Scared."

Then she bit her lip and shook her head. "I didn't mean that. Well, maybe I did. I still can't believe that a girl I really didn't even know would actually try to kill me."

Abruptly, Reese got up and moved over to the sofa. Hamlet all but flew off, hopping onto the dining table and coyly peering around the fragrant blooms. As for the detective, Reese settled beside her and grasped Darla's hand, giving her digits a gentle shake.

"I don't blame you for being scared. Out-of-the-blue things like this can really throw you for a loop. And running into a psycho like that kid is a one-in-a-million bit of bad luck. Just remember that you have plenty of friends around here who have your back."

He chuckled a little, his smile wry.

"That Mr. Plinski is a pistol. While Mary Ann was busy calling Jake, he was on the horn to 9-1-1 insisting there was an emergency next door, and that one of his neighbors was calling for help." The smile broadened. "He neglected to mention that the neighbor doing the calling was Hamlet. But he knew something had to be wrong, and he wasn't going to take no for an answer."

Darla managed a smile back. "Hamlet knew something was wrong from the start. I just wasn't smart enough until it was almost too late to figure out what he was trying to tell me. And, like you said, he had my back."

She glanced down at his hand, still holding hers.

"So, do you have time to hang out for a while?" she ventured. "Mary Ann sent up a couple of homemade dishes, so we probably should give them a try."

Reese glanced down at their entwined hands, as well. Apparently realizing that the gesture had gone on too long, he abruptly loosed her hand and stood. Darla covered her rush of disappointment by giving Hamlet, who'd leaped back to his spot beside her, a quick pet.

Reese cleared his throat.

"Sounds good, but Connie's waiting downstairs in the car. Oh, I almost forgot, she sent this for you," he added and pulled a small gold gift bag from his jacket pocket.

Handing it over to her, he added, "I'll get with you tomorrow. The way this case has blown up, I'll have a lot of questions, so you might want to rest up tonight."

He was out the door again as quickly as he'd entered. Darla locked the door after him and then returned to the sofa. Hamlet had taken advantage of her momentary absence to stretch out to full length, leaving her just enough room to squeeze in beside him.

"Well, Hammy, I guess it's just you and me," Darla told him. She gave him another scritch, and he returned the gesture with a rusty purr. Then, brow knitted, she reached for the gift bag. "Let's see what Connie sent me." She reached into the bag, and her fingers closed on something cylindrical. *Mace?* But when she pulled the object out and saw what it actually was, Darla shook her head and rolled her eyes.

"Lipstick," she muttered. This probably meant that Connie had been with Reese when he'd shown up at the hospital, and the woman had seen her in all her not-so-wonderful glory after the stomach pumping.

"But, hey, at least she didn't cheap out," Darla told the cat as she saw the name on the tube. "I could buy five of my usual brand for what she probably paid for this." Pulling off the top, she smiled a little at the vibrant color. "Now *that* is red."

Hamlet gave a *meow-rumph* of agreement.

Darla's smile broadened. "Poor Connie," she told him. "She keeps bringing up the old chestnut about diamonds being a girl's best friend. Well, she's wrong. Cats are girl's best friend."

At that, Hamlet leaped from her lap and sauntered over

to the bookshelf. Then, glancing back with wide green eyes, he reached out a deliberate paw and used a claw to snag a book, which promptly toppled to the floor.

"Hammy, I've never actually seen you do that," Darla exclaimed as she rose, too, and went to retrieve the book.

Then, glancing at the title, she laughed in delight. It was a nonfiction book she'd bought soon after her divorce, and which she'd always meant to toss into a garage sale, but somehow it had followed her there to Brooklyn. And now, she didn't need the book, she realized . . . not with Hamlet in the house.

"So, Hammy, you want to try some of Mary Ann's casserole?" she asked as she tossed the copy of *Soul Mates* into the wastebasket by her desk.